They found _____ t
have seen an _____
nobody. The _____ stones, panting
a little now, __ found no one. There was only
the crackling fire, now dying down and short of
fuel. Earnshaw and his party came rushing in, and
they, too, had seen no one. They stood in the heat
and glare of the fire, getting breath again and
wondering what had happened. The fire had been
big. Someone had taken some trouble over it, and
it must surely have had a purpose. They looked at
one another, puzzled.

'Look carefully,' said the vicar. 'They'll have left the
signs of their hellish work, as they did at Lammas.
Look everywhere.'

WITCHFIRE
AT LAMMAS

Robert Neill

ARROW BOOKS

Arrow Books Limited
62–65 Chandos Place, London WC2N 4NW

An imprint of Century Hutchinson Limited

London Melbourne Sydney Auckland
Johannesburg and agencies throughout
the world

First published by Hutchinson 1977

Arrow edition 1979
Reprinted 1988

Printed and bound in Great Britain by
Anchor Brendon Limited, Tiptree, Essex

ISBN 0 09 919560 7

To ARCANUS;
and to one like him, who was my friend.

Contents

1
Lammas

In the sleepiness of the summer afternoon Sir John Mallinder was sleepy. He had hoped for some peace and quiet, and instead he had the vicar; which, to his way of thinking, meant trouble. He did not see eye to eye with the vicar.

'I don't know why you come to me with this,' he was saying irritably. 'Climbing up there in the night to light a bonfire—' He waved at the high moors, the foothills of the Pennines, that rose beyond the garden. 'I'd call it pretty silly, but it won't harm anyone. So why come to me with it?'

'But on Lammas Day—'

'I *know* it's Lammas Day.'

His irritation was open, for it was Monday the 1st of August 1715, an anniversary he did not like. Exactly a year ago, on the 1st of August 1714, Queen Anne had died, and the country had not been the same since. He thought it was now a sink of Whiggery, with Whig ministers, Whig bishops, and pestilential Low Church parsons. This vicar was one of them.

He tried to come to grips with things. He had been sitting in his garden, peacefully waiting for his wife to join him, when the vicar had called, and there had been nothing for it but to invite the man into the shade and offer him a chair. Out of the shade the garden drowsed in the sun, its heat kept in by the walls of mellow brick.

The grass, now parched and brown, left borders by the walls, and here in close array were the flowers and herbs that the still-room was for ever calling for; thyme and sage and marjoram, mallow and elder, jonquils and violets and lily of the valley, marigold, cowslip, gilliflower, tansy, fennel and feverfew. Here, above all, were the roses, red and fragrant, that were needed by the hundred for rose water, perfumes and pomanders, and the pickled flowers that would float in a bowl of water to brighten a winter day. In the heat of the afternoon their mingled scents were soporific, and from all along the borders came a steady drone of bees to remind him of the hives in the fruit garden. He waved at a hovering wasp, and turned again to the vicar.

'What's wrong with Lammas?' he asked truculently, 'A fine old day, and it's in the prayerbook too. It marks the height of summer, and that's something we should be thankful for.'

'Midsummer's day is in June, as well you know.'

'Heaven help you!'

Sir John was exasperated. Any man must be a fool who thought the height of an English summer came in June. A Whig must be a fool too, and this man was both.

'Lammas is not a Christian festival, whatever the calendar says.' The vicar's clear voice was incisive. He had uncrossed his long legs and was sitting tensely upright, his bands and black coat looking out of place in the colour of the garden. 'The Church may have tried to give a Christian look to the pagan festivals, but it has not succeeded with Lammas. It's as pagan as ever it was — here.'

'What *are* you talking about? Are you saying that our people are pagans, after all your sermons?'

'Who's to say what they are in heart and mind, even if they sit in a Christian church on Sunday? Old beliefs die hard, and some have not died at all.'

'You build a great deal on a bonfire.'

10

'There's more to it than that. And if, sir, you would give me a proper hearing—'

'I'm trying to. Ah!'

Sir John broke off with relief in his voice as his wife and daughter came down the garden to join him. Lady Mallinder was still graceful and elegant, and in this summer afternoon she was looking cooler than her husband. She had discarded the high head-dressing of a year ago, and had only curls that pressed close to her head and tumbled down her neck. Her gown of cream-coloured muslin was cut low enough to have brought a startled grunt from Sir John when he had first seen her in it, and it hung open in the front to display the petticoat of pale green silk, embroidered with flecks of gold. Jane, her daughter, had turned seventeen, and had gown and petticoat alike in the new cloth from the Indies called calico, in a clear pale yellow. It suited her years, and it set off admirably the healthy tan of her face and the brown of her eyes.

The men were on their feet at once. The vicar was tall and slender, and his bow to Lady Mallinder was quick and vigorous, done as if for all his forty years he had by no means lost his eye for a woman's charm. Sir John did not bow at all, finding himself in a quandary. He had been alone in the garden, and in the heat his full-bottomed wig had been intolerable. He had pulled it off to show his close-cropped hair, and then he had discarded his long full-skirted coat, with the gilded buttons and enormous cuffs. It was lying on the grass beside him. So how could a man, without making himself ridiculous, bow even to his wife when he had lost his wig and was in waistcoat and shirt sleeves? He decided not to risk it, but to get back to business at once. That, he thought, offered a chance that the vicar would first make himself ridiculous, which would be vastly preferable.

'The vicar seems put out,' he said when they were

11

seated. 'He says it's Lammas and there's been a bonfire, and he fears his parish is turning pagan. At least, that's how I understand him.'

He sounded sardonic about it, and he might have had a sharp answer. But Lady Mallinder spoke quietly.

'A bonfire? Where, please?'

'Up yonder, on the moor.' The vicar turned at once, and answered her clearly. 'You'll know the ring of old stones our people call the Sisters?'

'Put there by druids, were they not?'

'They're older than that, and I think they're evil too. It's time they were rooted out and done away with.'

'Why?' asked Sir John. 'We don't know what they were for.'

'We might guess. Twelve stones in a circle, all tall and slender, and then, at the eastern side, just where the rising sun will strike, a different stone, long and flat and smooth. What would *that* be for?'

'Have their dinner on, I should think.'

'Dinner!' The word snapped back, and then the vicar controlled himself again. 'What sort of dinner? What kind of flesh, and how killed? What sort of rites were these, and to what gods were they offered?'

'I don't know, and nor do you. Nothing may have been offered at all, and they may have been only for dancing round.'

'Only!'

'Please!' Lady Mallinder intervened suddenly, as if she would keep the peace. 'Mr Loveday, were you not to tell us of a fire last night?'

'Indeed yes.' The vicar nodded as if he accepted the reminder. 'I was first told of it by my housekeeper. She had woken in the night, she said, and heard the clock strike two. Her window looks to the moor, and through it she saw what she called a patch of light, red and quavering. It got her from her bed to see more clearly,

12

and she had no doubt that it was a fire, and a big one. The moon was bright, lighting the whole sky, but she had still no doubt that it was a fire. She could see the flicker of the flames, so fiercely did it burn.'

'How far away?'

'She thought it was by the Sisters, which would be near three miles away.'

'Hmm!'

Sir John sounded as if he were reluctantly accepting this. Richard Loveday had come as vicar only six months ago. He had been fourteen years a widower, and he had brought his housekeeper to the parish with him, where she had become known as a woman of clear mind and good sense. What she had said about this fire might therefore be taken as true.

'All right.' Sir John seemed to concede the point. 'Three miles, then. But who made the fire?'

'I don't know. I did not learn of it till breakfast, or I'd have gone up at once to catch them at it. As it was, I could do no better than go up mid-morning.'

'In this sun? You must be tired?'

This was from Lady Mallinder, and she was looking at his long black coat, his black breeches and woollen stockings. He was keeping to his cloth despite the heat, and he certainly looked tired.

'It was necessary,' he said simply, and he spoke now to Sir John. 'The possibilities were all too plain. Lammas, you will remember, and the night of full moon also. If any of our people look to a horned god —'

'A what?'

'Say the devil, if you will. I do not know the difference.'

'Heaven help you! Do you babble of witches again?'

It was by no means the first time that this vicar had spoken of witches. He had come from Hertfordshire, where some three years ago a woman had been arraigned

13

of witchcraft and found guilty by a local jury. But this, in the year 1712, had been too much for the judge, who thought the whole thing a silly superstition. He had sent the matter to the Privy Council, and the woman had been released and sent home, where a neighbouring squire had given her a cottage and a trifle to live on. But it had soon appeared that even in 1712 there were still men of education who believed in witches, and a fierce war of pamphlets had quickly broken out. It had filled the newsletters and spread to the whole country, and Mr Loveday, from his Hertfordshire parsonage, had taken a prominent part in it, writing furious denunciations of witches and of all who now disbelieved in them. Nor had he changed his mind in his new parish, where he had more than once preached against witches, which Sir John had thought insufferably silly. Hence his impatience now, though he had perhaps not expressed it very courteously.

'I beg your pardon,' he said stiffly. 'But do you suggest all that, just because someone was fool enough to be out in the night to light a fire?'

'It was more than that.' The answer came crisp and firm. 'This morning I went at once to the Sisters, and the ashes of the fire were between the stones, all hot and quivering, with smoke wisps still rising. The stones form a circle, some thirty paces across, and the ash was in the centre. Further out, near the stones, the grass was bruised and trodden in a ring, right round the circle, and by feet that were doing more than walk, I could see some heel marks, dug deep as if there had been some capers and some leapings in the air. This had been a dance, a ring dance round the circle, time and again, and all done wildly, perhaps in a frenzy.'

'Oh?' Sir John was looking puzzled. 'By how many, do you think?'

'A score at least, if I may judge by some leavings of

14

food I found there — some gnawed bones, mutton and chicken, some crumbs of bread and a few apple cores. A meal, you see, after the dance, and perhaps at daybreak.'

'Very pleasant, if you think it's worth losing your sleep for. But I still don't see that it's evil.'

'There is something more. You will remember the flat stone at the east of the ring, call it table or altar or what you will?'

'I'll call it a stone. What of it?'

'You will find this odd.' For a moment the vicar paused, and his face seemed tighter. 'Round that stone a circle had been drawn, cut in the turf, and I thought it had been done with a knife. And at four points on that circle, the east and west, the north and south, some blobs of wax could be seen. Candles had been there and had guttered, the wax running down.'

'Oh?' Sir John sounded baffled. 'What for, if you please?'

'I don't know. But I have heard of magic circles, so called.'

'The devil you have!'

'Devil is perhaps the word. For on that flat stone I found a little patch of ash of charcoal, and from it came a scent, sweet and sickly, which I had certainly smelt before. You may find it in churches, of a certain sort. Incense, beyond a doubt.'

Sir John stared blankly at him, irritated because he could no longer brush this off as nothing. Then the wasp came suddenly back at him, humming round his head in a way he thought threatening. Again he drove it away, and for a moment that brought him to the peaceful garden, with its fragrance of flowers in the summer afternoon. But the vicar had other thoughts.

'I had not known that witches use incense,' he was saying, 'so that's something I've learned.'

'Witches?'

'Take, please, the whole of this together. Lammas, a day noted for sabbats. Then a gathering in the night, no doubt to meet the dawn, and done in that ancient circle, put there for rites we can only guess at. A fire in the moonlight, and a ring dance, wild and abandoned, with shadows flickering across the stones to turn excitement into frenzy. Above all, that altar stone, with a circle cut round it, and the charcoal on it, and the smoke and a scent of incense. It was indeed an altar last night, but what sort of rite was done? What ritual was this, and to whom performed?'

'There's no proof.'

Sir John answered stubbornly, knowing by now that there was more in this than he liked. He knew his country people, and he did not think they had much changed their minds about witchcraft, whatever the learned might think. Belief in it was too old and too deep rooted. There had been an outbreak of it in the parish fifty years ago when a woman had died, supposedly bewitched, and another had been hanged for it. There had been nothing since, as far as Sir John knew, but the grand-daughters of those women were now in the village, mothers themselves, and believing as fully in charms and spells and images. It was all there, waiting only for the moment, and Sir John stirred uneasily. He believed in none of these things, but the vicar might still be right that a meeting had been held and some sort of ritual gone through. It was very possible, if someone had found the knowledge and the force of character to arrange it and take the lead; and if it were so, Sir John could see some trouble coming.

He struck again at the hovering wasp, setting it buzzing angrily, and then he turned directly to the vicar.

'Why do you come to me with this?'

'Because you are a Justice of the Peace, the only one near to us.'

'What can I do as a Justice? You've not forgotten Jane Wenham?'

This was the Hertfordshire woman whose conviction and release had caused such a stir, and the vicar had certainly not forgotten her.

'I think her pardon an encouragement of evil,' he answered firmly, 'and without it these people might not have dared what they dared last night. But if a Justice cannot proceed on one charge he may sometimes proceed on another. Also, as the squire and the Lord of the Manor, you are heeded when you speak to people, and I've no doubt you could greatly discourage this madness.'

'At the moment I can't do even that. I don't know who these people are who were gnawing bones and burning incense. Can you name even one of them?'

'They were all gone when I reached the place.'

'Then we'll have to wait for it. I can't discourage anyone till I know who to discourage.'

'But—'

'You must keep your eyes open, and so will I. If nothing more happens, well and good. If it does, we'll hope to get a name or two. For the present, that's all.'

It seemed to be. There was silence, and the vicar's reluctant nod showed that he, too, could think of no more for the moment. The silence held till Lady Mallinder spoke again.

'If you were up there this morning, Mr Loveday, in this heat, you must be very tired by now.'

'But it had to be done. I did not think anyone else would go — to those stones.'

'With the name they have?' She met his eyes for a moment. 'But I don't think people fear them in the sunlight. It's at night they're said to be dangerous.'

'People were there last night none the less, and I'd like to know who persuaded them to it.'

'A feast and a dance could attract many in a summer night, and there may be no more to it than that. But I still think you should take some rest.'

'You are right in that, Lady Mallinder. I'll be better for an hour or two at home.'

He took his leave at once, and Sir John, not regretting this at all, went round the house, still without coat and wig, to see him on his way across the park. Then he went back to the garden and flopped into his chair.

'The man's mad,' he said tersely. 'There's a witch behind every tree. You remember how he gibbered about that Wenham case? Now he sees a whole coven of them, just because someone thought to have a fire and a dance.'

'At the Sisters? An odd place to choose. And what about incense and a circle in the turf? John, what do you make of it?'

'I don't like it. I'm not going to believe in witches, but most of our country folk know a wise woman who'll charm their warts and keep them from the evil eye. That's halfway to witchcraft, and this could make it the whole way.'

'So what will you do?'

'What *can* I do? I don't know the name of even one of them.'

'I think I do.' Jane, who had been following the talk with a bright-eyed interest, spoke suddenly and cheerfully. 'At least, it could have been.'

'It could what? What do *you* know about it?'

'It just might be.' She was not at all disconcerted by his stare, and she returned it brightly. 'I woke early this morning, and I heard the clock strike five. It was getting warm, and I thought I'd open my window.'

'Jane, you know very well that the night air is dangerous.'

18

'But it wasn't night. The sun was up, and it was a lovely morning.'

'I dare say it was. But go on.'

'I opened the window and I had a look out. And I saw someone walking past.'

'Who was it? At that hour?'

'Agnes Elton.'

'Who?'

'Agnes.' She pronounced it Annis, in the north-country style. 'Don't you know her? She's Aunt Sophie's parlour-maid at the Dower House.'

'That fair-haired girl with the blue eyes?'

'Deep blue.' Jane nodded cheerfully. 'I thought you'd have noticed her.'

'Don't be silly. And go on with this, please. What was she doing?'

'Just walking past, by the trees on the edge of the lawn. And I did wonder why, at that time of the morning.'

'You might well wonder. But —'

'But if she'd been at the Sisters and was walking home to the Dower House, this would be her nearest way. It would be her short cut, and she wouldn't expect to be seen — then.'

'No.' He was terse, but he seemed thoughtful now. 'It's only a guess she'd been to the Sisters.'

'Where else had she been? Was there anywhere else? And if she'd left about sunrise she'd have been here about when I saw her. So it might be a good guess.'

'And about what we could expect from your Aunt Sophie's—'

'Ouch!'

A shrill yelp from Jane cut him short. The hovering wasp, perhaps irritated already, had stung her neck as she attempted to brush it off, and there were some moments of confusion before she was taken by her mother to the still-room to have a salve applied. Sir John

19

got his breath back and settled in his chair to think this out. Sophie was his sister-in-law, and he had no high opinion of her. She was the widow of his younger brother, who had gone the way of so many younger sons, into the Army. That had been in 1685, at the age of seventeen. Five years later, under King William, his regiment had been sent to Ireland, and as a young lieutenant he had been in the battle of the Boyne in 1690. He had emerged unhurt, but a young brother-officer, Charles Bancroft, with whom he was in close friendship, had been wounded too badly for a quick return to England. He had been carried into Drogheda, and then to a house in Armagh, where he was given care and hospitality by an English settler who had long known his family. Here he had been joined by his sister Sophie, then a vivacious and attractive girl of twenty, who hurried from England to help in caring for him. To this house, also, came Kit Mallinder, who was still with his regiment, and he and Sophie had taken to each other at once. The end of it had been a precipitate marriage, to the great happiness of both of them and the great annoyance of brother John, who had heard of it only after it was done. He had heard also that the Bancrofts were a family of Whigs, whom a Mallinder should avoid, not marry. But it was done, and he had had to accept it and make the best of it.

He had certainly tried. The regiment had been sent to the Netherlands, and Kit had had to bring his Sophie to what had then been his father's house and leave her there. John had thus seen a good deal of her, and had found her little interested in country ways and works, or in anything but social diversions; and for these she was soon in much demand, whether her husband was away or not. She danced excellently, played a fine hand at cards, and was allowed to be the best horsewoman for miles around. In those same years Kit was seeing some hard service, the battles of Steinkirk and Landen and the siege and storming of Namur. But in 1697 had come the Treaty of Ryswick, and in the ruthless disbanding of the Army that had followed he had been one of the many officers who were retired on half pay and left to fend for themselves. For him this had not been difficult, since his father had now died and had left him enough to live on. From his brother John, who now had the estate, he had also the use of the Dower House, which was standing unused; and here, by the summer of 1698, he and his Sophie were living very gaily, making their house the social centre of the neighbourhood. They had done it for five happy years, until in 1703 Kit broke his neck while hunting. He had died instantly, and Sophie had been inconsolable. All meaning seemed to have gone out of life for her. She had lost all taste for gaiety, and had seemed to wish for nothing but to sit alone, brooding on it. Sir John and his wife had done their best, but with no success. She had stayed in the Dower House, seldom going out or asking anyone in, and acquiring, as the years went by, a worse and worse name for bad housekeeping, for a dirty and untidy house, undirected servants, and meals ill cooked and ill served. Sir John, hearing these tales, fulminated. It was the opposite of everything he found in his own house, and of everything he thought a properly brought up woman would see to in any house, and he thought it did no credit to his name. That was what mattered, for it was not to be denied that she did have his name. Whatever he might think of her, she was unquestionably Mrs Mallinder.

It was all in his mind as he sat now in the garden, waiting for Jane and her mother to return. If anyone's parlourmaid was so ill-disciplined as to go out in the middle of the night, it would be Sophie's parlourmaid. He had no doubt about that. And if it were allowed to go on, it would spread to the rest of Sophie's servants, and then there would be a scandal affecting the Dower House and the name of Mallinder. So it would have to be stopped. Sir John, however, had no wish to go himself to the Dower House to say so. He knew what it was like, arguing with Sophie.

He took the easy way, and he had it ready when the others came back to him,

'Jane,' he said briefly. 'You may now make yourself useful.'

'Me?' Jane, who had been ruefully rubbing her neck, looked surprised. 'What am I to do?'

'Go to the Dower House for me. Find your Aunt Sophie and tell her what you saw this morning. You know all about it, and you heard what the vicar said, so you know what to say if she asks any silly questions. Tell her from me that she's to put a stop to it, and quickly.'

'Ye-es.' Jane looked doubtful but not displeased. 'But suppose I can't see Aunt Sophie? She sometimes sleeps in the afternoons. Suppose it's Celia?'

'Ugh!'

This was another complication, and he had not wished to talk about it now. Celia was Sophie's niece and a newcomer to the Dower House. She had arrived only a few weeks ago, and Sir John, who saw little of the Dower House, did not yet know what to make of her.

'It might well be Celia,' said Jane calmly. 'Aunt Sophie doesn't like housekeeping, and she's told Celia to do it. Says she can work for her living.'

'Who told you that?'

'Celia. After church on Sunday. She said she was just starting it.'

'Then she hasn't got very far, if this is how she lets her servants behave. What the devil can *she* know about housekeeping, after an upbringing in an Irish Bog?'

2
Arcanus in Arcady

Jane set out cheerfully on her walk across the park. Her
father's dislike of Aunt Sophie meant little visiting
between the houses, and she had not been to the Dower
House since Celia had arrived. She knew her only from
a few politenesses in the churchyard on Sunday mornings, and she was quite willing to know her better. She
had thought Celia interesting, and this errand to the
Dower House might lead to some talk.

But that had to wait a little. Half-way across the park
she heard a gentle thump of hooves on the grass, and
when she turned she saw a docile country pad coming
lazily towards her carrying Tabitha Verey, daughter of
the late vicar. Jane came to the alert at once, ready for
anything.

'Jane, what are you doing here? Why walk the park
in this heat?'

That was in Tabitha's usual style, brisk and
authoritative, and with a general air of knowing best.
Jane took it calmly, and wondered if Tabitha could be
provoked into something amusing.

'Nothing much,' she said easily. 'Just a message to Aunt
Sophie. Our vicar's upset.'

'He would be. Is it this tale of doings round a bonfire?'

Jane nodded, not at all surprised that Tabitha knew
it already. Tabitha usually knew it already. Her father,
the late Charles Verey, had been vicar of the parish for

23

more than thirty years before his death a few months ago, and during his last years he had been a widower. In that time Tabitha had tried to fill her mother's place by doing all that would usually pertain to the vicar's wife, and when Mr Loveday had come as vicar, without a wife, she had seen no reason to change her ways. She was still, among much else, making what were almost parochial visits to the village folk, especially in times of sickness, taking them medicines and fruit, or perhaps more substantial contributions to a dinner. It may not have endeared her much to the vicar, whom she had not consulted about it, but to the village folk she was welcome. They knew her, and they liked her. She had grown up among them. She knew how to talk to them, and in return they would talk to her more freely than they would to most people. No one, therefore, was more likely than Tabitha to know what the village gossip was, and Jane was in no way surprised that she should know about the fire. There might, however, be some more, and Jane set herself to find out.

'Yes,' she answered cheerfully. 'But it's the doings round it that trouble the vicar. He thinks it's witches.'

'We haven't any witches. Our people have more sense.'

'The vicar thinks they haven't.'

'He hasn't any himself. What *were* these doings by the fire?'

'A dance, it seems, and then some eating and drinking.'

'Would anyone but the vicar scent a witch in that?'

'They'd enjoy it, I suppose?'

'Of course they would, and that may be what's upsetting him. Rejoice with them that do rejoice isn't his way at all. Sin and the devil are all he thinks of.'

Tabitha did not like the vicar. She followed her father in being Tory and High Church, and the new vicar was the opposite; and Tabitha, seeing him Sunday by Sunday in her father's place, now thought him everything a vicar ought not to be. But Tabitha was nearly thirty and still unmarried, which Jane thought a pity.

'But why the Dower House?' asked Tabitha sharply. 'What's it to do with them?'

'Oh, I saw Annis Elton.'

She explained it briefly, and Tabitha was as forthright as before.

'The little monkey!' she said. 'Going out at night like that. So I hope you succeed. No one has done yet.'

'In what?'

'Persuading Sophie Mallinder to order her house properly.'

'It may not be Aunt Sophie. I may get Celia.'

'Oh?' For a moment Tabitha looked thoughtful. 'What do you think of Celia?'

'I've only seen her at church.'

'So have I, except once when I called, and she wasn't very welcoming. So if you do learn more of her I'll be glad to hear it. Good luck to you.'

Tabitha, looking younger than her years, sat back for a moment, poised, confident, and very well turned out. Usually on her goings about the parish she wore country russets, old and comfortable, but today, perhaps as a concession to the heat, she had a riding habit of pale yellow taffeta with a black tricorne hat, exactly like a man's but smaller. It all suited her admirably, and Jane, taking in the details, thought that Tabitha always knew what she was doing. Even with her clothes, she always seemed to get things right.

Tabitha shook her bridle, and the pad went ambling off at his own easy speed. Jane, left on the scorching grass, felt the heat come suddenly back to her. She had forgotten it while she talked with Tabitha, but her only wish now was to get into the shade. She felt limp. Her clothes were sticking to her, and in the glare of the sun the wasp sting on her neck was throbbing and burning.

25

It grew worse as she went on, and when she came at last to the Dower House she felt her mouth dry and her head beginning to swim. The house faced south, and it seemed deserted, silent in the sun, its walls of the pale millstone grit flinging the light and heat back into her face as she plied the knocker. Then, sooner than she had expected at the Dower House, the door swung open to show Annis Elton, looking unwontedly trim and neat. She was crisp and polite when Jane, too limp now to be crisp about anything, asked vaguely for Mrs Mallinder.

'I think she's busy. She has a visitor,' was the surprising answer. 'But I'll ask Miss Bancroft.'

That, of course, meant Celia, and Jane, not much caring what Annis did, thankfully took a chair in the cool and shaded hall, where the walls were of small oak panels and a long-case clock ticked noisily. Annis disappeared, and Jane shut her eyes. She began to feel better, and when she looked up again she saw that the narrow table of oak, which she remembered as dull and grimy, was now clean and polished, and had a great bowl of white and fragrant roses. The panelling, too, had been cleaned and waxed, and some new curtains, blue and white, were drawn across the open windows to keep out the sun. Even the clock was different, with its case gleaming, its dial washed, and the blue and gold of its sky and moon looking fresh and new through the shining glass. Jane sat up, making sure that she was awake. Annis, too, had looked as if she had been washed and polished. So someone was certainly getting things in hand at the Dower House, and it could only be Celia — brought up in an Irish bog, as her father had said.

But that was not true, and Jane knew it was not. It was just one of the exaggerations he was apt to use when he was out of humour. Celia, in fact, was the daughter of Sophie's brother, the Charles Bancroft who had been wounded at the Boyne. He had never again been fit enough to rejoin the Army, but instead, since it was thought he might make a good settler, he had been offered a grant of land near Enniskillen. He had accepted it, and there, in 1692, when Sophie had married Kit Mallinder and gone with him to England, he had settled and made a home. It was remote indeed, and far from Dublin, but he had an English neighbour or two, and it had been excellent farmland, certainly not bog. What had followed was obscure, for his letters to Sophie had become shorter and fewer as time went by, but certainly he had married the daughter of another settler — though there were grounds for thinking that the girl had in fact been half Irish. But they married, and to them, in 1695, a girl had been born — Celia. Again the tale was vague, but Celia had herself told Jane that when she was ten years old her mother had died. All that Jane knew after that was that earlier in this present year Charles Bancroft had died too, and that someone had decided that Celia, who was still only nineteen, could not stay there alone. She had been uprooted forthwith and shipped over to England and her Aunt Sophie, and here she now was. Her upbringing had been in Ireland, but certainly not in a bog.

'Jane, what brings you here? Whatever it is, I'm glad to see you.'

The crisp pleasant voice cut into her thoughts and brought her to her feet. Celia had come quietly in, and was standing still and straight, looking positively cool in a clear pale green set off by a petticoat of golden yellow. It was unusual, and perhaps a contrast that few would have chosen, but for Celia it seemed exactly right. She was slim enough to seem tall, and her fair hair had a distinct tinge of red, not aggressive, but certainly there. Her young face had firm lines, as if she could stand up to trouble if she had to, but she was in no such mood at present. She looked friendly and welcoming.

'I'm sorry about Aunt Sophie,' she said cheerfully. 'She's in the garden with the vicar.'

'Who?' Jane had forgotten her manners in surprise.

'It's a little odd, I agree. I'd not have thought that either was the other's dream of heaven. Did I tell you I'm housekeeper now?'

'Yes.'

'It was put on me. But at least it's let me call the housekeeper's room my own, and I've told Annis to bring a dish of tea there. So come along.'

It was not quite the reception Jane had expected. It was not the Celia she had expected, and when they reached the housekeeper's room it was not the room she had expected. She remembered it from earlier days, a room of some size, looking to the side of the house, with only some odds and ends of old furniture, and offering no comfort. Now it had been transformed. It had rugs on the floor, a polished table, some cushioned chairs, and two oak presses against the wall, fitted with locks. The copper canopy over the hearth was bright and gleaming, and under it was a wide bowl of yellow sunflowers, bringing summer to where a fire would be in winter. On the table was a bowl of marigolds, ringed with blue forget-me-nots. But it was to the long low window, facing east to the garden, that the eye was drawn. A long window seat ran below it, of bright clean oak, gay with cushions in cream and blue. On one of these a cat was sleeping, stretched full length below the open window, with his head between his paws. He looked up sharply to see who was in the room, but Jane for the moment ignored him. She was looking above him, almost to the top of the window, to where a ball of shining glass was hanging from the ceiling in a fine silk net. It was perhaps six inches across, and the glass had been so treated that it had become a mirror, shining and gleaming and reflecting. It was bright enough now, in the afternoon, but in this eastward window it would have the morning sun to make it blaze and dazzle; and Jane, looking through the window, saw the distant moorland, and thought at once of the Lammas sunrise there, of smouldering ash — and of Annis Elton, who had so decorously opened the door for her. Then she looked again at the shining ball.

'What is it?' she asked impulsively.

'That?' For a moment Celia seemed to hesitate. 'Some people would tell you it protects from the evil eye.'

'How?'

'It reflects. So if the glance comes in at the window, that will throw it out again.'

'But please —'

'You don't have to believe it, Jane. It's just what some people say. At least it's good to look at, and it brightens the room. What's happened to your neck?'

The change of topic was abrupt, but it had to be accepted, and Jane was still explaining about the wasp when Annis came in with a teapot and cups. She was again quiet and proper as she set them on the table and tiptoed out of the room. Celia grasped the teapot thoughtfully.

'Bohea tea,' she said. 'I hope you like it?'

'We don't have it too often. It's too expensive.'

'You should know a good smuggler. Here you are. Now sit down, and I'll get you a salve for your neck.'

'I've had one.'

'You've had the sun on it since then, so I'll get you another. I'm good with salves. You can drink your tea while I get it.'

She went out, and Jane, left alone, savoured the excellent Bohea and tried to collect her thoughts, which were all of Celia. She was beginning to think there was something odd in Celia. She had grown and lived in the depths of Ireland, yet she seemed wholly English. Her speech was English, her manners English, and her housekeeping seemed to be the best of English. Her dress was impeccably English — except, perhaps, for her choice of colour. Green was called unlucky, and few women, whatever they might say about nonsense, would have worn it so distinctly. But Celia seemed to like strong colours, and Jane looked again at the flowers and the blue and white cushions. Then she saw that the cat had lifted his head and was watching her with a steady and unblinking stare. His eyes, she noticed, were yellow-green.

Celia came back with a jar of salve, and dabbed at Jane's neck with it. The effect was immediate. The throbbing and burning died away, and something like comfort returned. Jane gasped with relief.

'That's better,' she said. 'What *do* you make it of?'

'Pennyroyal and other herbs, and ashes from a fire of wood, all taken up in water. Let it stand in warmth till it's thick.'

'It sounds easy.'

'That depends on how you make it. You should pick your herbs and have your fire in the wane of the moon, and it's better if the moon may be with Mars, he sinking too.'

'But—'

'Didn't you know? If you would have a salve to make something grow less, you take the wane of the moon. For an increasing salve, take the waxing moon.'

'I've not heard that before.'

'Perhaps you wouldn't, in England. But I grew up in Ireland, where it's different. Now, Arcanus, are you waking up?'

She was speaking to the cat, who had come suddenly to his feet. He stretched forward, then arched his back, flopped to the floor, and came to Celia. He stood for a moment with his tail erect and the tip curling over,

30

and then he jumped, landing in her lap and settling there, purring as she rubbed his head. She was smiling as she turned to Jane.

'This is Arcanus,' she told her, 'and we're old friends. He came from Ireland with me, and *he* knows something too. More than you'd think.'

'Oh?'

Jane was beginning to think she liked Arcanus, but the mention of Ireland had started her thoughts again.

'I'll guess what you're thinking,' said Celia. 'Am I Irish or English?'

'I did wonder.'

'I'm both. I've had to be. We were deep in Ireland, in the heart of it. It wasn't a cabin in a bog, mind you. It was a pleasant house in good farmland, but the women who came in were Irish — and I saw a lot of them. I came to know them and talk with them. I learned from them, and you *can* learn in Ireland, whatever the English may think — though it won't be the things you'd learn in England. They learn from nature in Ireland, and they aren't in a hurry. They make mistakes of course, but there's something of truth in what they tell you.'

'I don't quite—'

'I'm sure you don't.' The brisk note came back to her. 'My father didn't wish me to learn too much of it. He liked the Irish, but he said he was English and he wanted me to be English too, and when I was eleven he sent me to Dublin to a boarding school. I think it was a good one, but it was meant for daughters of the English, and it was very English. It taught us English ways.'

'And English housekeeping?'

'Oh, you've noticed, have you?' She laughed outright. 'Yes, I did learn English housekeeping. We had to, and plenty of trouble it got us into, but I'm glad of it now. This aunt of mine had five servants in the house to see

31

to things, and they weren't doing one body's work between them. They are now, though.'

'Yes.' Jane looked round her and could believe it. 'But I've been sent here by my father to tell you of one of them.'

She explained it carefully, telling of Annis, and then of the vicar's vehement suspicions, backed by what he had found at the Sisters. Celia's young face tightened, but she listened intently, showing nothing of her thoughts. Then she spoke easily.

'She's a careless creature, Annis. But leave her to me, and I'll try to put some sense into her. Tell your father so. But this vicar of ours, what does he think was doing up there?'

It sounded as if she was coming to what mattered, and Jane had to grope for an answer.

'He talked about a fire, and chicken bones, and—'

'Oh, I'll believe all that. But what was it for? *Why* were they doing all this?'

'He talked about sacrifices and nameless rites, and he thought the flat stone was an altar, and—'

'Devil worship, I suppose, or some such nonsense. Has he learned nothing?' Celia was sharp, and then she relaxed and showed some signs of amusement. 'He's such a contradiction. He showed a good clear mind when he was up at the Sisters, putting the little signs together to see what had been done. And I suppose it took courage to go up there alone, believing what he believes, so we'll give him credit for that. But then the good sense leaves him, and as soon as he's down he's blathering as his grandfather would have done. Did he talk of witches?'

'Yes.'

'Devil worshippers, of course, and they'll all be muttering and cursing and then turning themselves into cats and hares to run about at night. He's a man who believes such tales, and that's the contradiction. Good sense at the

32

stones, and then such talk when he comes down here, and all from the same head. I can't put him together.'

Nor could Jane, and she did not much wish to. She was more interested in Celia, and she tried to turn the talk accordingly.

'What do *you* think happened at the stones?'

'Oh, pretty well what he said. A feast and a dance, and perhaps a little more.'

'Do you think it was evil?'

'Of course I don't. Would anyone worship a devil?'

'Then why were they doing it?'

'To enjoy themselves. And why not? Why shouldn't they play at times, even if it has to be at night? Have more tea.'

Jane sat baffled while Celia filled the cups again. It was not only the vicar who had disliked this tale of the night. Her father had thought it should be stopped, and her mother had seemed to agree. Yet Celia seemed quite unperturbed; and the thought occurred that her upbringing with Irish women might have had something to do with this. Jane looked steadily at her.

'Did you have things like this in Ireland?' she asked.

'Yes.'

'Oh!' It had been very terse and clear. 'Did you call them witches?'

'Not as this man meant it. Call them wise women. They were certainly too wise to worship devils. But they could do some odd things.'

'What sort of things?'

'Jane, I mustn't talk to you like this. I don't want to upset you.'

'You won't.'

'Then say I don't want to upset your father, because I'm quite sure he didn't send you for this kind of talk. I don't really know him, though. I've met him just once or twice, in the churchyard on Sundays, and when he's spoken to me he's been pretty short about it.'

33

'He's been short with everyone lately.'

'Any good cause?'

'Oh —' Jane pulled a wry face for a moment. 'I think perhaps it's politics. He's been growling every time he's had a newsletter. He doesn't like the King, he doesn't like the Government, and he doesn't like anything. He wants everything as it used to be.'

'He can't have it.'

'And he thinks the country's going to ruin, and the Church as well.'

'Poor man! Do *you* read the newsletters, Jane?'

'When he leaves them about. I'm not supposed to.'

'Then what in particular will bring us all to ruin?'

'I think it's these riots, and this new Riot Act. He keeps talking about them.'

'A good old Tory. High Church too, I suppose?'

It was not hard to understand. Almost all the Tories called themselves High Church, but what they really meant was that the Church of England was the Church by law established, and therefore a part of the State; and that all offices of the least importance in the State must therefore be held only by members of the Church of England. Otherwise, they said, the Church would be in danger. They thought the Toleration Act of King William pernicious, and in recent years they had worked up a great deal of popular feeling against it. The coming of King George, who was everything a High Church Tory was not, had been fuel to the fire, and when he had declared himself determined to keep the Toleration Act inviolate the unrest had turned into rioting. Throughout June there had been riots all over the country, the most dangerous being in Manchester, and the Government had become thoroughly alarmed. It had used troops to restore order, and had then rushed through Parliament a Riot Act which made it a felony to pull down buildings or to refuse to disperse when formally commanded to by a Justice. It had come into force this very day, Lammas, and it had been a main topic of political talk. Sir John, like others, had had a good deal to say about it.

'He's all fussed and heated,' said Jane. 'He says people will be so angry that the riots will be worse than ever, and it won't be safe to go anywhere. That's how he's talking, and I don't think he'll take me to London after all.'

'London?'

'Oh —' Jane sounded rueful. 'He was to take me there this winter. I've never been, and he says I'll not be properly accomplished till I have. He talked of a house for a month or two, and meeting people, and some balls and concerts of music, and the theatre for one of Mr Handel's operas.'

'And isn't he to take you?'

'He hasn't really said he won't, but he talks so much about riots, and nothing safe anywhere that I don't think he will. I wish I knew.'

'Ye-es.' Celia nodded sympathetically. 'You're disappointed. Who wouldn't be? But —' She looked searchingly at Jane, as if she wished to be sure of her. 'I might be able to tell you something, if this is a right hour. Have you finished your tea?'

'Yes, but—'

'Arcanus, you must wake up. There's work to do.'

Celia, half laughing, lifted him from her lap and put him gently on the floor, where he stood looking up at her indignantly and lazily waving his tail. She leaned forward and took into her hand the thin teacup that Jane had used, and for a moment she peered into it. Arcanus stood alert and still. Then he sank into his sitting position, with his tail curled round his legs and his head thrown back as he watched her every movement. She swirled the cup three times round, then quickly poured away the dregs of tea. Arcanus flicked the tip of his tail and Celia looked down at him, meeting his eyes. Then she turned to Jane.

35

'It doesn't always work,' she said. 'But I can sometimes see a picture in the tea-leaves.'

'I've heard of that.'

'I'm sure you have, even in England. And Arcanus can often help.'

'Arcanus?'

'Cats see more than we do, and they sometimes know more, so a cat can help if he will. Usually he won't, and that's why Arcanus is such a treasure. He nearly always will. Won't you, love?'

She leaned forward to rub his head, and Arcanus gave a momentary purr. Then he was quiet again, and Celia gave attention to the tea-leaves which were splashed all over the cup, a few at the bottom but more round the sides. Arcanus sat watching intently, his big yellow-green eyes unblinking and unwavering. Celia was as still as he, with both hands holding the cup.

'I see something now,' she said slowly. 'The leaves form pictures — if I'm seeing true, and don't imagine.'

She turned her head, glancing for an instant at Arcanus, and at once he flicked his tail and broke into a deep rich purr, strong and reassuring in the quiet room. Celia nodded, and was intent on the tea-leaves again.

'He approves,' she said quietly, and without taking her eyes from the cup, 'and he's telling me I may continue. But this is hard to read.' She had half shut her eyes, as if direct sight was not important now. 'There's something that keeps trying to look like a range of buildings, tall ones, perhaps even a church or two. It's fancy if you like, but that's what scrying is, and it can be true for all that. Is it?'

She flung her question at Arcanus, who had stopped his purr and was sitting intent and watchful. He reared up in response, putting his front feet on her knee and quivering with pleasure. Celia nodded.

'He says we're chiming together, and his sight's worth

three of mine. So this should be London. But it's at the bottom of the cup, which is far off things, so don't expect it just yet. You'll get it, Jane, but you'll have to wait a little.'

'Oh!'

'I'm afraid so, because here's another group at the side of the cup, right at the top, which is present things, and it looks—' Again her eyes half closed, as if she waited for what would rise within her. 'It looks like our moor here, with the stones and a winter sky. I'm afraid it's your winter, Jane.'

Arcanus jumped, landing neatly in her lap, standing for a moment and then settling down and curling comfortably. Ceila tickled his chest, and he rolled on his back, with his legs in the air.

'He likes this,' she said. 'But what he means is that there's no more for today. No more scrying, so there's probably no more to see, and you'll just have to accept it.'

Arcanus rolled back, curling himself again and giving a soft sleepy purr. Celia seemed about to speak, but she was interrupted. A quick knock sounded on the door, and Annis came in, showing her best manners as she stood demurely in front of Celia; which was not how Jane remembered her.

'The vicar's gone,' she announced, 'and Mrs Mallinder's asking for you.'

'Oh?' Celia did not sound very pleased. 'Very well, Annis.'

Annis slipped out of the room, and Celia gave something like a grunt.

'That's Aunt Sophie,' she declared. 'I take the whole management of the house off her hands, and do it better than she's ever done, and she hasn't a thing to do. So she fills her time by sending for me, in season and out, for anything or nothing. Mostly it's nothing, but I suppose I'll have to go to her.'

'Then I'd better leave you.'

'I don't know how long she'll keep me. But I hope I've been of some little help to you, in my odd way?'

'Oh yes. And thank you.'

Jane's thoughts had gone back to the divining with the tea-leaves, which was not what she would have expected from this brisk and cheerful Celia, who was so good a housekeeper. There was the cat too, Arcanus, which now seemed an odd name. It might mean something. She had said he saw things, and could help in divining. She talked to him, and he seemed to understand her, almost to answer her. He had come from Ireland, and Celia was from Ireland too. Jane remembered it suddenly, and for a moment the summer afternoon seemed to fade. It was Ireland, a dark little cottage room with the door shut tight, and Celia was sitting with Irish women, talking of secret things in the silence of a winter day. She had a kitten on her knee which they had given her with some whispered words, and he was purring softly while a peat fire smouldered and the sky was grey with rain.

Jane shook herself and tried to have some sense. But thoughts were running wildly, as if sense and nonsense were the same, and Arcanus had come close to her, watching her with eyes that seemed to understand. She lifted her head and tried to put it all into one confused question.

'Celia,' she asked impulsively. 'Do you believe in witches?'

Celia sat very still, and then nodded.

'Of course,' she said quietly. 'I am one.'

3
A Search for Loyalty

Jane, walking home across the park, thought she had an awkward problem. Was she to tell her father of that startling admission, or not? Celia would not have called herself a witch if she had not thought herself safe from the law, but neighbours had to be thought of too, and there could certainly be some trouble. Jane had no wish to be the agent in this. She liked Celia, and she thought that Celia might very well have supposed that they were talking confidentially, which was how Jane wished to think of it. So what was she to say? She had still not made up her mind about it when she got home.

But she was spared an immediate decision. Her father had a visitor, who was with him in the little room he liked to call his study. Jane asked questions, and was told he was Major Ansell. He had stayed at the vicarage years ago, when Jane had been only ten and Mr Verey had been the vicar, and he had been easy and friendly to everyone. So why had he come again? And what did he want?

That was just what her father had asked when he had been told of his visitor.

'What the devil!' he had said. 'I thought we'd seen the last of the fellow. Didn't someone say he'd quarrelled with Tabby?'

'That goes too far,' his wife had answered. 'We don't even know that he wanted Tabby. He was Charles's guest, you'll remember, not hers.'

'Not when he came the second time. Charles was dead, and that's when they say he fell out with Tabby.'

'Tabby can be difficult.'

Charles Verey had been Tabitha's brother, two years older than she, and when he talked of a life in the Army, Sir John had helped him to a pair of colours in a marching regiment. A few years later, when he had come home on leave, he had brought Jack Ansell with him, his friend and brother-officer, and everyone had thought the visit a success. They had certainly enlivened the neighbourhood. But in the next year, which had been 1708, Ansell had come again to the vicarage, this time alone and unhappy, to tell of the Battle of Oudenarde. Charles had been killed, and Tabitha had never quite got over it. Ansell had gone back to his regiment, and nothing had been heard of him since — till now. Which was why Sir John was puzzled.

'What's he come for?' he asked. 'If he wants anyone round here, it should be Tabby. Why isn't he with her?'

'Use some sense, please. Tabby's unmarried, and he can't lodge with her.'

'Oh, I see. Yes.' Sir John nodded and began to sound genial. 'I'd better go and talk to him.'

He went stumping off, and in his study he found his visitor standing by the open window, getting what air he could. He was not in uniform, and his brown coat, long cream waistcoat, russet breeches and dusty riding boots would have suited any man of affairs. Yet he did not look it, and he never would. He was a soldier who had served through the wars, the Schellenberg, Blenheim, Ramillies, Oudenarde and Malplaquet, a seasoned officer who had learned much about himself and others. He was wholly unassuming as he stood in the window, a quick smile of recognition coming to his face, but he could not now, whatever his dress, look anything but what he was.

'Ha, my boy! I'm glad to see you.' Sir John spoke in

his best bluff and hearty style. 'You'll stay for a while, I hope?'

'I'm afraid I can't, sir.'

'That's a pity. But a glass of wine, Jack? You'll need it, if you've been riding in this heat. And a chair too. Sit you down.'

He saw to the wine, then settled into his own chair and loosed a waistcoat button. He lifted his glass.

'Your good health, my boy!'

'Yours, sir.'

'Thank you. Now — er —' He paused, wondering how he could bring Tabby into this. 'Who do we drink to next?'

'The King, sir.'

'Oh yes. Very proper. But Jack — you don't mean this German, do you — this George?'

'I don't, sir.'

'That's well said.' Sir John nodded vigorously. 'So — our lawful King, God bless him!'

He meant James Francis Edward, who to the Whigs was either the Pretender or the Chevalier de St George. The tale that his birth had been spurious, that he had been a child carried into the royal bedroom in a warming pan, had died away, and almost everyone now allowed that he was indeed the lawful son of the late King James. But the Act of Settlement had reserved the royal inheritance for protestants, and had picked as the heir a cousin of King James, Sophia, who was as German as could be and was the wife of the Elector of Hanover. She had died, at the fine age of eighty-four, only two months before Queen Anne, and her son, who was already Elector of Hanover, had overnight become King George as well. He spoke no English, had no graces of any kind, and was heartily disliked by his new subjects. So between those who still believed in Divine Right, those who still had a sentiment for the House of Stuart, and those who

41

merely disliked King George, there were plenty who were willing to drink to the Chevalier. Sir John was one of them.

'Our lawful King!'

The glasses touched, clinked, and were drained to the end. Major Ansell was smiling.

'How is it among your neighbours, sir? The same good loyalties?'

'Oh yes. You could dine in any house round here and not see silver on the table.'

Ansell nodded, evidently seeing the point. In the Great Rebellion there had hardly been a gentlemen in western Lancashire who had not sent his silver, his spoons and beakers, jugs and dishes, to the King to be melted into money. But all that followed had been disaster, and though a receipt for silver, signed by a King, might now be a prized possession, it had no value in cash; and it had been hard enough to pay off mortgages and buy back land without replacing plate. Pewter had stayed on the tables.

'Aye, aye. So that's how it is, Jack. We don't apologize for our pewter, since that's how we had it. We're a loyal county, always have been, and please God we always shall be. Hmm!' This was one of Sir John's favourite sentiments, and he had produced a fine rich tone as he said it. Then he cleared his throat and tried to come to present matters. 'But we're glad you've remembered us, Jack, and come to see us. We'll make you welcome. And there'll be others too. Tabitha Verey for sure. You'll remember Tabby?'

'Indeed yes. But really, sir, it's a little awkward, because I've already met her. She was riding in your park as I came.'

'And why not? She's free of the park. What's awkward?'

'Tabby. She jumped at things. She thought I was here on her account, just to see her again, and it's not easy

42

to tell a woman that it isn't so. But truly, sir, I haven't leisure for her at this time. I mustn't linger.'

'Then what the devil did you come for? Why can't you linger? Leave ending, is it, and back to your regiment?'

'No.' Ansell spoke sharply. 'I haven't a regiment now. I've quit the Army.'

'You've what? But what's wrong, my boy? Not a wound, I hope?'

'Oh no. I've been lucky that way, luckier than many. But —' He paused, and then spoke firmly. 'I've had a doubt or two about loyalty. I think I gave an officer's loyalty to the Queen, but I couldn't quite forget, even then, that she had a brother who was by rights the heir.'

'Yes, yes. But we have to be practical, my boy. She was a very good Queen, and if she wasn't the first heir she was certainly the second.'

'That's what I told myself. And there was the Duke of Marlborough too. He led us always to victory, and he so cared for us and watched over us that the whole army had no thought but to do what he would have us do. It was loyalty to him, as much as to the Queen, that carried us along.'

'Aye, aye. A great captain.'

'The greatest in the world. But what have we now?' The tone became suddenly sharper. 'He's dismissed his command, and we don't know why. A dozen tales are told, but none thinks we have the truth. The Queen's gone too, and in her place we have this George, who is not of us at all. He knows nothing of us, so what can he care for our ways, and our laws and Church?'

'No, no.' Sir John nodded, finding this easier. It was a good Tory sentiment. 'He's no more than a dupe of the Whigs, and the country's going to the devil.'

'So perhaps are we, if we serve this George and deny our King, and that's why I quit the Army.'

'Well — that was right, I suppose.' Sir John was more

used to men who spoke loyal sentiments than men who acted on them. 'Yes, we must call it right. But what now, Jack? You'll have to make a whole new life for yourself.'

'But there's work to do first. Sir, do we speak in confidence?'

'We speak in wine, and that's enough.'

'Thank you.' Ansell looked steadily at him. 'Sir, I have news for you.'

'Oh?'

'One of my brother officers, selling out also, hastened to Bar-le-Duc, where the Chevalier had his court. He spoke his loyalty, offered his sword and service.'

'Honourable, I suppose.' Sir John hid a thought that it might have been foolish too. 'How was he received?'

'Graciously. He is now back in London, and he brought me news indeed. Sir, the swords are sharpening.'

'What — what the devil do you mean?'

'The Chevalier and his ministers had known a year ago, when the Queen died, that it was their moment, before this George had settled in. But what could be done? The Chevalier had no ships, no soldiers, and no money, and the King of France was too weak from war to offer anything.'

'Thanks to you and Marlborough.'

'True. But he has now had a time of peace. He has recovered something, and now he has promised help before the year is too late. A ship or two, and some money. So the Chevalier is making ready. His friends are flocking to him, the swords are sharpening — and in short, sir, we hope that before the summer is out he will be in Scotland with his standard raised, calling for his own again.'

'What!' Sir John stared blankly at him, not quite taking this in. 'Invasion, do you mean? Why Scotland?'

'Safer for landing. There's hardly a frigate in those waters. And quicker for raising men. The clans obey their chiefs, and you don't have to beat recruiting drums. We'll do that here, as we march.'

'Here?'

Sir John's tone was of less than rapture. Twice in the last century Scottish armies had marched through Lancashire, one to be stopped at Preston, the other at Worcester, and Lancashire had forgotten neither of them. The Scots, who had set out provided with almost nothing, had sought food, clothes, and horses in every house and village within miles of their march. Sir John struggled for words, knowing that his house was about six miles from the Preston road. To talk of loyalty and lift a glass to the Chevalier was one thing. It showed that a man was of good family and had his heart in the right place. An army on that road was another thing altogether.

'Certainly we must enlist men here,' said Ansell briskly. 'So great an enterprise is not to be managed by a few thousand Scots. They can give us a start, but that is all. Thousands more will be needed, and where should they be found but here, in this county of Lancaster? Is it not known for its loyalty?'

'Huh!'

Sir John stifled a hasty answer. Ansell must be badly out of touch if he thought it was as simple as that. Too long by the Danube, perhaps. Lancashire, in the main, was Tory and disgruntled, detesting alike the Whigs, the dissenters, the Government, and King George. There was plenty of seditious talk and drinking to the Chevalier. But Sir John, knowing his neighbours, could think of none who would welcome an army of Scots at his door, with their demands for carts and horses, food and forage. As for enlistment, they would think, one and all, that the county had done this twice, and it was someone else's turn this time. They would give politeness and a glass of wine to any Jacobite officer who might come to the door, and they would have reason after reason why they must stay at home. Sir John was sure of it; and again he wished he had not said so much about loyalty, or drunk that health to the Chevalier.

'Yes,' he said, and tried to speak heartily. 'I hope we'll ever be a loyal county. But it's a great matter, of course, not to be taken lightly, and in these days, when there's so much to think of, men would need a little time. Arrangements to be made, and so on.'

'I understand that, sir.'

'You spoke as if it would be a short warning, and I'm telling you that it mustn't be. Men need time.'

'The Chevalier understands that, and that is why I have come to you. I have his precise command to do so, in a Commission under his hand and seal.'

'What!'

'Just that, sir. I am here to *bring* you warning. I am to visit gentlemen known to be loyal, telling them the day is at hand and loyalty at test. It's swords and service that are needed now, their own, their sons', and their tenants', and I bring good warning, so that all may be planned and ready — and promised.'

Sir John sat aghast, all but speechless. This was not the visit of goodwill and kind remembrance he had thought it was. The man was a Jacobite agent, a determined one, who would not be easily put off. He was asking for promises; and Sir John twisted in his chair, wishing yet again that he had been less free with his loyal sentiments. The afternoon was too hot for this sort of thing.

'Are you expecting the whole county to rise?' he asked unhappily.

'Only those who are loyal, and of these I'm to call on as many as I can. And here's where I must ask your advice. I don't know who's loyal and who isn't, and if I open this to the wrong man and he turns against me, my mission's at an end. I'll be clapped into Lancaster, and as like as not hanged for it.'

'You'll be safe enough with most of them, all the papists and pretty well all others. Some men may ask you, though, whether the Chevalier is to change his Church. Indeed—' Sir John caught at his breath as he suddenly saw how he might escape with dignity. 'I'm going to ask you that myself.'

'His Church?' Ansell spoke slowly, and did not try to evade it. 'I hope indeed he will, but I haven't heard of it.'

'Then it's going to be difficult. We know whose son he is.'

'But—'

'It's twenty-seven years since his father took ship to France, and I doubt if you'd been breeched. But we'd four long years of King James, and it was one long persecution of the Church, with the Indulgence and the Dispensing Power and the Commission to oppress the clergy. Don't think we were disloyal. We were not. But desperation drove men against the King who were as loyal as their fathers had been. I was one of them.'

'To your honour, sir, in those days. But need we fear it again? We've a new King now, and he's spent those twenty-seven years in exile. He'll surely have learned something.'

'His father never learned anything. He was high and mighty to the end of his days, all threats and fury and lists of those he'd hang. Not a hint that he'd been unwise. And what sort of tutors will he have put about the boy in France? Priests and Jesuits, I suppose, and we can guess how they've filled his head.'

'I know, sir. But—'

'Arguing won't help. I'm telling you there's a doubt, and the doubt will hold men back. A man who's loyal in all his heart may say he won't ride out in arms to bring King James back again. There's a loyalty to the Church as well as to the King, and the one can be as deep as the other.'

Sir John had surprised himself. He had begun by merely seeking an escape, and he had ended in full sincerity. He could not in conscience give help to a Chevalier who was all too likely to be his father come again, and here was his reason for refusing; loyalty to the Church, and he must leave no doubt about it.

'Does this mean, sir, that you will not take sword for the King, even though he be here himself?'

'I hope I'm as loyal as my father was, but I will not turn from the Church. If the Chevalier will turn protestant, I'll join him as soon as any, but we must not have a papist King again. I've those four years to tell me what it means, and it will not come again by my doing.'

'I understand.' Ansell looked him in the eye. 'I'm of the Church of England too. You'll remember me in the church here when I was guest at the vicarage.'

'Of course I do. You and young Charles, who's dead, and Tabby sitting with you. And her father in scarf and surplice, reading the service for us.'

'Aye, sir.'

'But what the devil, Jack? If you feel that way for the Church, why come on an errand like this?'

'I promised it before I'd quite understood about the Chevalier. So now I must do my best, and hope. That's something I've grown used to, in war.' His face tightened for a moment, and then he forced a smile. 'I suppose I can expect the same answer from other men?'

'Some, perhaps. The papists can't say it, of course, and the protestants aren't all alike. The Church means more to some than to others.'

'But more to you?' The smile was easy now, not forced. 'I remember, those years ago, Tabby telling me how much you did to help, and how good you were to the vicar.'

'Ah, well —' Sir John sat back feeling pleased, and could

not help enlarging on this. 'Something's always needed in a church — a flute or a viol, say, or sheets of music, or bibles at a Confirmation — that sort of thing. I took it as a duty.'

'But help to the vicar—'

'Oh, that's a matter of supporting him, being friendly, letting the parish see that you are on his side. That's what counts.'

'And very well you did it, from what I was told. No doubt you still do.' Ansell came suddenly to his feet. 'I'll have to go, sir. I've other men to call on. But there's one small thing I'll ask of you, if I may? Have a word with Tabby for me. I couldn't tell her what I was really here for.'

'You'd have been safe enough if you had done. Tabby doesn't like King George. But leave her to me, and I'll make your peace.'

They went out of the house together. The horse was brought round and Ansell swung into the saddle. For a moment he stroked the horse's head, and then he looked down, half-smiling.

'My thanks that he's been cared for. And for kindness to me too.'

'I've disappointed you.'

'Half.' Again for a moment he stroked the horse. 'This talk of Tabby and her father makes me understand it better. The Church owes much to you and means much to you. So while the King is papist — yes, I understand. God keep you all.'

'Keep *you* even more, in the work you've promised. Make an end of it, please, and then come back to us. We all wish to see you. Even Tabby, perhaps.'

'Oh?' Again, for an instant, he fondled his horse. 'When I can I will. There's a peace in this place I haven't known for years. so be sure I'll come — when I can. Tell Tabby so.'

He went quietly away, not hurrying the horse, and Sir John stood watching, thankful for his understanding. It had been difficult, and it could have ended very differently, but again Sir John was thankful. It had cleared his mind, and shown him what he must do if another Jacobite should call. He was of the Church of England, its prop and support in the parish, and he could *not* give welcome to a popish King. That was what he must remember, and he felt a glow of satisfaction at the thought that it was not an excuse. It was entirely true.

He went slowly round the house, and in the garden he met Jane, looking as if she meant to have a word with him.

'I'm just back,' she told him.

'Where from?'

'Where you sent me. The Dower House.'

'Oh yes.'

He had wholly forgotten it. There had been something about witches and a fire at the stones, but Jack Ansell had put it out of his head. He tried to bring it back.

'Oh yes. The Dower House and Aunt Sophie. You saw some girl of hers—'

'Annis Elton. You sent me to say to Aunt—'

'You needn't keep telling me. What did Aunt Sophie say?'

'I didn't see her. It was Celia, and she said she'd deal with Annis.'

'I should hope so. Why couldn't you see Aunt Sophie?'

'She was talking to the vicar. Celia says he goes there, and Aunt Sophie makes him welcome.'

'The devil she does!'

He had gone into his thoughts again. Making the vicar welcome was what he should be doing himself, and was certainly not doing. A chill courtesy, blending into hostility, was the best he usually achieved, and it was not good enough. He was to be the prop and support of the Church, and he must come to better terms with the vicar, supporting him and letting everyone see he was supporting him. Then the thought came that this must now mean supporting him in this alarm of witches, little though he wished to. He did not believe in them. Still, he had promised the vicar he would try to discourage it, so he had better show some zeal at finding someone to discourage.

'I didn't think it would matter,' said Jane, 'not seeing Aunt Sophie. She wouldn't have known about Annis.'

'Who? Oh—'

The thought came at once. Annis had been at the fire, so he did know someone to discourage. She had probably not been important, but she could at least be asked what she had been doing there. Even the vicar would have to call it a beginning.

'I like Celia,' said Jane. 'I want to see more of her.'

'By all means.'

He was terse about it. He was thinking of witches, or women who thought they were witches, and he was not interested in Celia.

4
Justice in Pickle

Two days later Sir John announced at breakfast that he would be sitting as a Justice that morning; which was his way of saying that his family were to keep out of his study and not disturb these proceedings. He did not say who was to be brought before him, or why, so Jane found some duties at the front of the house. She liked to know.

It turned out to be Annis Elton, who was brought across the park by Jack Earnshaw, the elected constable for that year. A minute or two later the vicar arrived. Then, to Jane's surprise, came Celia, looking rather as if she had left home in a hurry. Jane, hearing her father's voice, kept prudently out of sight till all was quiet again. Then she found Celia standing by the shut door of the study.

'Celia, what is it? What's happened?'

'Annis.' Celia glanced at the door, and sounded angry. 'Earnshaw came for her suddenly and said he must take her. No warning given, or I shouldn't be looking like this.'

'It doesn't matter.'

'Doesn't it?' The answer snapped, and then she calmed herself. 'I'm sorry, Jane. It's from that affair on Monday, when you saw Annis in the morning. I'd not have thought it a crime, but if she's to be questioned about it I'd better be here too. She's in my service.'

'She seems to be,' said Jane carefully. 'Celia, I suppose

52

she *was* at the stones for that fire?'

'Of course she was.'

'And so were you. You've told me you're a witch, so I'll guess you commanded at that meeting. Did you?'

'Yes. Have you told your father?'

'Of course I haven't, and I wish now I hadn't told him of Annis.'

'Why shouldn't you? The girl was a fool showing herself like that. All the same, if she's in trouble I must help her if I can, but I'm not being allowed to. I'm sent out, on your father's orders.'

'He does sometimes see people in private.'

'Then what's the vicar doing in there? He's made welcome, and I'm shut out.'

'Oh, come away and I'll get you some tea.'

They had it in the parlour with the door left open, and Celia was on her feet the moment they heard voices in the hall. She hurried out, and Jane stood listening, knowing that she must not appear at such a moment. Instead she went to the window, and almost at once she saw Annis being marched across the park by the constable, with Celia close to her other side, perhaps in talk with her. Then the vicar came into sight, some way behind, and Jane took little notice of him. She was thinking only of Annis. If this walk with the constable meant the stocks, as it usually did, she was going to have an uncomfortable time, and she would need all the encouragement that Celia could give her. Jane considered some possibilities, and decided to make a neighbourly call on Tabitha Verey. This would take her through the village and across the green where the stocks were.

The weather was changing. It was still hot and sultry, but no longer with a blue sky and blazing sun. There was cloud everywhere, darker in the east and becoming murky, and as Jane came out of the house a wind puffed in her face, snatching at her hat and setting the dry dust swirling. Then it had gone, and the air was still again, but the signs were plain to anyone. The heat wave was coming to an end, and thunder clouds were rearing. Jane looked at the murk, and thought of her summer hat.

She came to the green and found that she had guessed right. Annis was already in the stocks, with the constable and Celia a few paces away. The usual crowd had gathered and there was no reason to think they would be hostile, but anyone in the stocks was reckoned to be an entertainment, and even from a friendly crowd Annis could expect to have a few things thrown at her. This should have started already, but everyone was quiet and orderly, and Jane wondered why.

She pushed forward, thinking that Annis was lucky to have dry ground to sit on, and then she saw that the mud by the stocks had been baked as hard as a rock, with all the lumps and ruts still in it. Annis, sitting helpless with her ankles a foot or more above the ground, would have been uncomfortable on any surface, but on those unyielding ridges she was already writhing painfully as she tried to find a better place to sit on. Celia seemed to be in argument with the constable, but she broke off as she saw Jane.

'Why's this?' asked Jane. 'What's she sitting for?'

'Being pert, from what Earnshaw says. She was sent for because of that fire, and she's admitted she danced there and ate a chicken leg. But they wanted to know who else was there, and she wouldn't tell them. She may also have given a pert answer or two, at any rate to the vicar, and perhaps that's why she's here. Teach her a lesson. No impudence.'

'Is it lawful?'

'What does that matter? You can't argue with a Justice. If he says stocks you're into them, and the constable must do as he's told.'

'I think he's a decent man, Jack Earnshaw.'

'If he'd go away I could slip a blanket under her. But he says he must keep an eye on the crowd, or they'd take to pelting her.'

'They might, for sport.'

'They won't quarrel with *me*.'

A moment later she had a chance to show what she meant. Half a dozen children squirmed through the crowd, clutching handfuls of wet and slimy weed they had pulled from a ditch. They dodged past everyone, and the first of them hurled his fistful of weed at Annis. It missed narrowly, and then Celia was in their way, directly in front of Annis. She looked at the crowd, and at once two women and a man came pushing forward to seize and slap their offspring. The rest of the children ran for safety, and then silence came again, broken by a low rumble of thunder. Jane glanced at the east, where the murk was ominously closer, and then her thoughts came back to this; and slowly they became clearer. Celia's junketings at the stones had probably been a huge success, wildly enjoyed by everyone. If, moreover, she had added to her feasting and dancing some sort of ceremony round that big flat stone, she could have passed the whole thing off as a rite of religion, and perhaps not a new religion. It might have been a very old one, and, with Celia leading it, a gay and exhilarating one. That Celia was a witch, and a very knowledgeable one, would therefore be known to everyone. It would be the common gossip, carefully hidden from the squire and the vicar and a few others, but the free talk of everyone else; and no one with any sense would quarrel with a witch. It was as simple as that, and Jane took another glance at Celia, wondering what she had indeed been up to in the Lammas dawn. A memory came of incense, and a circle cut in the turf.

'Jane, what's this? What's she done?'

Jane spun round to see Tabitha Verey standing next

to her. She gave a hurried explanation, and Tabitha looked dissatisfied.

'That fire again?' she said. 'Our vicar makes himself ridiculous. All the same—' She looked down at Annis, twisting helplessly in what was now more than discomfort. 'What's she in for? It's not a crime, is it, to watch a fire?'

'No,' said Celia. 'But there's talk that she was impudent.'

'I can believe it, of Annis, but I still didn't know it was a stocks offence.'

'Then perhaps Sir John let the vicar call the tune.'

'Nonsense. Sir John won't be guided by this witch-babbler.'

'You don't believe in witches?'

'Does anybody?'

'Yes.' Celia looked calmly at the crowd. 'About half these people do. And those that don't are not quite sure they don't.'

'Oh!' Tabby was sharp on it, and then her innate good sense took hold. 'I suppose it could be. Some of these folk haven't much in their heads.'

'Perhaps it will be put in.'

'What?' Again she was sharp, and again she turned thoughtful. 'I think you're right, Celia. This nonsense would drain out of them if it wasn't put back, but this fool of a man with his sermons and questions is putting it back every day, and—'

A flash of lightning, blazing across the sky, cut her short. The bang of thunder was deafening and ominously near. The crowd swayed and shifted, and mothers began to take some frightened children home. Tabitha looked again at Annis.

'How long's she in for?'

'Two hours. And it's long enough, with what's coming. She'll get a drenching.'

'She won't be the first, and it will at least be warm. Some have had it in the winter. Who's this?'

She had turned her head as a thick-set middle-aged man came hurrying across the green, as if he had only just learned what was going on. He was Joe Parker, the cobbler and clogger of the village, and known to be an awkward truculent fellow. His wife was hurrying after him, looking as if she was in pursuit.

'Is she a witch?' he bellowed. 'Is it true?'

He sounded so angry that startled women recoiled, giving him a lane to the stocks. He stopped a few paces from Annis, glaring furiously at her.

'Try this,' he shouted. 'Then get back to the devil and lick his breech.'

He grabbed a lump of mud, and hurled it viciously. It was hard as iron, heavy enough to have blinded her if it had hit an eye, and Annis flung herself flat as it went hurtling past her. Then the constable intervened.

'Stop that, Joe. No more of it. We don't want anyone hurt.'

'You speak for yourself, Jack Earnshaw. Some of us know about witches if you don't. I do, and my grandmother knew, by the time she—'

'Give over, Joe.' His wife clutched at his arm, trying to pull him round. 'Come home, will you?'

'Hold your tongue. If you folk don't know how she died, I'll tell you. I'll tell the lot of you. She—'

The sky seemed to explode. Lightning ripped across it from end to end, and the thunderclap deafened, rolling and reverberating to the moor and back. A woman shrieked, more children began crying, and were hurried away by their mothers. But some men stayed, and some women too, unwilling to miss so entertaining a quarrel. Joe Parker was standing his ground, and they wondered what he would say next.

It shocked all of them. Celia had now moved in front

of Annis, perhaps to protect her, and at sight of her Joe forgot Annis and his grandmother and all else too. He stood quivering, glaring wildly at Celia, and then he burst out.

'You?' he bellowed. 'She's sitting there for you, when she's just a whelp witch, and you the dam. That's what you are, the dam, a devil's hag with his marks all over you if we could see them for your fripperies. *You* taught her, you with your smoke and stink. You tell 'em they'll enjoy it, don't you, till you've got 'em in, and then it's the devil's—'

'Shut your mouth, will you? *Now* — till you find your manners. And find 'em quick.'

This was Earnshaw, striding furiously up to him, then grabbing his arms and shaking him. He looked as scandalized as he was angry, and faces showed that this was the general feeling. Witch or not, Celia was niece to Mrs Mallinder. She was therefore in the squire's family, and should be spoken to accordingly. They could say what they pleased behind her back, but not to her face, and they did not approve of this from Joe Parker. It was a question of manners, not of witches.

But Joe twisted round again with Earnshaw holding one arm and his wife pulling at the other.

'And your cat's out of hell like you,' he bawled. 'Black as sin, and you can see the devil in his eyes. *We* know what work you keep him for, you—'

Earnshaw jabbed him in the stomach, knocking the breath out and setting him to gasp and splutter. Celia had not moved. She was still in front of Annis, erect and silent, with her face tight and angry. Men went quickly to Earnshaw's help, grabbing Joe's arms and turning him away, and at that moment the lightning blazed again, jagged and blinding. Thunder detonated like a cannon shot, startling everyone and hurting ear-drums, and before hearing had returned the rain came down as a seething deluge. Houses disappeared in a mist of water, and the patter on the grass became a roar. The water was through their clothes before they had a chance of shelter, and it was too much for them. The lightning streaked again, and in the shattering thunder they ran for any house they could get to. Joe ran with the others, all thought of witches washed out of him, and Jane felt her arm clutched firmly.

'Come on,' said Tabitha. 'My house, quick. Run.'

Jane ran. Already the green was deserted, except for Annis in the stocks, and Celia, who had stayed with her and was sitting in a pool of squelching mud. Even the constable had dived into the alehouse, and no one minded where anyone was. Tabitha butted a knee into Jane to get her moving faster, and together they plunged into Tabitha's snug and comfortable house at the end of the village, both of them drenched and dripping. Tabitha was brisk about it, hurrying Jane upstairs and finding her some dry clothes, and then, in her parlour, there was hot spiced ale with nutmeg. They drank it by the window, staring at the sheets of rain and the flashes in the murk, and talking as best they could between bangs of thunder.

'Do you think it was true?' asked Tabitha abruptly. 'What Joe was saying about Celia making that fire and playing at witchery? Was it true?'

'It — it might be.'

'I think it is. I visit these people a good deal, and I've had a hint or two about Celia which I didn't believe. But I'm changing my mind. She's an odd creature, and I'm wondering what Ireland did to her.'

'I think she knew the women there.'

'I'm sure she did, and now she's putting it to use for her amusement. I can understand that she might need amusement, living with Sophie Mallinder in that gloomy house, and she might well think that a fire and some more tomfoolery would be liked. But she's found more than she expected. Jane—' Tabitha turned, putting her back to the seething rain and the vivid forks of lightning. 'Jane, did you understand why Joe was so upset?'

'Not really. What was he shouting about his grandmother?'

'Did you know we had witchcraft here in King Charles's days?'

'I've heard tales of it.'

'It must have been horrible, because that was when they all belived in it. There was nothing they wouldn't believe, and when a woman called Lizzie Bell took a fever and died, they remembered that she'd just quarrelled with Alice Openshaw. Alice was a widow. She was old, and lived alone, she walked with a stoop and muttered to herself, and she kept a cat and talked to it. She was everything a witch should be, and when Lizzie Bell died they were saying in no time that widow Alice had made an end of her with the help of the cat — the familiar, of course. I've never learned quite what their nonsense was, and it doesn't matter. What's certain is that the widow was charged with witchcraft and sent to Lancaster, where they hanged her for it. Then they hanged her cat as well, to make sure. The people did that here, on the green, by the stocks.'

'Oh!'

'You may well pull a face. But go back a minute. Lizzie Bell, who died, was Joe Parker's grandmother, the one he was raving about just now. He must have been brought up with it, and taught as soon as he could toddle that he must hate and curse all witches.'

'Oh dear!' Jane was beginning to see some possibilities, and Tabitha nodded.

'Exactly,' she said. 'And as a further detail, just to add sauce to it, this Annis who's in the stocks is a descendant of Alice Openshaw who was hanged. So she's the other side of the quarrel. It can happen like that, in a village.'

'Yes.' Jane was staring out of the window, seeing the rain still splashing down, though the thunder was moving away. 'But how about Annis now? She'll be sitting in water by this time.'

'That's part of the stocks. You get a stated time, and you take what weather comes. It's worse in winter.'

'I didn't know about Joe and his grandmother. Or Annis either. Nobody told me.'

'And nobody told Celia. That's the trouble.' The words came sharply. 'Celia's been too clever. Jane, do you think she started this witch nonsense?'

'I don't think she meant any harm.'

'Then it's what I've told you. She came from Ireland with her head stuffed with this trash, and she thought it would divert her to see a dozen silly women playing at witches. She knew nothing about us, and if she'd ever heard of Lizzie Bell and the widow she doesn't seem to have thought that they could have left any descendants. It's said that if you call the devil you get worse than you expect, and that's more or less what Celia's done — and got. So what will she do next? And what of your father?'

'Father?'

'Somebody's sure to tell him about Joe and what he shouted at Celia, so he'll soon know that one of his own family started all this. And he'll no doubt have the vicar frothing at him too, trying to make it worse. It's a pretty pickle for a Justice to be in. So what's his way out?'

5
The Witch-cat

That was what Sir John was soon asking. His troubles
began that same afternoon when the storm had drifted
away, leaving dripping trees and sodden grass, and Earnshaw came to the house to report that Annis had done her
two hours in the stocks. That was routine. But Earnshaw
went doggedly on to tell of Joe Parker and what he had
shouted, and this brought Sir John to boiling point.

'Is he from his mind?' he crackled. 'Gone all lunatic?'

'But he's like that, sir, is Joe. A bit crabbed, and always
has been.'

'It's his mouth I'm asking about, not his legs. Devil's
hag, did he say? To Miss Bancroft?'

'That's it, sir.' Earnshaw began to sound soothing. 'Of
course he was beside himself just then, about his grandmother.'

'Devil take his grandmother.'

'That's the trouble, sir. Joe thinks he did.'

'Did what?'

Took his grandmother. Joe believes in witches.'

'He can believe in boggarts too, if he likes.'

'Yes sir. But that's why he's upset. A man mightn't like
thinking the devil has his grandmother.'

'He can have Joe too, if he wants him.'

'Yes sir. But they did think Joe's grandmother was
bewitched, and there was a woman hanged for it too.
That's fact enough.'

'But why talk about it now?'

'Because Joe's brought it all back to them, and now they're taking sides about it — mostly against Joe.'

'Oh?' Sir John had understood at last that Earnshaw was trying to tell him something. 'Go on. Why against Joe?'

'It's the way of them, sir. Joe believes in witches, but he hates them too, and he's scared of them till he shakes. But most folk aren't like that. They half believe in witches, because they always have done, but they'll take a witch as they find her. They'll be careful, of course, because they wouldn't like her to turn nasty, but if they find her friendly they'll be friendly too. And I think that's how it is here.'

'Then now we come to the point. Who is it? Who do they find friendly?'

'Hard to be sure, sir. But it all came out of that fire the other night, and whatever they were doing round it. I don't quite make out what they *were* doing.'

'And it's time we did know. But who planned the fire? Who thought of it?'

'Till this summer, sir, I'd have said there wasn't anyone who could do it. But as we are now —' Earnshaw paused, and looked him straight in the eye. 'Putting it together as best I can, a bit I've heard here and a bit there, I'd say everything about that fire came from the Dower House.'

'Good God!' Sir John sat up and thumped the table. 'Who are you talking about, at the Dower House?'

'Of course, sir, there's more than one living there.'

'That girl Annis didn't plan a fire. Are you saying it's Miss Bancroft?'

Earnshaw made no answer. He stood silent, and that was answer enough. Sir John tried to speak, and achieved only a splutter. Celia was niece to Mrs Mallinder, and it was *his* Dower House. He tried to resist belief, but it forced itself upon him. She was from Ireland, where they surely had witches. There had been nothing of this until she came. She had stayed by the stocks with Annis, and—

'How about Joe, sir?' said Earnshaw cheerfully. 'What do we do with him?'

'Eh?' Sir John shook himself as he tried to get hold of this. 'You deal with him, Earnshaw. Tell him if we've any more insolence there'll be trouble of a sort he won't like, and I'll see he gets it. Make that plain to him.'

'I'll try, if he'll listen. But his mouth's bigger than his ears, and too much spit in it.'

'You're the constable. Deal with him, and don't make difficulties.'

He spoke briskly, like a man of decisive mind who knows what to do, and it at least got rid of Earnshaw. Then he sat back and tried to think this out. He could certainly not deal with it as a Justice. To charge Celia with witchcraft, in this year 1715, would be ridiculous. Besides, there was the family connection. The affair must be kept quiet, and he would have to deal as head of the family, pointing out to Celia the disgrace she would bring on them all if she went on like this. That should be enough, and he could say it with authority and a proper dignity. So he would send a note to her, written in family terms, asking her to come to see him at once.

But events moved differently. By six o'clock the last of the storm had gone, and they had as pleasant an evening as summer can bring, a blue sky, golden sunlight, and a soft westerly breeze. Sir John sat by the open window and wrote his note to Celia. He was just sanding it when he was told that Mrs Mallinder had called in and wished to see him, and he was so surprised that he spilled the sand. He did not remember when she had last come to his house. Then the explanation came to him. Someone must have told her what Celia had been

64

doing, and she had come to apologize for her niece. This was better, and Sir John sat back.

'Bring her in,' he said cheerfully, and hastily felt his wig to make sure that it was straight. He cleared his throat and pulled his waistcoat down.

She came sweeping in, not with the diffidence he had expected, a woman now of forty-five, who had by no means lost the poise and vivacity that had made her the wife of Kit Mallinder. Nor had she lost her good looks, as he quickly noted. With her deep gold hair, her blue eyes and white teeth, she had always taken the eye, especially the masculine eye, though Sir John had never given full approval. A pretty face and an empty head was what he had always said about Sophie, and he saw no reason now to change his mind. Still, it would be something if she had thought to apologize for Celia, and perhaps more than he would have expected of her.

'Sit down, Sophie,' he said gruffly, and waved her to a chair. 'It's good of you to remember me.'

'Not entirely.'

It was not quite the tone he had expected, and he glanced sharply at her. But she was untying the light cloak she had worn across the park, and pushing its folds aside to show a dress of cool ivory that was all simplicity. It made no attempt to take the eye. It was merely a background for her eyes and hair, but it fitted perfectly and she was wearing it with a confident ease. Sir John's surprise grew, and he was less sure than he had been.

'Not entirely?' He echoed it. 'Why not, pray? It's certainly good of you to remember me.'

'I had no choice this morning but to remember you. And I have come, sir, to hear your explanation.'

'What the—'

She ignored his splutter and calmly seated herself, flicking her cloak left and right so that she could sit in ease and dignity. Sir John stared blankly at her, not

65

understanding in the least. He dropped into his chair, and tried to get a grip of things.

'Sophie, what are you talking about? I don't understand you at all.'

'Then your understanding must be very poor. This morning, sir, your constable came to my house, being so ordered, as it seems, by you.'

'Oh, that? Yes, I see.' Sir John coughed, and began to think he did see. 'But that was necessary. As a Justice, and from what—'

'I dare say it was. I do not know of these things. But would it not have been proper that I should be told of this first — and not hear of it afterwards?'

'Eh? What? Weren't you?'

'I was not. Your man went straight to my kitchen, more or less seized my parlourmaid and took her away, making no attempt to see me or even send a message to me. I had to learn of it from Celia, whom my other servants told.'

'Oh!' Sir John was uncomfortably aware of the blunder. 'It's unfortunate. Not intended, Sophie. But—'

'Futhermore, sir, my parlourmaid, I am told, was put into the stocks, no doubt at your orders also.'

'Why yes. Only for an hour or two. She—'

'I said I was told of it, and so I was — by Celia. Would not the most ordinary courtesy have required that I be told of it by *you*? Annis is my parlourmaid, living in my house, and I am not even told, before or after. Do you show such discourtesy to others, pray, or only to me?'

Sir John sat speechless. This was the woman he had thought come to apologize, and now she had left him to make the apology himself. For he knew she was right. It had been a shocking discourtesy, which he would never have offered, even to Sophie, if he had not been so used to thinking of her as one who took no interest in her servants or anyone or anything else. But Sophie as he had known her would not have taken him up like this, or even have been dressed like this. She had become almost what she once had been, and he found himself asking what, or who, had changed her.

He was not given time to think of it. She flicked her cloak back over her knees and adjusted it for tying; and her way of doing it somehow suggested that she would waste no more time on a stupid man who could not answer a question. Sir John saw it, and with a deepening annoyance he knew there was nothing for it but to make his apology. He stumbled through it somehow, and she accepted it with the same air of superiority. Then, when she had at last gone, he was in trouble with his wife, who asked why he had not brought Sophie to see her.

That had been bad enough, but what came the next morning was even worse. Its sheer craziness defeated him. He had scarcely finished his breakfast when Earnshaw arrived again, this time looking ill at ease. Sir John asked what was wrong.

'It's Joe, sir. Joe again. He's had—' The constable hesitated, and then plunged at it. 'I'll call it an accident, sir. He's broke his leg and broke his nose, and his head's cracked too by the way he's talking.'

'What's the fool done?'

'It was last night, sir — or evening I should say, and Joe had his door open to let the sun come in. It's a bad stair in that house, sir, with oak treads, and they're pretty narrow.'

'Polished?'

'That's it, sir. His wife's that sort. Won't leave off. So you'll guess the rest of it, except for one thing. Joe was just starting down the stair when a cat came in by the door and looked up at him. A black one, and Joe didn't like it. It put him in mind of the devil. He could see the devil in its eyes, he says, and he was so scared of it — thinking it had come to get him — that he slipped.'

67

'On the stair?'

'Aye. Those polished treads, and his wife found him at the bottom. Of course he's in bed now, leg in splints and his nose a bit puffed.'

'I dare say it is. But people do fall down stairs, and I've known them scared of cats. So why come to *me* about this?'

'It's the way Joe's talking, sir, now he's had time to think about it. He's remembered how he went on at Miss Bancroft yesterday, and he knows she wouldn't like what he shouted at her, so what's in his head now is that she sent the cat to break his leg, or kill him if it could — she being a witch, of course.'

'What!' Sir John sat up angrily. 'Then he'd better stop this. I won't have it. Is it what you came to me about?'

'Not quite, sir,' Earnshaw stood hesitating for a moment. 'I don't think it matters much what Joe says. Everyone knows him. It's the way other folk are talking now, and that's the way you'd guess. Miss Bancroft *must* be a witch, and a pretty strong one too. She's just shown what she can do if you cross her, so you'd better keep right sides with her. That's how they're talking.'

'What damned nonsense!'

'Yes sir. Of course she does have a cat, and a black one too, and I did think its eyes are a bit odd. A sort of golden yellow, and they stare at you.'

'Damnation, Earnshaw! You're not telling me that you—'

'Oh no, sir. Not me. I was just saying how folk are talking.'

'Why shouldn't she have a cat if she likes the things? *Was* it Miss Bancroft's cat?'

'That's what Joe says, but I don't know that it's true.'

He stopped as a tap came on the door. Jane appeared and said that the vicar had come and was asking urgently to see Sir John. What was she to do? Sir John stared at her and then at the ceiling, having no doubt that the vicar would be worse than Earnshaw. He grunted, and told her to bring the man in.

Jane brought him in, carefully shutting the door behind him and leaving herself inside. Then she slipped quietly into a corner, hoping that she would not be noticed.

The vicar had no trace of a smile for anyone. He took the proffered chair and he looked grim. Then he began the tale that Earnshaw had told already, and Sir John soon stopped him.

'I've heard enough about this cat,' he said. 'Are *you* saying it was the devil?'

'Devil?' The vicar answered carefully, as if he wished to get the right word. 'Not quite. Parker said so, I believe, and in the main he has a proper view of these matters. But I think he is wrong in that detail.'

'That's a relief, and I hope you told him not to be a fool?'

'I don't say he's a fool. I merely say he errs in a detail. He has not studied the details of witchcraft.'

'And you have?'

'Exactly. And I therefore cannot doubt the malignance of that cat, or that Parker was right in supposing the devil to be involved. But I do not think the devil was in the cat. It was the witch who would be in the cat. Or, more precisely, the witch *was* the cat. Or the cat was the witch.'

'What — what in heaven's name do you mean?'

'It's hardly in heaven's name. However —' Again he seemed to be seeking the right word. 'There is no doubt that a witch may from time to time transform herself into the shape of an animal. Many witches have owned to doing this. And I tell you, sir, that in all probability this seeming cat that entered the house of Joe Parker was in reality —'

'What!' Sir John was staring at him in sheer incredulity. 'Are you saying that this witch — you mean Celia Bancroft, I suppose?'

'I fear so, most unhappily.'

'Then you are saying that Celia is a cat?'

'Of course not — usually. But from time to time, by these hellish arts that are all too real, she may assume the shape—'

'Don't be so daft!'

Sir John exploded at him, and then sat silent, trying to understand how the man could talk such nonsense. It was beyond Sir John, and he had made nothing of it when the vicar spoke again.

'I'm sorry you should take it so. But I do assure you that shape shifting is not new. It is as old, no doubt, as the devil. And it is not always the witch who is transformed. She may instead transform another, as with a boy in Pendle Forest, who had a bridle cast round his neck, and was by that transformed into a horse, and in that shape ridden by the witch on her way to—'

'I'll not listen to this moonshine blather.' Sir John banged his fist on the table, and decided that the man must be clean out of any mind he had ever had. 'A grown woman turning to a cat! And back again, I suppose? Use your common sense, man.'

'Sir, this is not over-courteous.'

'I dare say it isn't, but I can't help that. Think what you're saying, and try to put some sense into it.'

'Very well.' The vicar sat for a moment with lips pressed tight, and then he rose to his feet. 'I hope you'll soon change your mind. And I much fear you'll have cause to.'

He turned to the door, and Jane left her corner and saw him from the house. She returned to find Earnshaw speaking in his slow and deliberate way.

'No sir,' he was saying. 'Joe just said the devil was in the cat. This about Miss Bancroft turning to a cat, that's the vicar himself.'

'What about folk in general? Will they believe it, or is it too crazy for them?'

'I wouldn't like to say, sir. They're sure enough that Miss Bancroft is a witch, and—'

'It's plain damned nonsense, and they'll have to be told so.'

'Yes sir. I'm not sure they'd take much heed of me, though, in a matter like that.'

'Why not?'

'It — it might come better from you, sir.'

'Me?' Sir John viewed it with distaste. 'No, I can't do that, Earnshaw. I'm supposed to support the vicar, uphold the Church and so on, and I can't go round saying that he's too daft to listen to. He is, but I mustn't say so, and we'll have to think of someone else.'

He looked vaguely round the room, as if hoping to see someone, and he saw Jane, who was still standing by the door, listening with interest. She did not wait to be ordered out, but came forward at once.

'Think of Tabitha,' she said easily.

'Tabby? What the devil for?'

'They listen to her in the village, and they might listen to her about witches.'

'Eh?' He stopped, hanging in thought for a moment, and then his tone changed. 'I think they might. What do you think, Earnshaw?'

'I think they would.' The constable sounded emphatic. 'They think a lot of Miss Verey. She's in and out of their houses all the time, this new vicar not having a wife, and they do think well of her. So—'

'*She* doesn't believe in witches, I suppose?'

'No sir. She's said a few things already.'

'Then she can say a few more, and I hope they listen to her.'

'Yes sir. Though they might listen more to Miss Bancroft.'

'I'll deal with Miss Bancroft. She's going to hear a few words from me that she won't like. Now then —' He sounded very firm and decisive. 'Jane, you've suggested this, so now you can give some help with it. Don't argue. Go to the Dower House and tell Celia she's to come here some time today. Make it clear that I expect her. When you've done that, go in search of Tabby and tell her the same but more politely. I'd be glad if she could — that sort of thing. You understand?'

'Yes.' She answered brightly, thinking that this might be even more interesting. 'I'll go at once.'

6
Sophie Resurgent

Jane set out carrying the bundle of clothes she had come home in after the thunderstorm. They ought to be returned to Tabitha, so she passed the Dower House and went on through the village, which was now quiet and orderly, with children playing on the green and a woman or two washing clothes in the brook. She even had a glimpse of Joe Parker's empty workshop, and she wondered when he would be cobbling shoes again.

Tabitha was ready to go out, but she put that aside and offered a pleasant welcome. Jane delivered her message, and went on to explain what lay behind it. Tabitha listened with incredulity.

'It's not possible,' she snapped. 'I can't believe it.'

'I don't think anyone believes it except Joe.'

'Joe's village born and he's never been out of the place. He's never learned anything except how to stitch shoes, and he has this family tale as well. So he's still in his grandmother's day, when they believed in the devil possessing cats. We can excuse Joe, but what can we say of the vicar? He's of education and good learning, and in some things he's of good sense too, but as soon as he scents a witch he's crazier than Joe. He's not content with just the devil in the cat. He says it's Celia who turns into a cat and then back to Celia, and *he* is the educated man. That's what I can't understand. It's two minds in the same head. What does your father think of it?'

'Much what you do.'

'That's a relief. Tell him, please, that I'll certainly call on him, and I'll certainly do what I can in the village to make an end of this nonsense. As for Celia, she seems to have loosed all this on a peaceful village just for her entertainment, and if that isn't plain stupid it's downright selfish. I don't know which to say.'

But half an hour later, when Jane was at the Dower House, she began to think that Tabitha, for all her forthright good sense, had not yet got the full measure of Celia, who was in the kitchen when Jane arrived and looked anything but a witch. She made no difficulty about leaving it, and she brushed Jane's apologies aside.

'It's no matter,' she said easily. 'They can manage without me for a while, and they'll hear about it if they don't. I'm glad to see you. Annis, a dish of tea to my room.'

Annis went limping away, and Jane turned to Celia.

'How is she? She's not walking well.'

'You wouldn't, if you'd been in the stocks with the mud as hard as that. She can't sit down, and the others keep laughing at her. But I've been rubbing a salve into her, and she'll be all right in a day or two.'

'Poor Annis!'

'Poor nothing. I've told her it was her own fault for letting herself be seen. Really, though, she's done well. She didn't tell them anything, and I'm pleased with her. I've told her that too. Now come along.'

She led to her own comfortable room, and it was not as it had been in the afternoon. This was morning, and sunlight was flooding through the long eastward window, giving a glow and sparkle to the room, and making the most of Celia's strong colours. Yet Jane hardly looked at anything but the silvered ball that hung above the window seat. It was in full sun now, sparkling and dazzling, swaying and turning in the breeze from

74

the open window, giving a pattern of dancing light on the walls and ceiling. Jane stood staring.

'Don't,' said Celia. 'It will hurt your eyes.'

'It does.' Jane blinked, and made herself look away. 'Did you say it was for the evil eye? To keep it out?'

'I said some people would tell you so.'

'Meaning that you don't?'

'Not really. And it can be soothing, in a dim light. It takes your eye, and gives you something to look at. You go on looking at it, and you forget the thoughts that trouble you. It can make you quite sleepy.'

'Oh?'

'*You* don't need it, Jane, so forget about it. How are things this morning?'

She had suddenly turned brisk, and Jane had to deliver her message. She put it as politely as she could, but it was still a summons to the Manor House, and Celia raised an eyebrow.

'What's this about?' she asked. 'Joe Parker and his troubles?'

'You know about them?'

'Of course I do.'

Annis tapped at the door and came in with the tea, carefully and uncomfortably. She went out, and Celia turned to the teapot.

'Joe's broken his leg,' she said carefully, 'and he thinks I did it. I sent a cat and the devil was in the cat. Is that right?'

'Yes, for Joe. But the vicar says *you* were the cat.'

Jane explained it, and Celia sat very still and quiet. She took time for thought before she spoke.

'It's going to be difficult,' she said at length. 'Of course I didn't do any of these things, and I hope you didn't think I did. I'm not malicious.'

'I'm sure you aren't. It's only Joe—'

'And the vicar. They're in the last century, those two, and all witches are wicked and more or less mad. And

75

perhaps they *were*, in the old days. Think how they were treated — cursed and kicked by everyone, beaten, swum in ponds, pricked with pins, and on the least excuse hanged while a crowd hooted and pelted filth at them. It was every hand against them, and not a gleam of mercy or understanding. Do you wonder they turned near mad, and hit back, blindly and anyhow, if they thought they could?'

'Oh! I hadn't thought of it like that.'

'No one ever has.' Celia stopped, and seemed to steady herself. 'But it's different now, Jane. The law has had enough of it, as your father plainly knows. We shan't be hanged now, and I don't think a witch will ever be swum or pricked again.'

'Joe Parker would do it.'

'But there aren't many of him, so we're fairly safe. What Annis had yesterday is about the worst any of us can expect, and that won't happen often. So we can be our proper selves now, thank God!'

'That's—' Jane stopped, all perplexed again. 'Celia, does a witch thank God?'

'This one does, and it's something I'm trying to teach my people. Most of them are plain heathen, even if they do go to church on Sundays. But I was telling you, Jane, that I did *not* send a cat to Joe Parker. What do you think would happen if you told a cat to go to anybody? How much notice do you think he'd take? As for this notion that I turned myself into a cat, I can't understand how even the vicar can believe it. But he does, and it's going to make trouble.'

A soft thud came from the window. Arcanus had jumped from the garden and was standing on the sill, arching his back and looking querulously at Celia. She laughed softly.

'He's heard us talking,' she explained, 'and he's come to see who it is. He likes to know things. Come along, then.'

Arcanus flopped down to the window seat and lazily stretched himself. Then he gathered himself up, stood swaying for a moment while he judged his distance, and took his leap. He landed neatly on Celia's lap, and at once rolled on his back, inviting attention. She laughed as she rubbed his chest.

'Soft old thing,' she said happily. 'Imagine him scaring Joe!'

'You don't mean it was Arcanus who—'

'Of course it wasn't. I don't think he goes so far, and anyway he was in the garden with me. But Joe seems to say it was Arcanus, so I expect he'll get half of the blame. I'll get the other half.'

Arcanus looked up at her, purring noisily, and she tickled his chin. Then she turned again to Jane.

'I don't like it,' she said slowly, 'and I know I've made mistakes. I let Annis go home as she pleased that morning, though I knew she was a careless creature. And I never even thought that the woman who was hanged could have left descendants, and that they'd still be here. It was downright silly of me, and I'll have to do better. What does your father want me for?'

'He didn't tell me.'

'It's an easy guess. First of all I'll get the rough side of his tongue, and when he's finished with me that way he's as like as not to expect a promise that I won't have any more fires, or do anything else for these people. And that's just what I can't give.'

'But why?'

'Why?' It was on a note of surprise. 'Jane, why do you think I'm doing this?'

'It's a diversion, isn't it? You find it pleasing?'

'But hardly a diversion. Didn't I say that these people are pretty well heathen, and I'm trying to teach them? They should have something better, and they need it too.'

'Better than what?'

'This reverend man with his talk of sin and misery and the devil always after them. They try not to believe it, or anything else he says, and that's how they're becoming heathen. And that's why I'm trying to teach them better. Any witch would, if she's been properly taught and isn't in fear of being hanged each day.'

'But—' Jane felt baffled, wondering yet again what Celia really was. 'What *do* you tell them?'

'That they can forget this dismal talk, that there *is* a God, who wishes his people to be happy and bless his name, and has given them the means to do it.'

'But, please—'

'I mustn't talk to you like this, Jane. All I'm really telling you is that I'm not doing this as a diversion, whatever people think. I'm not saying I don't enjoy it, because I do, but I'm still doing it because I must. And that's why I can't promise to give it up, however pressed I am to do so. When does your father want me?'

'Soon, I think.'

'Then I suppose I'll have to. I must look into the kitchen again, and then I'll make ready. Tell him, please, that I'll be across in about an hour's time.'

Jane could make no sense of this as she walked home. It fitted very badly with everything she had ever heard about witches. But so did Celia. Then the thought occurred that a God who wished people to be happy might have fitted very well into whatever had been done round the fire at the stones. Everyone had been very happy.

Tabitha was already with Sir John when Jane returned, and their talk must have been going easily. She left within a few minutes, and he sounded very cordial and friendly as he went to the door with her. Then Celia arrived, and this was different. She was more than half an hour with him, and he sounded anything but cordial as he saw her away. Jane kept out of sight, but later, from the talk at dinner, she gathered that Celia had apologized politely for causing such trouble in the village, and had promised to be more careful in future. Which had not satisfied Sir John at all. He wanted a clear promise that she would drop this witchcraft nonsense altogether and have no more of it, and this she firmly had refused to give. Sir John growled about her at dinner, and it was plain that he was surprised and annoyed. He was the Justice and the squire, and he was not used to people who would not do what he told them to do. Jane wondered what would come next.

It came the next morning in a letter brought from the Dower House by Annis. She gave it to Jane who took it to her father. He ripped it open and then stared at it as if he could not properly take it in. He ended by going to his wife, and Jane carefully went with him.

'Read that,' he snapped. 'What the devil does she take us for?'

'Who?' His wife stayed calm as she took the note. 'Who's it from?'

'That damned woman at the Dower House. She's madder than I thought she was.'

'Then I'd better read it.'

To Jane's relief she read it aloud. It was from Celia, who in polite and friendly terms, and 'at the wish of my aunt Sophie', asked that Sir John, with his wife and Jane, should go to the Dower House on Sunday, for dinner at two o'clock.

'Excellent,' said Lady Mallinder. 'And high time too. It's years since we dined at the Dower House.'

'It can be more years yet, after the way that girl's behaving.'

'Celia?' She looked at him carefully. 'The invitation is from Sophie, and she's your sister-in-law.'

'Then I wish she'd remember it. By the way she spoke to me the other night—'

'You told me of it. And now it's Celia. You've fallen out with both of them, it seems.'

'I've fallen out with nobody. I've only—'

'They've asked us to dinner, which can only mean they wish to make their peace. It's an olive branch, and you'll have to take hold of it.'

'They can't ask us to dinner after—'

'They have done. So you'll have to accept.'

'I'll not dine with Celia.'

'What's wrong with her? Do you think she'll poison the gravy?'

'If she does, she can drink it. I don't care if—'

'John, we must accept, even if it's a little difficult. We've hardly seen Sophie for years, and this is a chance to mend all that. And your troubles may be mended too, for they'd hardly have asked us if they hadn't wished for peace. So you'd better write a note at once, and Jane can take it over.'

'I'll not write to Celia.'

'Of course not. You must write to Sophie. But go we must. Besides—' She hesitated, and then spoilt it a little. 'I'd like to see what Celia's done to that house.'

In the end she had her way. Sir John growled and grumbled, but he wrote the note and told Jane to deliver it. Being still in his awkward mood he added that she was to give it to Aunt Sophie, and on no account to Celia.

Annis, looking recovered, received Jane politely and said that Mrs Mallinder was in the drawing-room. This was in the front of the house, and it had begun as the big parlour. It had become the drawing-room when Sophie and her husband had re-panelled and re-furnished it for their parties and social gaieties. Sophie, sitting alone in the window at a delicate writing table of glowing walnut, was now writing a letter, and she had drawn one of the damask curtains to keep the dazzle of the sun from the whiteness of the paper. Her pen gave a loud scratch as she flung it down and pushed back her chair.

'Ah, Jane!' She had an air of relief, as if this was much better than writing letters. 'You're a surprise after all these years. I'm glad you're here again.'

'Thank you, dear Aunt. I'm glad to be here.'

'Annis, a chair for Miss Mallinder. Now sit down properly and be at ease. What brings you?'

'I've a letter for you, from my father.'

'Oh, that?' She had evidently guessed it. 'What does he say, I wonder?'

She broke the wafer and read quickly. Then she nodded.

'That's good, though I must say he sounds a bit stiff. Was he surprised at being invited?'

'Yes,' said Jane briefly.

'Poor man! He's always a little behind what's going on.' Sophie rippled with amusement, and looked very attractive as she did it. Then the amusement faded, and she spoke quietly, with a touch of hesitation.

'It's been my fault,' she said slowly. 'I've shut myself up since I lost Kit, and I've lived in myself, and my memories. It was silly of me to do it for so long. But then I was told of Celia, and asked if I would have her here, and I knew I must. I had to give her a proper welcome, but it wasn't easy after so long, and when she arrived I was so muddled that I don't wonder she was exasperated, especially with what she found in the house. But she was really splendid, and her company was just what I needed. So everything's all right now, and we get along excellently, she and I.'

'I'm so glad.'

'Yes. You seem to like Celia?'

'I do.'

'She likes you, which is fortunate. You're almost of an age, and she needs someone, with all the trouble she's run into. I'm afraid that's getting difficult, and it's why I'm asking you all here on Sunday. Wine and a pleasant meal can ease hard feelings, as I remember from the old

81

days. It wasn't strange to us then to give a dinner here. But this won't do.' Her tone sharpened abruptly. 'I'm talking of those days, and I mustn't. I must live in these days now.'

'I'm sure we shall all be glad.'

'Tactfully answered, Jane.' The smile came again for a moment, and seemed to be of amusement. 'But talking to me won't be what you've come for. Do you want Celia?'

'Yes, really.'

'Go and find her. She went up the garden to cut flowers, so you may look there first.'

Jane had been finding it difficult, not yet knowing how to talk to this new Aunt Sophie, or even what answers to make, and she seized on the chance to get away. She made her best curtsey and slipped out of the room. There was a side-door, she remembered, by which she could reach the garden.

Celia, basket in one hand and scissors in the other, had finished cutting her flowers and was standing by the rose border looking at Arcanus, who was sitting on the grass looking at the border. He came to his feet as Jane approached, lifting his tail and watching suspiciously till he decided that he knew her. Then he sat again, and Celia laughed.

'He's keeping an eye on me,' she explained. 'He says you never know with mice, and I'll be safer if he's about. But has your father had my letter?'

'He certainly has, and I've brought an answer.'

She explained about it, telling what he had really said, and what Aunt Sophie had said. Celia took the last point first.

'Yes,' she said thoughtfully, 'and I don't wonder you're a little puzzled. I'll admit I prodded her into life. I had to, if she was to be fit to live with at all, but I've got more than I expected. She's remembering all the things she used to be, and getting them back as fast as she can. So don't think she's being guided by me, because she isn't. She's going her own way now. This dinner was *her* thought, not mine. She just told me she was doing it, and she'd need dinner for five on Sunday, please. I don't mind seeing to that, but I do wonder how it will go. I don't even know what she intends.'

'To make the peace, from what she said.'

'But what sort of peace? Your father's sort would mean I give up everything I believe in, and become what he'd call an accomplished young woman.'

'How about Aunt Sophie?'

'That's a surprise. She's been calling me every sort of a fool for letting things get known and not being more careful, but she hasn't asked me to give it up. And there's more even than that. When I knew that something was leaking out, I thought I'd better tell her about it myself. She'd better hear it first from me, though I thought she'd have the vapours or something. But after about a minute she stopped me and said if I was telling her I was a witch I could spare my breath, because she'd known it for the last month or so.'

'But—'

'Exactly.'

'How did she guess?'

'One or two things I'd said. And a few things in my room. I didn't think she'd know enough.'

'Do you think she really had guessed?'

'I'm quite sure she had. And there's Arcanus too.' She stopped and looked down at him, and at once he came to her, rubbing his head against her knees and purring. 'That's what he does with Aunt Sophie, and he jumps on her lap too, just as on mine.'

'But does that matter?'

'Arcanus knows things, and if he treats her the same as me it must mean he finds her the same as me. Anyway—' She stooped, rubbing his head as he reared against her legs. 'From one thing and another I'm beginning to wonder about Aunt Sophie.'

7
Dinner for Five

Sir John was noticeably restive in church on Sunday, making it plain that he thought the psalms too long and the sermon much too long. Jane thought the same, but had to be more careful not to show it. Celia, she noted, was not there, which might have been because of a dinner for five, or because she had thought it better to keep out of sight this morning. Anyone could guess what the sermon would be about.

But it was better than Jane had expected. Mr Loveday showed restraint. He did not shout or rant, and he did not use texts against witches. He did take one from Exodus, but it was not the notorious 22, 18. It was from Chapter 20: *I am the Lord thy God. Thou shalt have no other gods before me,* and Jane heard it with relief. If he kept to this he might have less to say about cats and people, and Celia in particular.

But he was in no hurry to come to it. He recited the events of the week, which he called an opening of the gates of hell, and he went back fifty years to remind them of the widow Openshaw and Lizzie Bell. Here he stopped, in a calculated pause that gathered the attention of all of them. 'If we extend our text a little, the Lord our God is a jealous God, visiting the iniquity of the fathers — or the mothers and grandmothers if you will — upon the children unto the third and fourth generation, and this very week we have seen it so. Iniquity there was,

84

and now upon this generation it is visited. Hate and strife have been loosed upon us.'

Then he came nearer to his text. 'The devil may speak us fair, offer us jollity and feasting, the delights of nature, the air of a summer morning, all this and more, and no chilling thoughts of sin. It is all simple and easy, and tempting — for, remember, that is his trade. But —' Again there was that careful pause. 'For this there is a price. He requires allegiance. Call it worship or not, as you will, for *he* will not mind which word you use. For when he does these things he does not call himself the devil, or let *you* call him the devil. That would give warning. So he takes to himself some other name — invent it as you will — and now there are *two* gods in the firmament. One sitteth between the cherubim. And the other — aye, what is the other?'

He took a longer pause, looking round the church, perhaps giving them time to think, and Jane wondered what was coming. She had no idea what the man was talking about.

'What is the other?' His clear voice came sharply as he brought them back to it. 'What you will be told is that this other is a benevolent god, found in the sun, the rain, the springs and wells, the seed and the growing corn, bringing fertility and happiness to all — and especially to you. Wherefore, heed our text. Thou shalt have no other gods before me. Or after me for that matter. There is *one* God, only one. There can be no other, and you are in the most mortal sin if you harbour such a thought at all.'

He spent the next twenty minutes enlarging on that, and Sir John showed open signs of impatience, while Jane wondered again what he was talking about. She had heard nothing of another god. Then he came to something new, and her first thought was that she had not heard him right.

'The devil cannot in truth hide himself. He may set himself up as another god. He may persuade you to give him another name. But by the wise ordering of providence he cannot hide his horns. They are plain to see, if only you have the will to see. And how can you follow a god with horns, and not know he is the devil?'

Sir John snorted and sat upright. He was fidgeting and spluttering through the rest of the sermon, and he spoke his mind about it as soon as they were in the sunlight of the churchyard again.

'The man's mad,' he said pungently, 'and he's getting worse. Jane, what did you think of it?'

'Did he mean the devil can be looked at?'

'Horns and all, or so he said. Hey, Tabby!' He turned as he saw her come from the church. 'What do you say to that?'

'I doubt if there was ever so stupid a man.' She was speaking angrily, and not troubling to hide it. 'I've been trying to do as you wished, telling these folk it's nonsense and best forgotten, and that's been hard enough with the amount that's been put into their heads this week. And now he must needs loose this horned god tale among them. I doubt if they even knew it till this morning.'

'Knew what?'

'This silly tale that witches used to have a god with horns.'

'The devil, do you mean?'

'The head of a goat's more likely, but I haven't heard of it in *this* village. They probably didn't even know of it, and now they all do. They'll think about it, and talk about it, and that will be enough to set somebody playing at it. He wishes to be rid of witchcraft, and he spends his sermon teaching it to them. That's what I call stupid. We might be rid of it if he'd forget his cats and horns, and join with us in laughing at it. I can't think what my father would have said of him.'

She went off, looking as disgruntled as she sounded, and Sir John seemed to share her mood.

'She's ruffled,' he told his wife, 'and who's to blame her? Why the devil couldn't she have stayed in Ireland?'

'Celia? She was sent here. She couldn't be left to live alone.'

'So she's at my Dower House, and I'm expected to sit at dinner with her.'

'Of course you are, and it's time we were getting ready.'

'I am ready.'

'You'll have to have your wig combed before you can go to dinner.'

That did nothing to soothe him, and he was still querulous when they arrived at the Dower House. Then he had to pull himself together and show good manners, for it was plain at once that the Dower House had remembered what hospitality should be. Annis received them, greeting Sir John as if there had never been an awkward word between them, and she was no more than helping Lady Mallinder from her summer cloak when Sophie appeared, elegant in cool pale yellow, and showed at once that she was hostess and knew exactly how to do it. She had had practice enough, in earlier days.

'Ah, Lydia!' She was addressing Lady Mallinder. 'It's years since you were here for dinner, and I must own it to be my fault. So I'm trying to make amends, and I'm very glad you've come.'

'We're delighted, Sophie.'

'Thank you. And John, I hope you're pleased also?'

'Oh, er—' He was perhaps trying to get used to this. She had hardly called him John since his brother had died. 'Oh yes, of course.'

'I make you very welcome. But here's Celia.'

She had just come in, and for an instant she glanced at Jane, as if to say that they understood each other. Then she showed something of her boarding school as she curtseyed to the elders. She greeted Sir John as if she had no memory of anything difficult between them, and she gave him no chance to remind her. She turned quickly into talk of the dinner.

'I'm new to it,' she told him frankly. 'It's my first dinner for guests, so I must hope it's well chosen, and that you'll enjoy it.'

He did, once he found himself in front of it. Celia, sensibly for a summer meal, had kept it to two courses, and he was soon watching with approval as Annis put the first of them on the table: a chine of mutton, spit-roasted and then skinned and floured; a dish of chickens in gravy; fried trout in a sauce of lemon and butter; a side dish of beans and cabbage, another of a sweet veal pie, and a tart of gooseberries, currants and pears. Sophie looked at the table and tactfully asked Sir John to carve the chine for them. He agreed at once, and he looked almost genial as he chose a knife and flicked it expertly up and down the steel. Then he carved for everyone except himself, and to Sophie's look of surprise he answered that he had not seen a sweet veal pie for years. Nobody ever made him one; and if he could only find another knife he would start on this one.

'It's here,' said Celia, handing him a knife. 'Will you have beans?'

'With this?' He had lifted a slice of pastry and was peering into the pie. 'It has artichokes, I suppose? Or is it grapes?'

'Both.'

'Good. And potatoes?'

'Plenty. With raisins and citron.'

'Then why do I need beans? Give them to Jane. She likes the things.'

'Claret, then?'

'With this damned duty on it? *Is* it claret?'

88

'Did you think I'd give you Oporto?' asked Sophie calmly. 'Of course it's claret, and it's in decanters you may remember. You gave them to us — once.'

'Eh? So I did.' He leaned happily back as Annis stretched forward to fill his glass. 'Why then — to you Sophie! Aye and Kit too! I gave 'em to both of you.'

'Yes.' She looked down for a moment, then faced him easily as she lifted her own glass. 'But this is of today. Your good health, John! And Lydia's and Jane's! There! Now I won't keep you longer from the pie.'

For a moment or two they ate in silence, and then Sophie decided that she must get some small talk going. She took what might have seemed the easy way.

'A pleasant morning,' she said. 'Did you like the sermon, Lydia?'

'Not very much. And I didn't properly understand it.'

Lydia answered briefly, as if she had suddenly found this awkward. Sophie said nothing. Sir John finished his claret and began to cut a second slice of pie. Then Celia said what they were all trying to avoid.

'What did he preach about?' she asked. 'Witches, I suppose? Or was it me?'

'No,' said Sir John, as Annis leaned forward again with the decanter. 'He never mentioned you.'

'I'm glad of that. But witches, surely?'

'I didn't know what it was. I wish you'd tell me.'

'I didn't hear it.'

'You've set yourself to teach everyone, haven't you? Ah, thanks, Annis. That'll do.' He lifted his glass again, drinking with a nod of appreciation before he turned back to Celia. 'He was talking about witches with a god they say isn't the devil though he really is, and this creature has horns, so they ought to know better. Tabby says she's heard this tale before, but I don't make sense of it. So perhaps you'll tell me.'

'Horns?' Celia answered him quietly, and as if she would

not evade it. But she put it back a little, perhaps to have time for thought. 'Jane, will you have more mutton? Or is it chickens now?'

'Please.'

Celia glanced at Sir John, and he observed the truce while he carved a chicken. Then Celia was ready for him.

'Are there enough chickens?' she asked.

'Plenty.'

'You could call it the horns of plenty, and that's one meaning I've heard put on horns.'

'It wasn't the vicar's meaning. About the one plain thing he said was that horns mean the devil.'

'I haven't seen the devil, so I don't know.'

'That's off the point. I'm asking whether witches have a god with horns.'

'There can only be one god, so they couldn't have another. And the Bible speaks well of horns. Will you have more pie?'

'No. Er — thank you.'

'You're quite sure?' said Sophie briskly, taking charge for a moment. 'Lydia? Jane? Then we'll have the second course.'

She had timed it well. It changed the talk, and everyone could relax as Annis cleared the table and loaded it with clean plates and the second course: a cheese-curd pudding, a dish of ducklings in a sauce of shallots and cream, and one of sausages fried with apples; a side dish of a syllabub of cream and oranges, and one of a jelly of calves' feet with eggs and lemons. Sir John showed an immediate interest in the ducklings, and picked up a carving knife.

'Now who?' he asked, looking round. 'Sophie? Do you like it whole, or shall I split it for you?'

'A half will do. And make an end of the claret, John. There's some mountain for you now.'

'That's what Kit used to drink.'

'So did you, with him. So you may have it now with me.'

Annis had it ready, and he lifted his glass, letting the light come through the clear white wine of Malaga. He sniffed it, then drank appreciatively.

'Aye,' he said slowly. 'Pleasant and fruity. Kit knew what he was doing.'

'He always did. But Jane would like a duckling, I think.'

She liked the wine too. They all did, and it seemed to go as well with the syllabub and jelly as with the ducklings. Sir John sampled everything, and then was persuaded to have another glass. He was looking thoroughly mellow and content when he had ended it, which may have been why he said no more of horns but tried a different approach. He began by thanking Sophie for a meal he had obviously enjoyed, and then he said that they must now let bygones by bygones and see more of each other in future. Sophie was charming as she made the obvious answer. Then he straightened his chair and looked her in the eye.

'There's one other thing, Sophie, one service you could do for me if you will.'

'But of course.' Her voice had steadied, as if a touch of caution had come to her. 'What is it?'

'Use your position as you should, and make it clear to Celia that while she's in your house she's to stop this witch nonsense altogether. It's causing endless trouble to a lot of us, so make an end of it, please. Tell her positively that it's to stop.'

'Oh!' The caution was suddenly obvious, and she looked steadily at him. 'Why Celia?'

'Because she started it and she's continued it. Did she or didn't she plan that fire at the Sisters?'

'Oh yes. That's not a secret now. But you were talking about trouble, not the fire, and I'd have said it was

91

the vicar who made the trouble and has continued it since.'

'The man's a fool, of course, and I'll agree he hasn't helped. But it started with the fire, and if there'd been no fire there'd have been no trouble.'

'And if there'd been no vicar there'd have been no trouble either. So why not put the blame where it belongs?'

'Sophie —' He was staring at her in annoyance. 'What's the matter with you? Don't you know what's been happening in the village?'

'I know that Joe Parker shouted at Celia, and I'd have thought he was more deserving of the stocks than little Annis. But again I think the vicar had a hand in it. I don't understand that man, and I've tried harder than most. I've asked him here once or twice, and tried to talk to him. He's polite and friendly and very kindly, but I was wasting my time on him. Once there's a mention of witches he becomes as hard as flint, and you can't make him see one gleam of reason. He'll go on making trouble till somebody can learn what's wrong with him.'

'I'll not quarrel with that, Sophie. It's very likely true. But we can't go on like this, with the vicar raving about Celia walking as a cat, and if we can't quiet him by argument, we must do it by stopping Celia. She must find some other way to divert herself.'

'She does not divert herself. She does it to help these people.'

'Help them to what?'

'Happiness, and perhaps to know themselves. Then to some thought of God.'

'Sophie!' He was staring at her in amazement. 'You'd best take hold of yourself and not talk like that. You're asking for trouble.'

'Like Celia?'

'What!' The long stare came again. 'Are you saying she's talked you into her nonsense?'

'She didn't need to. I knew as much as this before she was even born. And half believed it too.'

'Believed what?'

'What Celia believes and is trying to show these people. You need not look so surprised.'

'If I were only surprised it mightn't matter.'

'Where do you think Celia learned it?'

'Ireland, for such a gammer's tale.'

'Where did I meet Kit?'

Sir John caught at his breath, and the jerk of his hand set the wine swaying in his glass. The young Sophie had gone to Ireland to nurse her wounded brother, and had found Kit Mallinder and married him.

'*You?*' he said slowly. 'You another.'

'Not quite. I'm not a witch, nor ever have been. But how do you think I filled my time in Ireland? I'd a lot of it to fill.' She looked down for a moment at a glass she had hardly used, then lifted it and looked at him across the wine. 'I made friends and I learned a good deal. And in this I stand with Celia.'

8
The Full of the Moon

An incident a day or two later caused some confusion. Jane was in the village when she met Tabitha, who was looking disturbed and annoyed. Jane promptly engaged her in talk.

'I've been to see Sally Parr,' said Tabby, with a nod to an outlying cottage. 'This madness is getting worse. Sally was grumbling about the weather.'

Most people were. It had been a dry summer, and the spell of heat before the thunderstorm had so dried and baked the ground that there had been fears for the fruit and vegetables, and for the potatoes in particular. The storm had largely put that right, but it had been so heavy that the standing corn had been bent and battered, and in places beaten down. So Jane was not surprised that Sally Parr should grumble.

'No,' said Tabby, 'but then she let something slip. She said they shouldn't have asked a witch's help, and I'd some trouble to get out of her what she meant. You'll remember that for two Sundays before the storm the vicar had been praying for rain? But it hadn't come, and somebody remembered that the old witches were supposed to be rainmakers. So they asked Celia to do it at that fire of hers, and it seems she did some hocus pocus round the flat stone and threw some incense about. And of course it worked. That's to say the rain came.'

'But you don't say —'

'Of course I don't. But these people do, and that's what matters. Celia did it. They're all sure she did, and it's done more than anything to set her up as a witch. She's proved it, you see, shown what she can do.'

'Oh, but—'

'I know, I know. But that's how they talk — or did. But Sally's old head has another thought in it now.'

'What?'

'That storm did as much harm as good. So was it wise to ask a witch? She may do some good, but can she help doing harm as well? That's the sort of tangle you can get into if you believe this idiocy. What will *he* say to it?'

She meant the vicar, who by chance was coming towards them. He stopped courteously, and at once and without invitation Tabby told him of her talk with Sally Parr. His first response was what might have been expected.

'Worse and worse,' he said gravely. 'A further working out of evil. It is well known that witches, or some of them, can call down rain and storm. In the reign of King James the First—'

'But this time, Vicar? Are we to believe it was the witch? You were trying to do it yourself.'

'I was *what*?'

'You twice prayed for rain in church. I heard you. So why must we believe that the witch did it? That's believing that evil is stronger than good.'

'Oh — er—'

He was plainly stumbling, not knowing how to answer, and Tabby stood waiting with a glint of satisfaction in her eyes. Then she summed it up for him.

'Most clergy would have known the answer. They have a lively faith in God, and none at all in witches. You could think on these things.'

Perhaps he did, but there was no sign that he had changed his beliefs in any way. Jane went for another talk with Celia, and asked her outright whether she had tried to bring down rain. Celia laughed, but she seemed a shade embarrassed too.

'I almost had to,' she explained. 'We *were* short of rain, they were all frightened for whatever they were growing, and they pressed me to it. It would have been a bad start for me if I'd said I couldn't.'

'But can you?'

'Only ask for it, and hope. But that seemed fairly safe. We'd had the heat for a fortnight, and that sort of heat almost always ends in a storm. So I did an invocation.'

'And then came the rain. Splendid. But what's this of incense?'

'Oh, it's strange scent, and there's the smoke as well. It sets a mood, and they begin to expect something.'

'I think you're sometimes a shade too clever.'

'I've been that once or twice already.'

'Then do be careful. Will there be anything more?'

'Not that anyone will know about.'

All stayed quiet for a day or two, or would have done if the vicar had left well alone. But in church on the following Sunday he gave out what he called a special notice. Apart from such occasions as Lammas, he said, witches held their meetings in the nights of full moon, and something could therefore be expected on the night of August 30th. He urged them all to be alert for evil that night, and not to stir from their houses. After this they must look forward to Michaelmas, a great night in the witches' calendar, and again they must prepare for evil, and resist it by every holy means.

If the talk of witches had ever stopped in the village, that was enough to start it again. Tabby went angrily to Sir John and told him that there was no chance of being rid of witchcraft in the village while the vicar insisted on teaching it. At this rate, she said, any girl who was a would-be witch would soon be getting a weekly lesson in what to do next, and Sir John had better do something about it. Sir John told her he could do nothing, and they parted on bad terms.

But on the surface all was quiet. There were no incidents and no alarms. Celia kept out of sight, the vicar found no more to say, and Sir John turned to his day-to-day affairs. Joe Parker was seen again in the village, hobbling with a crutch, and Sophie Mallinder, whose new view of social life had been known only to her family, caused some surprise by paying a couple of men to start painting the Dower House. It certainly needed it, and Sir John grunted his satisfaction.

The moon would be full in the late evening, a little before midnight, of the 30th, which would be a Tuesday. It turned out to be a fine summer day, pleasantly warm, with a blue sky, some high white clouds, and a light westerly wind. Jane, very much on the alert, went for a walk in the afternoon as she often did, but this time, once she was clear of the village, she took the track to the moor, easily and steadily, until she turned aside over the thick and tufted grass to the Sisters. The place was lonely and deserted, its tall stones shining in the sun, and when she stepped into the circle she could see no foot-marks or any other sign of anyone here of late. She sat on the flat stone, munching some cake she had brought with her, and wondering what it had indeed been used for those ages ago; then trying to imagine it in the glare of the fire that Lammas night, with the people pressed against the stones, the shadows dancing wildly, and Celia standing — or perhaps kneeling, or grovelling — in the smoke of incense as she called on some god with horns to give them rain. It became vivid, and Jane jumped from the stone, shaking herself to be rid of it. It was not the Celia she knew, and she did not like it.

She told her father how deserted the place had been, and he gave a nod of satisfaction. He said it fitted with what else he had been told. Earnshaw had been on the alert and had seen nothing, and Tabitha had heard of nothing. So

97

it looked as if Celia had learned some sense at last, and had made an end of her nonsense.

The next morning he was less sure of this. Earnshaw was the first to come, and what he had to say was not very startling, but was certainly odd. He had taken a late walk round the village, about eleven o'clock, when everyone should have been asleep. The night had turned cool, but it was fine and clear, with bright moonlight. He went as far as Sally Parr's cottage, and there at last he saw someone moving. He watched, trying to make out who it was, and the figure disappeared round the far side of the cottage. Then it appeared again, coming towards him on the near side, and now, in the moonlight, he could see that it was Sally's daughter Isobel, a girl of sixteen who was beginning to be attractive. He stood in the shadow of a tree, wondering what she was doing, and saw her pass the front of the cottage and then out of sight again down the far side of it. He waited, making no sense of this, and then saw her coming up the near side again. Then, as she turned to cross the front once more, he went forward, taking her by surprise and holding her before she could get away. He was further mystified when he saw that in one hand she was clutching a leafy sprig from a rowan tree.

But that was all he learned. She was plainly in confusion at being caught, but he could get nothing out of her. She said she had not been able to get to sleep and had thought a little air would help her, which he entirely disbelieved. As to the rowan sprig, she had seen it on the ground and had merely picked it up; which he disbelieved even more, since there was not a rowan tree nearby.

'And that's how it was,' he told Sir John, 'and what could I do? She doesn't break the law if she walks round the house. She was up to something, though.'

'What did you do?'

'I'd an ash stick with me, and I landed her a couple with that and told her to be off to bed before she got some more.'

98

'Quite right. I wonder if this vicar of ours will say what it was for. He's heard of a good many things.'

But the vicar, when he arrived a little later, could not explain it. He could only add another incident to it. Witches, he said, had been known to use a churchyard for their ceremonies, and he had therefore gone there at midnight to be sure. He had found no witches, but had seen a girl walking between the graves with a knife in her hand. He had seen the glint of it in the moonlight, and this had alarmed him. But all she had done was to cut a sprig from an elder tree and then return to the path and walk to the gate. Here he had stopped her, but, like Earnshaw, he had had no truth from her. She would only say that she did not know why she had done it, which he did not believe. But he, too, could do nothing. She did not seem to have done anything very wrong, and he had had to let her go. But he was suspicious, as Earnshaw was.

Sir John could do no better, so he went to consult his wife, who had a knowledge of village girls. This time, however, she could not help, and Jane, who had been carefully listening to all this, suggested Tabby, who also knew the village. Sir John thought this useful, and told her to go at once for a talk with Tabby; who might, he added, have seen something herself last night.

Tabitha was quite willing to talk, but she disposed at once of that last thought.

'Of course I saw nothing last night,' she said. 'I've more sense than to roam about at midnight looking for girls being silly. I was in bed, and stayed there. What's this about the churchyard?'

She listened carefully while Jane spoke again of the girl who had cut the elder twig, and then she was a little more helpful.

'She was hoping to cure a wart,' she said briskly. 'It's a well known charm and we needn't blame Celia for it. The girls knew it long before they knew her.'

99

'How's it done?'

'Oh, you cut your twig in a churchyard, and you must cut it under a waning moon, which is why she was there after midnight. She had to wait for the moon to pass its full. Then you rub your wart with the leaves and hang the twig to dry. And as the leaves wither, so will the wart. That's the way, and the odd thing is that it sometimes works — which I can't explain at all.'

'Oh?' Jane considered this for a moment, and felt no wiser. 'How about Isobel Parr, walking round that cottage?'

'Oh —' Tabitha became more thoughtful. 'I think that was a love charm, or something like it. It would be, with Isobel.'

'But how?'

'I think you walk round and round like that with your twig, and you say some sort of abracadabra over it. Then you go to bed and put it under your pillow, and you're supposed to have a dream that will tell you who you'll marry. It's something like that, and I've never heard that it works. But half the girls do it when they get to that age, and they don't think of it as witchcraft. It's just something they've heard from their mothers, who haven't learnt any better.'

'But why round the house?'

'Go and ask Celia. She may know, but I certainly don't.'

Jane liked a talk with Celia, and this seemed a fair excuse for one. So she walked across to the Dower House that afternoon, and at once she saw Celia with Aunt Sophie, on the terrace in front of the house. She crossed the grass to join them.

The house was on a slope, but in front of it the ground had been built up to give a level lawn. This meant a sharp drop at the end of the lawn, and here was a stone balustrade, ornamented by little statues of Venus and Adonis, each about two feet high, placed one at each end. The whole structure had been part of the improvements made by Kit and Sophie in their days of hospitality, and the flagged path by the balustrade had seen many a summer gathering. But since Kit's death it had been neglected, and it was now in a sorry state. At one end the retaining wall had given way and allowed the earth to fall, taking with it some twenty feet of balustrade, which still lay where it had fallen, a tangle of balusters, stones, and soil, all grown over with grass and weed. The statue of Venus, broken into three, lay further down the slope. What was left of the balustrade was green with moss, and the flagged path seemed to have more grass than stone. Sophie was standing with Celia, looking critically at this.

'It must all be put to rights,' she was saying. 'We can't ask people here to look at this. What would Kit have thought?'

She left that unanswered while she gave attention to an elegant little sundial in the centre of the lawn on a low stone pillar. It was forlorn and dirty now, and showed ample evidence of birds.

'That will have to be cleaned,' she told Celia. 'It can be done when they do the balustrade. Can you find someone to build this end up?'

'I expect so. The balusters don't seem to have broken. But how about that statue? It's in three.'

'Do without it, and knock the other one off as well. I never liked them. This path needs weeding. Ah, Jane!' She had suddenly noticed her, and she changed the talk with accomplished ease. 'I'm glad to see you. But how is everyone? Is all quiet?'

'I think so. Nothing that matters.'

'I thought it might be.' For an instant she glanced at Celia, then showed a twitch of an eyebrow as she turned again to Jane. 'How is my friend the vicar? He came to see me the other day, finding courage for it at last.'

'Oh?'

'He hadn't been here for weeks, and you'd have thought

he was entering a plague house. He'd hung a cross from his neck, and he kept clutching it. Celia was naughty.'

'How?'

'She brought us tea, and told him he could have a long spoon.' She rippled with laughter for a moment. 'Poor man! He was still trying to tell me what he'd come for when Arcanus jumped up to the window from outside, and you'd have thought by the way he pushed his chair back it was the devil come to grab him. An awkward moment.'

'What did Arcanus do?'

'Can cats laugh?'

'Yes.'

'That's what Arcanus did. Sat on his tail and laughed. I had to put him out before I could calm the man, and then he wanted me to do something to stop Celia. I don't think he minded what, so I had to promise him there'd be no trouble at new moon. That's why I asked if he'd found any.'

'Only a girl trying to charm a wart.'

'That's nothing. All girls do it. He didn't see anyone else?'

'I don't think so.'

'Then all's well. But I expect you'd like a word with Celia while I look at this.'

She went across the lawn to the sundial, and Celia stood watching. Then she turned to Jane.

'I like Aunt Sophie,' she said gravely. 'She was really very good with the vicar, and he was looking much happier when he left. I do wish I could understand why he's so frightened of witches. But let's go to my room.'

The afternoon sun had moved from her eastward window, and the room was cool and pleasant. The window was wide open, and the silvered ball was swaying gently in the wind, but the long curtains had gone. So had the cushions from the window seat, and Jane wondered why. They had looked clean enough a day or two ago.

'What's this of wart charms?' asked Celia.

'Oh yes.' Jane answered vaguely, still thinking about the

102

room. Something else was different, but she had not yet found what it was, and her mind was half on that while she explained about the girl in the churchyard. Celia took this easily.

'Pretty certainly wart charming,' she said, 'but nothing to do with me. I don't even know the girl.'

'But you know this way of doing it?'

'There are nine and ninety ways of charming warts, and one can be as good as another. But the other girl, Isobel Parr? *What* was she doing?'

'Walking round the house. She—'

Jane stopped, suddenly aware that the room was different because of a scent she had not known before. It was faint and elusive, and she found herself sniffing to be sure. It was sweet, fragrant, and perhaps a little sickly, and at once she guessed it.

'Incense,' she said suddenly to Celia. 'Is it?'

'Yes. I thought you might find it.' Celia seemed very calm about it. 'I had people here last night, in private, and the scent was strong this morning. Mostly in the curtains and cushions, so they're having a blow outside. Do you like it?'

'Not much.'

'Arcanus doesn't either. He's disgusted — upsetting his house like that — and he's sitting by himself in the garden. But more, please, of Isobel.'

She listened carefully while Jane told as much as she knew of this, and then she nodded thoughtfully.

'I'm surprised at Tabby knowing so much,' she said, 'but I think she's right. The girl wants a vision of her lover, and I don't think she'll get it. She's all muddled.'

'But why walk round the house?'

'She doesn't know why, but she's been told by somebody's grandmother that that's the thing to do. Really, she was treading a magic circle round the house, but she didn't know this. She didn't even know that with rowan she should have waited till next month for it to get berries. I don't think she'll see anything.'

'Poor Isobel!'

'I'll agree with that. But it was a good guess by Tabby all the same. Tell her so, with my compliments.'

Jane left the Dower House, but she did not go straight home. She walked slowly across the park while she thought things out. Celia had evidently had her witch meeting at full moon, but she had kept it to her coven only, and in the privacy of the Dower House; which, with that use of incense, must mean with the knowledge and agreement of Aunt Sophie. Jane knew she must not talk about it, but she could certainly talk about Isobel walking in a circle, and she found some amusement in the thought of Tabby being complimented by Celia. She was standing by the park gates, thinking of this, when Tabby came into sight, walking across the green. Jane went quickly forward, and Tabby looked none too pleased when she was told of Celia's compliments. Her answer was sharp.

'What's she surprised about? I'd have thought it common knowledge that village girls do as their grandmothers did, and it doesn't do any harm. Isobel could have walked round the house for the rest of the week without pulling Joe Parker from his cobbling or driving the vicar to a devil hunt. That was Celia, and then she sends compliments to *me*, as if nobody—'

She stopped as if breath had failed her, and then she was staring across the green, seeming to have lost all thought of Jane. Her face quivered, and Jane, turning in alarm, saw a horseman coming towards them at an easy trot, a man in a russet coat and a tricorne hat, with a valise strapped to his saddle. Jane did not at first recognize him, but he came closer, and then she recognized him from years ago, Jack Ansell, who had been at the vicarage with Tabby and her brother, and then had come again, sadly and alone. He had been here only a month ago, but she had not seen him then.

Now he came directly to them, sweeping his hat and finding a smile for both of them. He took a quick keen glance at Jane, but he addressed himself to Tabby.

'I'm glad to find you again,' he told her. 'It was difficult a month ago. I'd affairs, and little time.'

'Yes.'

It was toneless, as if she had found it hard to speak at all, and for an instant he was staring hard at her. Then, with no comment, he turned to Jane.

'Again I'm glad,' he said easily. 'It *is* Jane, surely?'

'Of course.'

'And I don't know how long since we met.'

'Seven years. I was about this high.'

'Oh, more than that. But now I'm here again, so perhaps—'

'Oh!' It came from Tabby, like a gasp, and it cut him short. Then she spoke wildly, all manners forgotten. 'Why do you come *this* day? Of all days?'

'Tabby, I—'

'I'll talk another day. I can't now.'

She was all but in tears, and then, abruptly, she turned, putting her back to both of them and hurrying away across the green. They stared after her, and then he brought his eyes to Jane.

'What is it?' he asked. 'What have I done?'

'I don't know.' She was looking across the green to where Tabby was turning out of sight now. 'Ought I to go to after her?'

'Someone should. And it can hardly be me.'

'Yes.' Tabby was out of sight now. 'Are you staying with us?'

'Your father did suggest it.'

'Go to the house, then. Tell them I'll come when I can.'

He nodded. Then he gathered his bridle as Jane went after Tabby.

9
Amulets

Jane arrived home to find that Jack Ansell was shut away in the study with her father. But her mother was waiting for her in the parlour.

'Jane, what's wrong with Tabby?' she said. 'Jack says you had to go after her. Did you find her?'

'Yes, but she wouldn't talk to me. She said she couldn't talk to anyone, not tonight. She kept saying that — not tonight. And she did ask, once, if nobody remembered Charles but herself.'

'Charles?'

'She meant her brother.'

'Of course she did.' Lady Mallinder sounded thoughtful. 'He was killed in July, at Oudenarde. But we didn't know of it then. There were no letters, and the first Tabby knew of it was when Jack came here himself.'

'I remember *that*. Everyone was miserable, and I had to creep about as quiet as a mouse.'

'I expect you had. But do you remember when it was? Jack had to get his leave and then make his journey, and it was the end of August when he came to us here. The last day of August, and that's the date Tabby has always remembered. Charles died to her at the end of August. So do you see now? What day is this? What date?'

'Oh!'

'Just so.' Her mother nodded. 'It's the last day of August, the exact anniversary as Tabby sees it. She'll have been remembering Charles all day, and Jack too, and the way he came riding across the green to her that afternoon.'

'Oh dear!'

'Yes Jane. And he comes to her again now, on this day of all days, riding across the green to her just the same. He'll have forgotten the date of course, but Tabby hadn't, and it was too much for her. I know that's a guess, but —'

'Can we *do* anything for her?'

'I'll walk across when I can. But I must see to our guest first, and he's still in the study there. I've hardly spoken to him.'

She had to wait a little longer for Ansell to come to them with Sir John, and then Sir John was casual about it, perhaps a shade too casual.

'He'll be with us for a little time,' he said. 'He's had affairs in the north, and he expects some more in a few weeks' time, so he'll stay with us till then. It's convenient for him here, and we're glad to have him of course, very.'

Jane said nothing, and wondered what affairs Jack Ansell could have had in the north, why her father had asked him to stay for weeks, and why indeed he had come at all. His friendship had been with the Vereys, but he would not see Charles again. It might, of course, be Tabby, but why had he taken seven years to come to her? Nothing seemed to fit, and Jane's curiosity was awake.

Later, when they were at supper, Ansell was a quiet and courteous guest, willing to take his share in the making of talk. But little by little, almost as if they could not keep away from it, the talk drifted to the upset of the last weeks, to Lammas, to the vicar and Celia and Joe Parker's outburst, and Ansell did not seem to take it very seriously. He was much more disposed to laugh at anyone who now believed in witchcraft. But when he added that he would none the less like to meet this Celia, Jane promptly determined that he should. This would be her work, and to take him to the Dower House would give her an interesting afternoon.

But the next morning her mother took charge. Tabby came first, she said, and everything else must be put aside. Then she turned to her guest and explained to him that his coming on the last day of August had been unfortunate. So he must now call on Tabby and calm things down with a few minutes easy talk; and on this occasion, since it might be a little difficult, he had best not go alone. In the next breath she appointed Jane to go with him, and Jane assented very cheerfully. She was quite willing to walk and be seen with Major Ansell on a fine September morning.

Their way across the park took them near the Dower House, and Jane, seizing what she thought was a chance, asked him if he would like to call on Aunt Sophie.

'I don't think so,' he answered. 'She was living shut away when I was last here. She didn't see anyone, so I've never met her.'

'But you did say you'd like to meet Celia.'

'So I did. And I will, at a proper time. But we have our orders, Jane, and it's Tabby first this morning.'

Jane had to agree, and they walked on through the village and made their call on Tabby. She received them politely, evidently recognizing that she must, though she held herself a little stiffly and was perhaps controlling herself. But Ansell gave her a firm lead.

'Tabby,' he said easily. 'I'm sorry I chose yesterday to come. I'm afraid I'd forgotten the date.'

'Forgotten?' Her voice was suddenly strained. 'I thought you'd have remembered Charles.'

'Of course I remember him. *And* the day he died. And my coming to you here. And the days after it too, that Sunday in the church, and—'

'Jack, don't. I can't—'

'I'm sorry. But I didn't remember which day in August it was. I'll own I didn't. Should I have done?'

'I suppose not.' She tried to summon a smile. 'But it's

108

been different, Jack. You've had the wars to think of, and much to do, and I'm left here to remember — remember alone, since my father went. Nothing to do but care for village folk and —'

'Yes.' Again he stopped her quickly. 'I should have remembered it, but I didn't.'

'Why should you? What do I matter?'

'More than you think, perhaps. Or I thought so once.'

'Once?'

It crackled back, and for a moment they were eye to eye, perhaps on the edge of a quarrel. Jane, forgotten by both of them, was utterly still, with an awkward feeling that she should not be hearing this. Then Ansell found his poise again, and spoke easily.

'Let be, Tabby. I came this morning to make my compliments, and to say I hope to see more of you in the weeks I may be here. For this morning, let it stay at that.'

'Very well.' She had recovered also, and she even managed a smile again. 'But why weeks, pray, in a place like this? Have you time on your hands?'

'No-o.' He seemed to answer carefully. 'I'd affairs in the north, which I think are now done, but I'll have to go back there in a few weeks time. So it's convenient to wait here.'

'It sounds odd. Affairs in the north, you say? You aren't of those parts.'

'It had to do with my leaving the Army. It's not important. So I'll hope for the pleasure again, before long.'

He was on his feet, obviously cutting this short and taking leave, and she had no choice but to accept it. She did it well, not forgetting a word or two with Jane, and she had her easiest manner as she went with them to the door. His manner matched hers, and he gave her a fine flourish of his hat in farewell, but Jane heard him take a deep breath as they walked back to the village.

'Tabby can be difficult,' he allowed himself to say. 'Like

an uncertain horse. You can expect anything, if the mood takes her.'

He had no more to say about her, and when they were back at the house he attached himself to Sir John, who was just setting out to see about some repairs to cottages. Jane went to her mother and poured out the whole tale.

'And I don't know what's going to happen when they meet again,' she ended. 'I suppose they will?'

'Of course they will, so I'll arrange something. If I don't, they'll meet by chance and who knows what they'll say? I'll invite Tabby to dinner. I think that will be best. They'll have to talk to each other then, and when we see how they get on we can decide what to do next.'

Jane said nothing. With fancies flying in all directions she was wondering if this was a process she had heard of called matchmaking. She had not suspected her mother of it before.

'Yes.' Lady Mallinder nodded sagaciously. 'That will be best. I'll have a word with your father, and then I'll arrange it.'

She did the arranging on Sunday, in the churchyard after service. The congregation stood waiting, as custom required, while she went out first with Sir John, followed by Jane and Jack Ansell, and then by Aunt Sophie and Celia. Sir John coughed, and did what was plainly needed. He presented Ansell to Sophie, who had no idea who he was but was not put off by that. She drew on her old skills and brought him to talk at once. Celia, finding little part in this, caught Jane's eye and stepped back.

'Do you know Bessie Neve?' she asked of Jane.

'She's a widow. In that white cottage there, beyond the pump.'

'I know. But what sort is she? Do you like her?'

'Not much. Nobody does.'

'Why not?'

'Oh —' Jane looked round, noting that her mother was

110

now in talk with Tabby. 'I think it's the way she looks at you. She can make you feel uncomfortable.'

'Or worse.' Celia nodded. 'Very dark eyes, and a glitter in them. She looks straight at you, and most of our people can't look back, or won't. They're downright frightened of her, and you can guess what they say. She has the evil eye, and you mustn't cross her. They believe this.'

'Oh? Do you?'

'Not really.' Celia was looking thoughtful now. 'I've not much belief in the evil eye. But being frightened isn't good for anybody. It can flutter your heart and turn your stomach wrong. It can upset your thoughts so that you can't think properly, and then you can soon find things going badly.'

'But why all this, this morning?'

'Oh—' Celia almost laughed. 'Because I've been having to deal with it. You remember Isobel Parr, who walked round the house to make a love-divining charm?'

'You said it wouldn't work.'

'It didn't. I went to the house and asked her, and I met more than I expected. She didn't dream of anything, and I was just trying to talk to her when her mother started about the evil eye.'

'Old Sally?'

'Yes. She thought I'd made the rain, you remember, and too much of it. But this time it was the evil eye. The charm had gone wrong, and it wasn't the only thing. Nothing would ever go right in the house while the evil eye was on them. And that's how we came to Bessie Neve.'

'Do you mean she'd done it?'

'Sally said she'd done it. According to Sally, she'd made a cake for Isobel's birthday, and it was in the hearth cooling when Bessie came and fixed her eyes on it. Sally says she knew Bessie wanted it, but it was for Isobel, so she didn't give it to her. So Bessie went away and put the eye on them, and everything's been wrong since.

111

Now — if Sally believes all that, who would she turn to for help?'

'You, I should think, as the Queen Witch.'

'Clever Jane! So would I put a curse on Bessie, please, and it wouldn't matter if it killed her. Sally was quite worked up about it.'

'And what did you say?'

'Jane!'

Her father's voice broke in, gruff and impatient, and she turned to see him standing with her mother, obviously waiting for her. Sophie had finished with Ansell and was probably waiting for Celia. Tabby had gone, and it was plainly time to stop talking. She grimaced at Celia, and went.

It was part of Sir John's routine to have a glass or two of wine after church on Sunday. He said he needed it to recover from the sermon. He hurried them home accordingly, and once he was at his wine his wife told him that Tabby was to come to dinner on Tuesday.

'She was a little shy about it,' she added, 'and I had to tell her firmly that she was expected. But she'll come.'

'Was she shy of *me*?' asked Jack Ansell.

'Just about your coming that special day. But of course you've called on her since then, and I expect that helped. She'll be all right on Tuesday if we take it easily.'

'Easily by all means. It's what I'd certainly wish.' He looked thoughtfully at his wine and then deftly changed the talk. 'Easy, do you say? She should take lessons from Mrs Mallinder, to whom you presented me this morning. She's charming and I've met no one easier to talk with.'

'I'm glad you like her, Jack. I hope you'll meet her again.'

'I shall. She's asked me to dinner on Thursday. You'll forgive me, I hope, that I've accepted?'

'Certainly. It's good that you should meet other people while you are here. And Celia too, I suppose?'

'Who seems charming also.' He laughed softly above

112

his wine. 'I haven't dined with a witch before, so she'll add something to the occasion.'

'Oh?' For a moment she seemed none too pleased, and then she found her smile again. 'I hope you won't find Celia a witch in two senses.'

It passed off, but Jane was left to wonder whether what had annoyed her mother had been the thought of Sophie as a hostess again. Sophie had shown in the old days what she could do. She now had Celia to help her. She was having that terrace repaired and the garden put to rights, and she had made a conquest of Jack Ansell in about ten minutes. It looked very much as if the Dower House was going to be known again; and Lady Mallinder would not like second place.

Jane heard a little more of it during the afternoon, when she walked across to the Dower House. Her main purpose was to let Celia complete the tale of Bessie Neve and the evil eye. But Celia had a question or two first about Jack Ansell, and Jane, in answering these, happened to mention that he had found Aunt Sophie charming. Celia laughed outright.

'So he should,' she said. 'She was sister to an officer, and wife to another, so she knew how to talk to this one. She says he's a good one, by the way.'

'Excellent. Now come back, please, to Sally Parr, where we had to stop. You'd told me she'd asked you to put a curse on Bessie. What did you tell her?'

'I told her I didn't put curses on people, and you should have seen her face when I said it. What's the use of a witch if she won't blast the other one? That's left from the old days of course, Joe and his grandmother.'

'But Sally?'

'I told her I wouldn't curse Bessie, but I'd protect her from the evil eye. I'd protect Sally and her Isobel.'

'Can you?'

'I don't really think there's much to protect from, except

being frightened. So I've given her an amulet, and another for Isobel, to hang round their necks.'

'What's an amulet?'

'This is.'

From a press against the wall she took a thin disc of baked clay, about two inches in diameter, and handed it to Jane. One side was smooth and glazed, but the other had a design of interlacing triangles which together formed a five-pointed star. It had been done quite simply by impressing the lines in the soft clay before it was fired. A small hole in the disc, near to the rim, must also have been made before firing.

'What is it?' asked Jane.

'An amulet. That star with the five points is the pentacle, which is a *very* old design, perhaps older than the Sisters up there, and it's always been said to repel evil. If you put a cord through that little hole to hang the thing from your neck, it will hang with one of the points at the top, and that's the right way up.'

'Do you believe all this?'

'What matters is that Sally shall believe it, so I made her come here to get it, and Isobel with her, and come after dark when I'd a fire burning. I'd no other light, but I'd some charcoal in a brass dish, lighted and glowing, and I sprinkled a whiff of incense on it. And between the scent and the smoke and the shadows from the firelight, they both fell on their knees. Then I took the amulets, one at a time, and held them in the smoke, as if it was charging them with power, and Isobel started squeaking. Then Arcanus helped. He didn't mean to, but he did.'

Celia was suddenly laughing at the memory. 'He'd been sitting by the fire, just keeping an eye on us, and Sally had looked at him as if he might be the devil come to help. The real witch's cat, all sleek and black. But he likes to know about everything, and when I held an amulet in the smoke he got up and came to me. He looked at the amulet

114

I was holding, and then he reared up and put his paws on it. He just wanted to feel it, but he looked as if he was blessing it, and that's what *they* thought. So I held up the other one, and he pawed that too. Then he sat on his tail and purred very loud, as if he was saying that everything was all right now. And so it was, of course. I gave them their amulets, and told them that if they kept them hung from their necks they'd never be trouble with the evil eye again, and they could laugh at Bessie. So off they went, and I don't know whether they're more frightened of me or Arcanus.'

'You think it will work?'

'Of course it will. They aren't frightened now, and that's because of me, and they'll tell everyone so. It couldn't be better.'

'I hope so.' Jane found herself admiring the cool way in which Celia had turned Sally's fears to her own advantage. 'A little more like this, and you'll have the whole village saying you're just the witch they want.'

'Joe Parker won't say it. Some others won't either, while Tabby keeps talking as she does. She's been here too long, Jane. That's the trouble. She lived here all her life, and they've known her and respected her all those years. That counts for a lot in a place like this.'

'Suppose she began to think of something else?'

'What?'

'Oh—' Jane's forehead puckered. 'Suppose she was looking at Major Ansell?'

'Jane!'

'I think she might, if he looked at her.'

'But will he?'

'I'm not sure. I might know better after this dinner on Tuesday.'

'I didn't know of this.' Celia nodded and looked thoughtful. 'It could certainly make a difference if Tabby forgot about witches, so I hope she enjoys her dinner.'

Tabby did seem to enjoy it. They all did, and what came

after it could have been forseen by no one. The September day had turned warm and sunny, and when dinner was over Lady Mallinder said that they would now sit in the garden for an hour. Sir John agreed, adding that he would enjoy it better with some brandy. So to the garden they went. Chairs were brought with the brandy, and they settled comfortably. Then, while Tabby was admiring the tall hollyhocks against the sunlit wall, they heard a horse in front of the house. Sir John told Jane to see what it was, and when she went round the house she found that a postboy had come with a newsletter. She took it back to her father, and he was plainly surprised.

'What's this?' he said. 'It wasn't due. News that can't wait, is it? Not the Chevalier?'

He had let his thought come out, and it brought them all to attention as he broke the wafer and unfolded the sheet. He read it and sat staring, though his face had eased.

'What is it?' asked Ansell. '*Is* it of the King?'

'It's the King of France. He's dead. Last Thursday, it was. The Sun King, didn't they call him?'

'*Le Roi Soleil.*'

'I could never get my tongue round that. But he's gone. What age would he be?'

'Seventy-seven, I think.'

'And he inherited when he was five. Seventy-two years as King of France. But we all go at last, and —'

'Please!' Ansell sounded as if he could stand no more of this. 'He's gone. Do you know who is the heir?'

'His grandson, isn't it?'

'A boy of five years. And the Regent, I think, will be Duke of Orleans, who is *not* a friend to the Chevalier.'

'Isn't he?'

'Do you not see what it means? King Louis had promised stores and arms, a ship or two to carry them, and some further help for a diversion against Devonshire. But now

116

there will be none of this. Orleans is not a friend, and our enterprise is dead, withered before it has grown.'

'Is it?' Sir John looked perturbed and seemed to cogitate on this. Then his face cleared, and he took a happier tone. 'Aye Jack, so it is. I think you're right, and perhaps it's as well. It was risky work, and you'll be safer out of it.'

'Do you think only of *me*?'

'I'd not wish you to come to harm. Nor would Tabby.'

'I would *not*,' broke in Tabby. 'And will you tell me what you're talking about?'

There was an edge in her voice, and she looked angry enough to have forgotten manners; just as the others, thinking only of this news from France, had forgotten what they were divulging. King Louis had been part of their world. He had been King for longer than they had lived, and his going would mean a different world. There would be new groupings in Europe, new ambitions, new centres of power, and it was too soon for them to grasp all this. Even in a first attempt to grasp it their minds had been so filled that ordinary caution had slipped. It could not be called back now, and Ansell turned to Tabby and tried to make the best of things.

'It isn't hard to guess,' he told her. 'There has been talk that the Chevalier is making ready to claim his own, and that's what we talked about. Such an enterprise is at an end. That's all.'

'Do you take me for a fool?' Her answer snapped, and she had certainly no thought of manners. 'I've been wondering since Lammas what brought you here, because it certainly wasn't *me*. You told me so. You said you had affairs that couldn't wait, and away you went to the north — doing nothing in particular, I suppose?'

'Tabby, I did have some affairs.'

'I'm sure you did, and Sir John had just told us it was risky work. Do you think I can guess nothing? You

117

always had leanings to the Chevalier, and called him King.'

'So did some others, in *your* family. However —' He stopped and looked steadily at her. 'It's out now, and I'll make no pretences to you. So what comes next?'

'Nothing, if you'll show some sense. But the only word of sense so far has come from Sir John.'

'Eh?' Sir John sat up sharply. 'What's this?'

'You said it was as well the thing had finished. You could have said that ten times over and still have talked sense.'

'Could I? But he's back here safe, so what more do you want?'

'Nothing, if he stays safe.'

'Tabby —' Ansell leaned forward, half smiling. 'Tabby, do you remember this?'

He sat for another moment. Then he undid a button, and from under his shirt he took a thin disc of silver, perhaps an inch across, hanging on a thin silk cord. He held it out to her, and Jane, stretching forward, saw a figure of St Christopher embossed on it. From Tabby she heard a sudden catch of breath.

'Yes.' He fingered it for a moment, and then slipped it back inside his shirt. 'You gave it to me, Tabby, the last time I was here. Your parting gift before I went back to the war, and I've worn it ever since. Do you know what you said of it?'

'Something silly.'

'Not silly. You said it would keep me safe and remind me of you — and it's done both. I've treasured it.'

'Oh!'

'It's my amulet — I think that's the word — to keep me from harm. Trust it now, as I do.'

10
The Forgotten Fear

Jane, setting out for a walk the next afternoon, had Jack Ansell with her at his own suggestion, and she took him to the rising track that climbed eastward to the moor. He sniffed happily at the cool fresh wind from the sea, and then he said he wanted to know about Celia.

'I'm to dine with her tomorrow,' he explained. 'I didn't even know we had witches these days, and if we do have them I'd not have thought she was one. She doesn't look it, so please tell me more of her.'

Jane was willing enough, though she knew she must say nothing of what Celia had shared with her in confidence. So she picked her way, finding plenty to tell him, and they were well up on the moor when she had finished. Then she thought he might as well see where it had all begun, so she led him to the Sisters, where he stood in silence, looking carefully at everything.

'I don't understand it,' he said at length. 'If we do have witches, I can think of this as a place for them, specially at night. I'd call it very suitable. But it doesn't match the Celia I met on Sunday. She can't be a witch. She's the very opposite of one.'

'She isn't the sort of witch they used to have.'

'I hope not. But I'm still puzzled.'

'Other people are, and not only by Celia. There's the vicar too, and my father says he's mad.'

119

'He was sane enough on Sunday. He preached a good sermon.'

'You should hear him about witches.'

'I expect I shall. Tell me more about him, please.'

Jane found this easier, and she remembered enough of the vicar and his doings to last her until they were almost down the hill again. It made a fairly full account, and a timely one, for they were scarcely in the village when they met him. He had a courteous greeting for Jane, and then he spoke to Ansell.

'I'm glad of this,' he said. 'The short word we had on Sunday was hardly enough. So permit me, please, to welcome you to the parish. I hope we still have some peace to offer you.'

'Indeed you have.'

'We are not as peaceful as we might have been.' For a moment he seemed to hesitate. 'You'll have heard, no doubt, of our affliction?'

'This talk of witches?'

'Of course, and it is more than talk. It is open and admitted. She does not deny it.'

'Oh, I see. But she is not, perhaps, a very harmful sort of witch.'

'All witches are harmful. What else could they be?' He stopped short, and then steadied himself to look Ansell in the eye. 'I know that I am much criticized for this. I am called credulous and superstitious, and by some I am called worse. Quarrels are everywhere, and I am blamed for these. Even Sir John thinks I am a maker of trouble. Believe that I am aware of all this.'

'Of course. But—'

'It is because I do believe that witches are harmful. I know them to be servants of the devil. So how can I be silent? But I must not pester you with this. I had meant only to hope that your stay among us will not be spoiled.'

'That is kind of you, Vicar.' Ansell answered slowly,

and he was watching the man carefully. 'But might I ask how you know so surely about witches?'

'It is what so many ask.' A note of despair had come into his voice, as if he could see little hope for a man who could ask that question. 'Have you not spoken with a witch? Do you not know the shudder that can come upon you when she speaks? Or how the evil in her eyes can strike your breath unsteady and your heart faster? Or the cold that may come to your forehead as you think of what may follow?'

'Yes.' Ansell nodded, and his eyes seemed even more alert. 'I do indeed know something of these. But you, sir —' you have known them, I think, for many years?'

'Since I can remember anything, and it amazes me that other men do not. I am pleased that at last I know a man who does.'

'For me it had nothing to do with witches. However —' He seemed very thoughtful now. 'Perhaps we might talk another day? At this moment —'

'By all means. I quite understand. But if we might indeed talk another day?'

'It might possibly be of help. So we must arrange it.'

They parted on that. The vicar went striding away, and for a brief moment Ansell looked at Jane. They resumed their walk across the green, and Jane, who had not in the least understood the talk, could keep quiet no longer.

'What do you think of him?' she asked.

'Your vicar?' He hung on it for a moment. 'A kindly man, and well intentioned. In most things of good sense, and probably of good attainment. I can think well of him.'

'But what was he talking about? I didn't understand him at all.'

'His breath unsteady, and so on? I'm glad you didn't.' He took another long pause, and then he turned his head to her. 'Jane, he's frightened. That's what it means. He's been very badly frightened.'

121

'By a witch?'

'I suppose so, and it must have been when he was very young, three or four years old, perhaps. When you're that age you can be scared out of your wits by something that wouldn't trouble you if you were older, and I think he was frightened so badly that he hasn't got over it yet. Mention a witch, and ordinary thinking leaves him. The old fear comes back.'

'Can it?'

Jane was puzzled. But she heard more about it that evening, when it came into the talk at supper. Ansell related the whole incident, clearly and deliberately, as if he thought Sir John should know about it.

'I'm quite sure,' he ended, 'that fear comes into it. He gave the signs of it very clearly, the breath, the heart, the cold forehead, and so on.'

'Is it so, Jack?'

'I've served in the wars. But it must be from something in his early years.'

'He's never said anything.'

'He mightn't know about it. Or not remember. That can happen, too. We had a man attached to us as an aide-de-camp — about Blenheim time, I think it was.'

He stopped, then sat toying with his glass, looking down at the table as memory gripped him. Sir John stirred slightly.

'Go on, Jack.'

'Oh, the aide. Yes. That's a mounted officer, of course, and it's his work to ride at his hardest from one post to another, carrying orders, or gathering news. They're shot at all the time, so it's dangerous work in action.'

'I'll believe it.'

'We liked the man, and he was as brave as another. But there was one thing he wouldn't do. An aide, you understand, must get through somehow, and if he finds a river in his way he must swim his horse across it, and that's what

122

he wouldn't do. He'd face worse dangers, but he couldn't bring himself to swim a river and we could none of us make out why. But one night when we'd had wine enough to free the talk he mentioned it himself. Then someone said *he* didn't like rivers either, and this was because he'd fallen into one as a child and had a nasty fright. He thought it might be the same thing again, but the aide said he'd never fallen into a river. The other man kept asking him to push his memory a litle further back. "Can you remember anything, anything at all when you were four years old? Good. Now is there anything — it doesn't matter what — a little earlier than that?" He went on like that, very quiet and easy, and suddenly the aide said, "Good God!" Then he sat staring as he remembered something. You could see it in his face, and after a while he looked at us again, and we could see he was breathing hard.'

'Aye, but what—'

'He *had* fallen into a river. It can't have been deep, because the horse was wading across, and he was sitting in front of his father. The horse stumbled and he fell in. They pulled him out almost at once, but it was enough to scare the wits out of him, and leave him with this fear of rivers. He couldn't put his horse into one.'

'Couldn't he?' Sir John sounded dissatisfied. 'I don't understand this, Jack. I'd have thought that if it scared him like that he'd have remembered it all his life. But you say he'd forgotten it.'

'So he had, and we didn't understand why. But then someone said he'd have hated that memory of falling in, and he'd have tried to forget it. And that's what he did. He forgot it altogether, till we helped him to get it back.'

'But if he forgot it, how could he still be frightened of it?'

'None of us could make sense of that, and I can only tell you that it was so. Once he'd remembered what he was frightened of, he knew he needn't be frightened, and that put him right again. He could swim a river like anyone else. I'll not forget that evening, and it came back to me this afternoon when I heard your vicar about his troubles. I think he may be another, and he could perhaps be helped in the same way.'

'Helped? How?'

'The man's in fear of witches, and since there's no open reason for it I'll guess he's like our aide-de-camp, frightened by something he's managed to forget. If he could be persuaded to remember it, then who knows? That's a guess, of course.'

'Aye. But if it worked with one man —' Sir John nodded sagaciously. 'It's worth trying, Jack. But whose work is it? Yours, perhaps, since you've seen it done?'

'As you wish, sir. He did ask to talk another day.'

'Then let him. If you fail, pass him to me and I'll see what I can do. But you first.'

'Very well. But I'm to dine at your Dower House tomorrow, with Mrs Mallinder, which will take my attention. And perhaps I should see something of Tabby too. She'll probably expect it.'

'She will,' said Lady Mallinder, who had been listening in silence. 'It's natural that she should expect something.'

'Ye-es. What would you suggest?'

'Take her riding. That's always reckoned proper. Jane can take your invitation to her.'

Lady Mallinder had her way. Jack went off the next day to dine with Aunt Sophie, and an hour later Jane got her orders. She was to find Tabby and deliver an invitation to ride with him the following afternoon. Her mother added a firm instruction that if Tabby should begin talking about propriety she was to be clearly told that a lady might usually ride with a man, even if she should not sit indoors with him. Jane looked dutiful, and carefully committed this to memory for future use.

Tabby was obviously pleased, and said nothing about

124

propriety at all. She said that on Saturday she was to go to Preston, where she would stay a few days with friends while she bought clothes for the winter, but she would spend Friday afternoon riding if Jack wished her to. Jane must therefore convey her thanks for the invitation. Jane, interested as usual, wondered how Tabby would spend her time in Preston, apart from her shopping, for Preston was notably a pleasant town, the first in the county for its inns and shops, its assembly rooms and finely built houses. In social life it so led the county that many of its houses were rented during the winter by country gentlemen who wished to give pleasure to their wives, and perhaps — as it was sometimes whispered — find husbands for their daughters. Jane had herself been there half a dozen times for shopping, and had always wished to stay longer. But she was not sure of Tabby, who might or might not look further than the shops.

'How long will you stay?' she asked.

'A week or so. Perhaps a little longer.'

'I hope there's plenty to do. They say it's October before Preston really starts.'

'Good enough for me, Jane.'

Jane went home and told this to her mother, who received it with plain annoyance.

'Going away?' she said tartly. 'Just when Jack begins to take notice of her? He invites her to ride with him, which is surely what she'd have wished, and then she'll go out of his sight the next day! Is that it?'

'She said she was going to friends, so it might have been an old promise.'

'There are friends and friends, Jane, and you have sometimes to consider which to put first. She could at least have said she'd be back as soon as possible.'

'She said a week.'

'Heaven help her! He's merely on a visit here, so you'd think she'd use what time she has. There are some people you can't help.' Lady Mallinder considered it for a despairing moment. 'I think, Jane, we'll say nothing of this to Jack when he comes in. She can tell him herself and make her own apologies. I hope he's enjoying Aunt Sophie.'

He came in at the end of the afternoon, saying he had indeed enjoyed Aunt Sophie, and Celia too.

'They're charming,' he declared, 'both of them, but especially the aunt. I've met no one who can talk so well and keep it so interesting. She knows something of the Army too.'

'Her marriage, and her brother's friends.'

'Just so. But she's certainly waking up. Celia too. They're buying horses now.'

'What!'

'Yes. It seems that in retirement she sold off and left the stable empty. But now she's buying again.'

'For Celia?'

'Herself as well. She says she'll need to ride if she's invited anywhere — as she means to be — so she's starting to get the feel of it again. I've been helping to choose a stableman.'

'*You* have?' Lady Mallinder again sounded none too pleased.

'Yes. Between three who wanted it. She'd told them to come today so that I could choose for her. She said a man would do it better.'

'Perhaps. But it was making use of you.'

'I was glad to help.' He laughed cheerfully. 'But that was nothing. I've been wine tasting since then.'

'You've what?'

'Yes, I have. She made some very pretty apologies and then took me to the wine cellar. There was quite a stock of wine when her husband died, and she's hardly broached a bottle since, so there it still is. But what's fit to drink, and what isn't? That's the question.'

'Did you know?'

126

'Not properly. Some of the wines, I suppose, will be the better for lying, but not all. A wine that was ready those years ago may have soured by now, and the only way to learn was by tasting. So that's what we've been doing.'

'You and Sophie?'

'Yes. And she knows more about wine than I do. Except bad wine, which is what soldiers mostly get.'

'You seem very cheerful about it.'

'That's Mrs Mallinder, a gift she has. She'd make anyone cheerful.'

'How of Celia?' said Jane.

'I should think she's very pleasant, but she didn't say much. I'd like to know what she thought of the wine tasting.'

Jane wished to know what Celia thought of everything, and she went to the Dower House the next afternoon to find out. She found Celia in the garden, watching the men who were repairing the terrace and cleaning the fountain. Already the place had been made tidy, moss scraped away and the fallen statue removed, and now the retaining wall was being rebuilt. A wooden pen had been built to hold slaked lime, and a man was mixing it with sand to make the mortar. A steady clink of trowels, mingling with some noisy talk, came from the wall, where two other men were putting the stones in place and bedding them in the mortar. Celia was on the lawn, and Arcanus was at the top of it, as far away as he could get, and contriving to look displeased.

'He doesn't like noise,' said Celia. 'Or strangers in his garden. Let's go in.'

She led to her own quiet room, where her silvered ball was swaying gently in the breeze from the open window. Arcanus, following unbidden, slipped past her at the door and got in first, jumping on the window seat and looking as if this was better. Celia waved Jane to the cushions at one end of the seat, and took the other end herself, where Arcanus promptly settled on top of her. She rubbed his head, and looked at Jane.

'I'm glad to see you,' she said. 'We had your Major Ansell yesterday. Aunt Sophie, by the way, called him Major throughout, with a fine air of ease. You could see she'd done it before.'

'He's much pleased by her.'

'So he should be. She worked hard with him. A real display of knowing how.'

'But why?'

'She likes to be liked. Also, she means to be a hostess again, and she was making sure that she remembers.'

'Is wine tasting a part of it?'

'That's what I asked her — afterwards — and she told me that what matters is to make a man feel useful and important. Which is just what her wine tasting did. You could see it in his face.'

'Clever of her.'

'She knows *all* the tricks. And when I said so she rounded on me and told me it was high time I learned a few of them myself, and now was the time to do it. Part of my education, she called it. Did you know she's buying horses?'

'Jack told me.'

'Jack, is he? Still Major to me. But of course she had saddles and bridles in the stable here, and they were left and forgotten when she sold her horses. They got damp, and now they're a mass of mould, ruined quite. So the saddler must make new for us, and it will be two weeks at the least before we have them. I'm telling you this because Sophie says we're to fill the time by going to Preston to buy some clothes. Perhaps next week.'

'You might meet Tabby there. She goes tomorrow, also to buy clothes, and Mother thinks she's lost her wits. Jack's taken her riding, and he doesn't know —'

She managed to explain what she meant, and Celia sat stroking Arcanus while she considered it. Then, to his annoyance, she pulled his ears.

'I don't know,' she said slowly. 'But tell Tabby she can come here for lessons, if she wants them — from Aunt Sophie. Otherwise leave her to it. But Sophie wants clothes, and so do I if we're to start entertaining. So we're going to Preston.'

'You're lucky. I like Preston.'

'I've heard well of it. And for another reason I shall be glad to be away from here for a while. Things are becoming difficult.'

'Why?'

'Me again, just a shade too clever. Do you remember what I told you about Sally Parr and Isobel, giving them amulets?'

'Against the evil eye? Did it work?'

'Rather too well, and that's the trouble. Sally was quite sure she was safe. She could spit at Bessie Neve, and I'm told she did. But then she started talking, telling everyone what I'd done for her, and that's where it went wrong. What I'd told her was that she and Isobel were now safe from Bessie's evil eye. The tale that's round the village is that I've destroyed Bessie's power altogether, so that everybody is safe from her, not just Sally. I don't know how it went wrong like that, but it did. Gossip can, I suppose.'

'Isn't it just as well? They'll all feel happy.'

'Except Bessie, and she's the trouble. It turns out that she's been living for years on the evil eye. It wasn't just that cake of Sally's. It's what she's been doing with everybody. She knows she frightens people, and she's been living on it. It hasn't stopped at cakes. It's been milk and cheese and flour, the best of the fruit and vegetables, meat when she could see it — everything she needed, and from one house after another, and everyone too frightened

129

to stop her. She's been very comfortable on it. But now they aren't frightened of her any more, and if she looks into a house she's told to get out. One man, I'm told helped her out with his boot. She gets nothing, and I don't think she ever will, now.'

'Just as well, perhaps. I thought she was a sempstress.'

'She'll have to be one again, and she doesn't like it. The eye was an easier living, so you can guess what a temper she's in with me. Taking the bread out of her mouth is the way she's talking.'

'Poor Bessie!'

'Why? She hates the sight of me, and she's been talking to Joe Parker, who's still quite sure I sent Arcanus to break his leg. So it's getting awkward. Joe and Bessie will be laying their heads together, and of course there'll be a few others who'll join them, people who don't like witches, or don't like me, and between them they could make some trouble. These country folk can be cunning when they're angry, so I shan't be sorry to be away for a few days.'

'I don't think they can do much.'

'There's the vicar, though. If a group forms against me, he'll probably take the lead, and that's more dangerous. He's forceful, even if he's mad. Is there any news of him, by the way?'

'Jack's been talking to him, and he thinks he's had a childhood fright. And then forgotten it.'

'What's this?' Celia was suddenly alert. 'Tell me.'

Jane did so, as fully as she could remember it, and Celia's interest was plain. She listened intently, and asked a question or two to clear some details. Then she gave it some thought before she spoke.

'It could be so,' she said at length. 'It could indeed. I've seen something like it in Ireland. A woman with a secret fear. But it took the wisest witch of all to find that memory in her, and *she* had to use her deepest wisdom.'

'A witch did it?'

'She's the wise woman, isn't she? But never mind that. You say Jack Ansell is to ask him if he remembers anything? Let me know what comes of it. I'm interested. And it *would* make things easier if the man could find some sense.'

But that had to wait. Jane had been home for an hour, and was strolling in the garden with her mother, when Ansell returned from his ride with Tabby. He came at once to the garden to find them, and it was plain that he was in high good humour. Lady Mallinder saw it with surprise.

'You've enjoyed it?' she asked.

'Excellently.' He had a happy smile as he looked at her. 'I'm most grateful, ma'am, for the hospitality you are giving me. None the less—'

'What is it, Jack?'

'I'm asking for your sufferance. I learn that Tabby must go to Preston tomorrow. She's to visit friends there.'

'A pleasant town.'

'Indeed yes. But there's a difficulty. She has no family with her now, and therefore none to escort her, and it would scarcely be proper for her to ride alone. She had intended to pay some lads from the village, but—'

'Oh no, no.' Lady Mallinder's wits had begun to work again. 'Hardly suitable, Jack.'

'Precisely. So I've agreed to ride with her myself, and see her safe to Preston. If you — er—'

'By all means, and you'll be welcome here again when you return.'

'Thank you. I shall stay a few nights at an inn. Tabby would have me meet her friends.'

'I wish you a pleasant stay.'

'So do I,' said Jane.

She was changing her estimate of Tabby; who would not, after all, need lessons from Aunt Sophie.

11
An Affair of State

Jack went off with Tabby the next morning. Jane, now much interested, had her own safe pad from the stable and rode with them through the village till they found the Preston road. Later in the day, feeling that she wished to talk about this, she went to tell Celia, who showed signs of amusement.

'I told Sophie last night,' she said, 'that Tabby was going away and leaving him to mope, and what do you think she said?'

'Tell me.'

'She said if Tabby had a grain of sense she'd be asking him what the road was like when he came here, and whether he thought she'd be safe alone. Hmm!' Celia laughed softly. 'So Tabby *has* a grain of sense. Let's tell Sophie.'

They found Sophie in the garden, telling the man who had been scraping moss from the sundial that he could now get soap and water and wash it. She heard them with interest.

'Good,' she declared. 'I don't like to hear of anyone being as stupid as she seemed to be, and I'm pleased she's not. What's the matter, Celia? Aren't you pleased too?'

'Oh, in that way, yes. But Jane told me that the man was to talk to the vicar, hoping to clear his mind a little, and I think it's high time someone did. Now, of course, it's put off.'

132

'It can wait. Though I agree there must have been something the vicar hasn't recovered from. Some of his sermons are very foolish. I wonder what he'll preach about tomorrow?'

'Me, I should guess,' said Celia. 'He'll have heard of Bessie Neve by now, and what she thinks I've done to her.'

It was a reasonable guess, but it was wrong. The vicar's sermon next morning surprised everyone. The Lord their God, he told them, had blessed them with sun and rain. The harvest would be good. In the next week the last of it would be carried in, and he had no doubt that every farm would observe the ancient custom of harvest-home. A procession would be formed to bring in the last load, and the youngest of the reapers would carry a fantastic doll made from the last sheaf of corn. There would be singing and cheering, and then, when the sheaves were at last under cover, safe from the winter rain, a festive supper, with music and dancing to follow it through the evening. This was good. There was a spirit of thankfulness in this, as well as of rejoicing, and that was right and proper. But it was a vague thankfulness. Thankful to whom? They should be thankful to the Lord their God, and to none other, and he had therefore decided that two Sundays hence they should offer a special thanksgiving during the morning service. Also — and here he looked carefully round the church — it would be very fitting if those whose yield had been plentiful would offer some small part of it to the poor, as an act pleasing to God. He would ask the churchwardens to receive such gifts for the poor of the parish, and he hoped they would be generous.

He ended abruptly, leaving his people to make what they could of this, and Sir John was heard to mutter that it was at least a change from witches. Outside, on the path, he told the vicar gruffly that he approved of it.

'A good old custom, a harvest-home,' he added. 'They all like it, and I'm glad you're not against it.'

'Oh no. If only they remember.' The vicar looked round as if his mind was not quite on this talk. 'I don't see Major Ansell today. I had hoped—'

'He's away.'

Sir John explained about Preston, and the vicar stood in silence as he took this in.

'I see,' he said blankly. 'I had hoped for a talk with him. He did say—'

'That he'd be talking with you. Aye. But he'll be back soon, and I'll see he doesn't forget.' Sir John sounded as if he, too, thought it was important. 'A good fellow, Ansell, and he's learned a lot in the wars.'

'Indeed yes. A man used to troubles, and able to overcome them. And at this time—'

'What of it?'

'Have you perhaps heard—'

He glanced round him, and Sir John was in a good enough humour to take the hint. He stepped off the path to the grass, where they could talk unheard, and the vicar went with him. Jane and her mother were left standing alone till Sophie came to them, bringing Celia with her.

'And what did you think of that?' asked Sophie. 'The sermon, I mean?'

'Oh —' Lady Mallinder hesitated. 'Sound enough, I should think.'

'The giving to the Poor? Excellent. But I don't think that's what he really had in mind.'

'What then?'

'The doll in the harvest-home.'

'They make it from a sheaf of corn.'

'And they give it eyes and a mouth and a nose, and they carry it lifted high. The men pull their hats off to it, and the girls dip a curtsey. So what do you think the doll is, or used to be?'

134

'Sophie, what are you talking about?'

'The corn doll.' Sophie wrinkled her forehead and looked thoughtful. 'Don't you understand? The doll is the old corn goddess, and when they carry her in procession, and shout and sing to her, they're thanking her for ripening the grain. They don't know that, of course. They've forgotten it. But the doll remains.'

'And a procession,' said Celia. 'With singing and dancing and feasting. It could all be put back.'

'Back?' Sophie's tone sharpened. 'By a witch, do you mean?'

'It's a part of the Old Religion.'

'What *are* you talking about?' said Lady Mallinder.

'The vicar,' said Sophie, with the calm of one who is used to steering talk to safety. 'I was saying he had more in mind than he told us.'

'And what, pray?'

'I think he knows well that the doll is what he'd call pagan. So what is he to do? He'd never persuade them to give up their harvest-home. It's too deep rooted. But if he can turn it into a Christian thanksgiving all will be well, and that's what he's trying to do.'

'Nonsense,' said Lady Mallinder tartly. 'You're making a mountain out of nothing. These things are forgotten now, and nothing is needed but to leave well alone.'

'He isn't a man to leave well alone. And he may have thought —' Sophie hung on for a moment, and a little pucker, which might have been amusement, came to her forehead, '— that if he didn't turn it into a Christian festival, someone might turn it into an older one. Did I tell you that my terrace is all made good again?'

She kept firmly to small talk until Sir John came across the grass to join them. But he showed no wish for talk. He was silent as they walked home, and he settled at once to his wine, saying tersely that he needed it. Then he had a question for Jane.

'Jane, what's this tale about young Celia and Bessie Neve? Something to do with an evil eye, or some such nonsense. I'm sure you know about it.'

Jane had to do her best, again with some thought of how much had been told to her in confidence. So she kept to the facts, Sally Parr's cake, Celia's amulets, and the abrupt end of Bessie's easy living. Her father listened with an occasional nod.

'Aye,' he said slowly. 'That's pretty well what he told me. Do you say Celia's bragging she's cured this evil eye?'

'She doesn't believe in the evil eye. She says all that was needed was to stop Sally being frightened.'

'There's some sense in that, perhaps. Better than I'd expected, from Celia. But she says all the others are safe too?'

'No, she hasn't said that. She doesn't know how that tale started.'

'The vicar says they all believe it?'

'Yes. So Bessie's getting nothing.'

'That won't harm. I've never liked that woman, but I didn't know she was living on the others like that.' He swung suddenly to his wife. 'I don't like the way the man's taking it. It's pulling him both ways, and he'll break in half if he's not careful.'

'What do you mean, both ways?'

'Oh—' He toyed irritably with his wineglass, and then tried to explain it. 'He believes in the evil eye, and he thinks it's very bad, about as bad as witching people.'

'Then isn't he glad it's been stopped?'

'He'd like to be, but it was stopped by Celia, with those amulets, and that was all wrong too. It was witchery.'

'But—'

'Don't you see it? If he says she did right he's approving a witch. If he says she did wrong, he's approving the evil eye, which is just as bad. So what's he to do?'

136

'What did you tell him?'

'I told him it was good out of evil, and he said that two evils don't make a good. You can't please the man anyway. I'm beginning to feel sorry for him. He's pulled both ways, and he hasn't had that before. He's always known the will of God about everything, but this time he doesn't, and it's just about pulling him in two.'

'Then what should be done?'

'I don't know.'

Jane, who had been sitting still and quiet, did not know what she thought of this. It seemed to her that the vicar had shown more sense than usual in his sermon, and that if he did share Sophie's belief about the corn doll he had handled it sensibly. He had not mentioned it openly, or put ideas into anyone's head, and his suggestion of gifts to the poor could surely cause no trouble. It left Jane wondering whether he could really be as distracted as her father had said.

There was a surprise during the afternoon. Celia came with a message for Sir John, saying that she and Sophie would be going to Preston on Thursday and would stay for a week. Sir John was surprised, but he appreciated the courtesy and sent a polite message back. Celia departed, and Jane chose to walk across the park with her. It was soon clear that Celia had this belief about the corn doll.

'Oh yes,' she said, 'and I'm sure the harvest-home is what's left of an old thanksgiving. Probably a very old one. And people *ought* to be thankful for the harvest.'

'That's what the vicar said. But he didn't mean thankful to a corn goddess.'

'What's that to it? There can be only one god, so it's only a matter of a name.'

'I don't think he'd say that.'

'But I do. So in this I'm with him, even if he isn't with me. But did the date seem odd to you, that he's fixed for this?'

'Why?'

'When will harvest be finished?'

'Two or three days, if the weather holds.'

'Then why wait a fortnight? Two more Sundays is what he said.'

'Oh?' Jane considered it quickly. 'What do you think?'

'I think he's being artful. Being what he is, he'll expect something from me at full moon, which will be on the 30th, early in the morning. Even more, he'd expect something at Michaelmas, which is the day before. So the night between them is the time when he'll expect all sorts of horrors to be let loose in his parish. They won't be, of course, but he'll expect them, and I think that's why he's put his giving as near as he can to that night. He'd like to turn their minds to something Christian just then.'

'And what will *you* do, just then?'

'Tell my people to support the giving. And perhaps go a little further in giving thanks for the harvest.'

'Will there be trouble?'

'There shouldn't be, but you know what he is. There'll be trouble of one sort or another as long as he's like this. Wasn't Jack Ansell to talk to him about his early days? When does he come back?'

'When Tabby does, I should think.'

But the fates thought differently. At noon the next day a lad came riding to the house with a letter. Sir John, who was at dinner, put down his knife in surprise, broke the seal, and looked first at the signature.

'From Jack,' he announced. 'What's wrong with him?'

He began to read, and then he caught noisily at his breath. His face changed, and soon he was staring at it in consternation.

'Good God!' he growled.

'What?' said his wife. 'Is he ill?'

'No, it's—' He stared again at the sheet. 'It's some fool

in Scotland. Where's Braemar? Have you heard of the place?'

'What's the matter?'

'He's out for the Chevalier. Out in arms.'

'Jack?'

'Don't be silly. The Earl of Mar, he says, and he must be mad. With the French king gone—'

'John, will you read me the letter, please.'

He picked up the sheet again and began to read it to her.

I must acquaint you of a great commotion suddenly come to Preston this Sunday afternoon. At about four of the clock an express came in from Edinburgh with news of swords drawn for the King who is across the water. It says that on Tuesday last gone, the 6th of September, at Braemar in Scotland, the Earl of Mar raised the King's Standard with as much ceremony as the circumstances of the place would allow. It is not yet known what forces he has, but it is supposed that he will soon be joined by many of the Scottish chieftains and their men. So the enterprise which I had thought abandoned has begun.

I feel some alarm at this. Such an enterprise was possible when we could look to France, but what can be looked for now, when France will send us nothing? I do not think we can blame Mar for this. King Louis died only on the 1st, and the news of his going can hardly have reached such a place as Braemar by the 6th. Mar must have raised his Standard not knowing that his support had gone, and by now he will have learned the truth.

But enough of that. It will all come clear, in God's good time, and my concern now is for the men I visited and talked with last month, simple gentlemen, not soldiers, perhaps not understanding that our hopes of success died with King Louis. I fear that some of them, hearing of a Standard raised, will declare themselves too soon, and may therefore lose their estates, and perhaps their lives, if a rising without proper arms should come quickly to an end. This, since they have trusted me and sat at wine with me, I must use all endeavours to prevent, and I see mothing for it but to go north again at once with some words of warning. I shall go tomorrow and complete this work as soon as maybe. Then, if you and Lady Mallinder will permit, I shall return to you.

I have spoke of this to Tabby, who shows at least some understanding of it. She sends her felicitations, as, of course, do I.

'Mad,' said Sir John again as he flung the letter to the table. 'I've heard before that Mar's a fool, but who said he was a general? What does he know of campaigns? It should have been the Duke of Berwick, who *is* a soldier.'

'John, will you come to earth, please? Who commands this affair is no concern of ours, and please God it won't be. I'd like to know what Tabby thinks.'

'Of what?'

'Use your wits. His going away, of course, when she's just got him to Preston.'

'He says she understands.'

'At least some understanding is what he says, and that sounds cautious.'

'It's an affair of State, and she'll have to put up with it.'

'Affairs of State may not be first in her mind, and I'd like to know what she really thinks.'

12
Thanksgivings

Tabby did not come back to tell them what she thought of it. She had arranged to stay for a week, and she did so. Sophie and Celia went on the Thursday, and Jane thought the village was empty. A newsletter said the Duke of Argyll had been sent to command the Government forces in Scotland against whatever rebels there might be, and since he was able and experienced soldier, who had been one of the Duke of Marlborough's best officers, this seemed to most people to be all that was needed. They took rebellion off their minds, and turned to their own affairs.

Tabby came back on Saturday, and she was in the church on Sunday to hear the vicar preach to the times, denouncing the rebellion as a popish plot, and warning his hearers to give it neither sympathy nor help. Sir John, who was still a mixture of new prudence and old loyalties, heard it with annoyance. Afterwards, on the churchyard path, he was at hand when his wife intercepted Tabby and asked her what she thought of Jack Ansell's new journey to the north.

'Oh—' Tabby hung on it for a moment. 'I can't say I was pleased, just when I had a chance to see him and talk to him, but it wasn't to be helped. I don't think he wanted to, but he was sure he must.'

'What did you say to that?'

'What could I say? If he thinks it can't succeed, I suppose he's right to keep these men out of trouble.'

141

She had plainly no more to say about it, and it had to drop. Sir John said nothing, but he certainly shared Tabby's wish that Jack would come back soon and safe, and he was still brooding on this when the vicar came to him a day or two later, asking for help with his thanksgiving for the harvest. He was anxious that it should succeed, particularly the giving to the poor, and asked that Sir John, as the squire, should give a lead in this. Sir John, seeing at once that he would have to, put a good face on it and answered that he would be delighted to give to such a cause. He was at his affable best when he said it, but it appeared later that he had no thought of doing any of it himself. What he had meant was that his wife would be delighted to do it, and he was very much at his ease when he told her so. She, also, could find no argument against it, and she told him she would see to it. Then she sent for Jane and told her to see to it.

Sophie came back with Celia on the Thursday, and Jane, going the next afternoon for a word with Celia, found her in a room littered with cabbages and cauliflowers, carrots and turnips, lettuce and cress, peaches, pears, plums and quince. Arcanus, comfortably asleep in his own corner of the window seat, lifted his head as Jane came in, and took a careful look at her. His nose quivered, as if he was taking a scent, and then he went to sleep again.

'He likes the scent of it,' said Celia. 'Especially the fruit. Can you guess what it's for?'

'I can. Has the vicar been to see you?'

'To see Sophie, not me, and she was as sweet as honey with him. She promised him all he wanted, and I suppose she was right. The man needs someone to be sweet to him. Is there any other news?'

'Only this affair in Scotland. It's taken Jack Ansell north again, to warn men to be careful.'

'What men?'

'Oh!'

Suddenly and acutely Jane was aware that she had blundered. Celia was a Whig, Sophie was a worse one, and they had not been told the truth about Jack Ansell. Nor should they have been, and Jane knew that she had now let it out, or as nearly as mattered. Celia nodded.

'So he *is* for the Chevalier? I thought he must be. But it's all right, Jane. I shan't talk.'

'But you're a Whig?'

'Leave that to the men. It isn't coming between you and me. We'll talk of something else. Have you heard of anything stirring in the village?'

'What sort of thing?'

'I don't know. My people think something could be brewing, but it's all very vague. So far it seems to be only women talking to women, half whispering, and watching you all the time to see if you're coming close. Then talking about the weather if you do. It doesn't sound much, but my people have noticed it as unusual, so I suppose it could mean something.'

'I'm afraid I can't help.'

'Then I'll have to wait and see. There's a hint, by the way, that Bessie Neve is deep in it, now she hasn't an evil eye.'

'Oh?'

'Exactly. So I'm just wondering. She might be trying something else.'

To Jane's surprise this came up again on Sunday, after the service of thanksgiving, which was a success. The bringing of gifts, led by the Manor House and the Dower House, had produced more than the vicar had even hoped for, and he said so from the pulpit. He thanked everyone, and he promised that he and the church-wardens would see to it that the flowers and fruit and vegetables were shared between those most in need. He was obviously pleased. But afterwards, on the path, his mood changed, and after a little hesitation he told Sir John that he must speak of something else. Then, slowly and carefully, he came out with almost the tale that Celia had told Jane. He admitted he could not be sure. He had only some scraps of gossip to go on, but he much feared it was another matter of witches, and he hoped it could be stamped upon at once. A quick glance at Celia showed where his suspicions lay, and Sir John seemed to share them. He went straight to Celia, told her what he had heard, and asked her in blunt words whether she was behind this and whether she was preparing some new stupidity. Celia caught at her breath, and then she spoke as bluntly as he had done.

'No,' she told him. 'I'm not behind it and I don't know who is. I don't even know what it's about, and I wish I did. And I'm not preparing a stupidity for Michaelmas or for any other time. Pray tell the vicar so.'

Sir John looked baffled and had to accept it. He told the vicar. But it evidently stayed in his mind, for when he was home and at his wine, he turned to Jane, asking her why Celia had mentioned Michaelmas. Was this tattle in the village about Michaelmas?

'I don't know,' said Jane. 'But Michaelmas is on Thursday, and it's said to be a witches' day, or a witches' night. So I suppose it's close enough to set Mr Loveday worrying.'

That, too, must have stayed in Sir John's mind, for the next morning he sent for Jack Earnshaw and asked him if he had heard anything of this muttering in the village. Earnshaw looked reluctant and then said that he had, though he did not yet know what it was about. He thought Bessie Neve had something to do with it, though she might not be the leader; and so far he had learned no more than that. Sir John grunted, and again had to let it drop.

144

His thoughts were taken off it when a newsletter came from London and told him that some four thousand men had now joined the Earl of Mar, who had already occupied Perth. Further north the Mackintosh was out. Seven hundred of his clan had joined him at the summons of the fiery cross, one of them being his kinsman Mackintosh of Borlum, a soldier of experience who had served in the armies of France. He had now taken command of the clan, and already he had surprised and taken Inverness; and it could hardly be doubted that he would now march south to join the Earl of Mar.

Whatever Sir John's thoughts on this may have been, he was taken out of them on Wednesday when the vicar arrived, again looking harassed. The next day would be Michaelmas, he said, and he had not forgotten Lammas. So if there was now to be a further outbreak of witchcraft he thought they should be ready to deal firmly with it. There were still men in the parish who had a proper understanding of these matters, and he thought that a small band of them should be out on Thursday night, patrolling like the Watch in a town. He hoped that Sir John would approve of this, and perhaps lead the patrol. Sir John hiccuped, and then made it plain that he had no intention whatever of walking about all night looking for witches. If the vicar chose to do so, well and good, and he could have Sir John's good wishes. But if there was any thought of arresting evil-doers they had better take the constable with them, since he alone had authority for that.

Michaelmas Day was dull and overcast, but by sunset the cloud was breaking and there was prospect of a fine night. The vicar had found half a dozen volunteers for his patrol, Joe Parker being the most zealous of them, and he had also the help of Earnshaw, who would much have preferred to spend the night in bed but had been too good natured to refuse. They went out at ten o'clock, and found the village quiet and deserted, all doors shut and not a gleam of light anywhere. To the east, above the moor, the harvest moon was bright in an all but cloudless sky, and under it the sleeping village was black and silver. In the light it would be impossible for anyone to move without being seen; in the shadows it would be easy.

They went carefully round the village, going into every shadow and to the back of every hedge, and they found no one. They went further out, looking for any gleam of light in a barn or shed, and again they found nothing. They returned to the green, and the vicar led them to the church. Witches, he told them, had been known to meet in churches, and they had better make sure, even though he had carefully locked it. They looked, and found no one. Nor, in the churchyard, did anyone lurk in the shadow of a tree. They made sure of it, and again they walked round the village, finding nothing.

It wanted a few minutes to midnight when an excited yelp from Joe Parker set them turning to look to the east. High above them on the distant slope of the moor, a point of light had sprung into being, flickering and unsteady, yellow against the silver moon. They stood staring, and saw it grow bigger, and a tinge of red come into the yellow. Thoughts of Lammas came to them at once, for this was a fire newly lighted, and it was at the Sisters or near to them; which made it a full three miles away, and all of it uphill. It would take them at least an hour to reach it.

It took them all of that, and the fire grew bigger as they went, and the heart of it redder. At two furlongs they could see the leaping flames and the sparks in the pall of silver smoke. It was certainly at the Sisters, and at one furlong the vicar stopped them. A few yards more, he told them, and they would be seen in the moonlight,

146

and the whole coven might then scatter and escape. So he sent Earnshaw with half the party to work round the stones and then close in from above. He and the others stayed where they were for five endless minutes, lying on the grass and hearing the crackle of the fire in the utter silence of the night. Then they came to their feet, a little nervous now, not knowing what they would find. They gripped their sticks firmly, and then they rushed at it.

They found no one. In the moonlight they must have seen anyone who tried to escape, and they saw nobody. They ran into the circle of stones, panting a little now, and they found no one. There was only the crackling fire, now dying down and short of fuel. Earnshaw and his party came rushing in, and they, too, had seen no one. They stood in the heat and glare of the fire, getting breath again and wondering what had happened. The fire had been big. Someone had taken some trouble over it, and it must surely have had a purpose. They looked at one another, puzzled.

'Look carefully,' said the vicar. 'They'll have left the signs of their hellish work, as they did at Lammas. Look everywhere.'

They looked, and they found nothing. Someone took a flaming brand as a torch to light the dark, and still they found nothing, no bones or crumbs of bread, no circle drawn with a knife, no whiff of incense, nothing to give a purpose to this fire.

'We must not expect it to be easy,' said the vicar. 'The devil is sly and cunning, and he knows well how to hide his works. Yet by the grace of God, and if we persevere, all will be made plain.'

'It's plain enough now for me,' said Earnshaw, 'and we needn't go on looking. We've been fooled and brought up here for nothing. That's what this fire's for, to get us out of the way. And while we're safe up here, there'll be summat going on down there.'

'Hell!' said Joe Parker, in a consternation that quickly spread to the others. The thought seemed all too likely, and even the vicar did not dispute it. He gave a last look round, at the ring of stones, the dying fire, and the great sweep of the hill, silent under the moon, and then he led them to the downward track. It was easier going this way, but they still had three miles of it, and it was past two o'clock when they came at last to a sleeping village that was as quiet and peaceful as it could ever be. Not a mouse was stirring, and the moon was bright and inscrutable.

They went to the parsonage for hot mulled ale, and then out again for another walk round, and they kept at it, patrolling in turns till six o'clock, when the sun was rising above the moor, and doors were opening and chimneys puffing smoke as the village roused for the day. They had seen nothing and heard nothing that should not have been, and Joe Parker, going for his breakfast, said that mischief could have been done earlier, when they were safely on the moor.

But Joe, hungry after his night of fresh air, was still of a mind for more of his wife's cold bacon when a neighbour ran in and began to chatter excitedly to her. Joe got up from the table with some noisy questions, and a minute later he was rushing out of the house to see for himself. He saw, and went for the vicar. The vicar saw, and hurried to the Manor House for Sir John. Sir John, now thinking they were all mad here but himself, clapped his hat on his head and went stumping off to see what they were talking about. Jane attached herself and went with him, uninvited.

Beyond the green, outside the village proper, was what they called the well, though it was really a spring that gushed from a fissure in the rock. It had never failed in the memory of any of them, and in times of drought, when the stream from the moor ran low, they turned thankfully to the well, sure that its clear cold water would still be splashing and gurgling into the little stone pool that an earlier Mallinder had built for them underneath it. Even in this year the women had washed their clothes in its pool during the Lammas drought.

Sir John, taken there by the vicar, gave a grunt of surprise and then stood staring. The well was as it had always been, the water still frothing into the pool, and the overflow still tumbling into the conduit that took it to the green. But the wide flat stones that capped the wall of the pool were covered now with fruit and flowers, big white asters, sunflowers, corn marigolds, larkspur and some late roses, with apples and pears, and in the centre some ears of corn. Someone had stretched a cord across the steep rock face above the fissure, and from this hung stems of bramble, thickly clustered with fruit. It had all been done quite simply, with no attempt at elaboration, and it perhaps looked the better for that. The well was simple, and this suited it.

'What the devil!' said Sir John. 'What's it for? And who did it?'

'We may guess what it's for,' said the vicar tartly. 'Is it not a mockery of what was done in church on Sunday?'

'Oh—' Sir John scratched his head and belatedly pulled his hat straight. 'It's the same sort of thing, but why call it a mockery? Somebody may have liked it.'

'Then I do *not*. It is an offering — but to whom?'

'Why call it an offering? It looks quite pretty to me.'

'Does it not seem pagan to you?'

'No. Why should it?'

'Why?' The word rang hard. 'Then will you please to walk to that field with me, the three-acre one behind the trees?'

This was part of Sir John's own farm. They crossed a field and passed round a line of trees that made a wind-break. They were in a field of stubble, short and thick,

149

trodden down by the gleaners as they had gathered for themselves the fallen ears the reapers had left; and here the vicar pointed dramatically. Near the trees, and hidden by them from the village, a sheaf of corn was standing, which had not been left by the reapers. It was firmly tied, and had perhaps a stick inside it to keep it upright. Round it, on the trodden stubble, a carpet of hay had been spread, and on the hay were potatoes, carrots, onions, and turnips, as if here was another offering; and half-way up the cornsheaf a little basket was hanging, looking strangely out of place.

'And what, pray, do you make of that?' said the vicar.

'I don't make anything of it. It doesn't make sense. What do *you* make of it? And what's that basket for?'

'I don't understand the basket. It will be a symbol, no doubt, of something hideous. But of the general meaning of the effigy I have no doubt at all. For an effigy, of course, it is. This thing—' He pointed to the cornsheaf in the stubble. 'What can it be but a pagan corn god, with the first fruits offered to it?'

'It looks damn silly to me. What's that round the top of it?'

'This?' The vicar touched a string that went round the top of the sheaf, with ears of barley hanging from it. 'The best they could do as a garland, perhaps. Another way of showing honour to the thing.'

'Oh?' Sir John looked carefully, and did not seem much impressed. 'And who do you mean by they? Witches again, is it?'

'Are they not pagan?'

'I don't know. But if this is what witches do these days, I don't think you need worry. They're not what they used to be, and you can be glad of that.'

'Glad?'

'Yes. And do think straight for a minute. In the old days, from the tales we've heard, witches were a pretty nasty lot, with their sabbats and their man in black and their images and dead men's teeth — even if most of it wasn't true. There were charges enough of murder against them then, even in this parish.'

'Do I not know it?'

'But they're not doing it now, and that's what I'm telling you.'

'At Lammas, by the Sisters, I found gnawed bones, a scent of incense, and—'

'I've gnawed a chicken bone or two myself, and so have you. And you'll find incense more in churches than anywhere else. So witches aren't what they used to be, and that's what I'm telling you. There's no talk of murder in these days, and none of dying cattle or blasted crops. There's only this, and I don't see what harm it does.'

'No spiritual harm?'

'Is it harm to give thanks, even in this crazy way? I've called it nonsense and you've called it pagan, and perhaps we're both right. But it could be better than no thanks at all.'

A foot moved in the stubble behind him, and a dry stem cracked. He spun round to find Celia with them, looking calm and cheerful.

'Exactly,' she said quietly. 'And that's the reason for it.'

13
The Grand-daughter

For a long moment Sir John stood watching her, perhaps wondering what was coming.

'Reason why what?' he said slowly. 'Did you put this thing here?'

'I had it put.'

'Then will you tell me the reason why?'

'Thanksgiving. And whether it's pagan or not, it will be better, as you've just said, than no thanks at all.'

'Aye.' He nodded slowly. 'I think that's true.'

'It is *not* true,' said the vicar, and his voice crackled with anger as he turned on Celia. 'Thanks have already been given in the church, so what cause had you to think that it should now be done again — by you?'

'We think that thanks for corn are best given in a cornfield.'

'And what, pray, do you call this thing you have made from a cornsheaf?'

'The name hardly matters. It is a reminder only, of God dwelling in the corn.'

'Now that's enough,' said Sir John suddenly, and his tone made it clear that he was the Justice and the squire and Sir John Mallinder too, and was now taking charge. 'Celia, if you learned this corn god blather in Ireland, I can't blame you too much for that. But it upsets the vicar, and you're not here to upset him. So just bear that in mind, and don't flaunt your moonshine under our

152

noses like this. And for you, Vicar, if you make a fuss about this you'll have everyone thinking it's important, which it isn't. Take no notice and they'll forget it in a week, and that's my advice to you. Now we'll go home.'

He was brusque and authoritative, very much a man who knows what is needed and will stand no nonsense. But when he was home again he seemed less confident.

'It's this nonsense of Celia's,' he said to his wife. 'It sounds all right as she puts it to you. Give thanks for the harvest, and this corn thing is just to remind you, but there might be more than that to it if she told you all she has in mind. I'm not surprised Loveday doesn't like it.'

'What did he say?'

'He thinks it's the road to hell, but he'd probably think the same of anything else she might do. You can't talk to the man.'

He went on grumbling. But an hour later he was pulled out of his disgruntled mood by the return of Jack Ansell, who came riding in from the north looking tired and cheerful.

'I think it's all done,' he said, when he had washed the dust off and been given wine. 'How's Tabby?'

'Alive and well, but keeping much to herself. You'd best go to see her.'

'I will, if I may stay here a little longer.'

'As long as you like, Jack. How is it in the north?'

'I've done what I could. I've warned them to be careful till they can see support from France, and I think they understand.'

'Aye, aye. But in Scotland, I mean. What's the latest from there?'

'Oh — Mar is at Dunkeld. His force is growing, and it must be six or seven thousand now. Argyll is at Stirling, commanding for Hanover, and at present he's weaker than Mar. But of course he'll be reinforced, so

153

Mar's obvious duty is to hit him *now*, with every sword the clans can muster. Instead of which, Mar stays comfortably at Dunkeld, doing nothing that I know of, and it looks to me like another enterprise being thrown away by muddle and incompetence. Still, war is full of the unexpected, so we must not lose hope.'

'No, no.' Sir John sounded a little more hearty than he perhaps really was. 'But if you're to be here for a while, Jack, I'm going to ask a small help of you. It's this vicar of ours. You'll remember you'd a notion of some witch or other giving him a fright when he was young, and you thought it might help if he could remember it.'

'So I did. But have you had more trouble?'

'About a corn doll, of all things.'

He went on to give an account of it, and Ansell listened carefully. Then he was cautious.

'I'll try if you wish,' he said. 'Your vicar did ask to talk with me, and he might be willing to talk of his earlier days and memories. Or he might not. I can't say, of course.'

'No, no. But if you'd try?'

'By all means, in due season. But I'd like it to be Tabby first.'

'Quite right, Jack. First by all means.'

Jane picked up the gist of this from the talk at dinner, and decided on a visit to Celia. She walked across the park to the Dower House, and Annis took her at once to Celia's room. Celia, sitting at the plain and sturdy table of local chestnut, looked up with a smile of welcome.

'I'm glad you're here,' she said. 'Our tea's waiting.'

'Did you guess I should come?'

'I knew you would. I've been doing some scrying.'

'Oh?'

Jane glanced round, and the room looked different. Michaelmas was gone, and this was the last day of September. The sky was dull and grey, with some spots

154

of rain and a chill in the wind, and the room had
responded to this. It was dull too, without the sparkle
of colour it had had in the summer. In the window the
cushions were less vivid, and the silver ball no longer
flashed and gleamed. In the hearth, under the copper
canopy, a fire was burning where sunflowers had been
in the summer days. The table, too, was different. It had
always had flowers in summer, and now it had Arcanus.
He was lying on it, awake and alert, facing Celia and
looking steadily at her. Between them, on the table, was
a shallow box of fine-grained sycamore, lovingly
polished, and he had his front paws pressed against it.
He took a quick glance at Jane, then gave a soft purr of
content as he turned again to Celia.

'He likes scrying,' she explained. 'He thinks he's a help.'

'How?'

'If you look into a mirror and hope to see something,
you probably will. But it's hard to know whether it's
true and real, or just your fancy. The two things look
the same. But Arcanus always does seem to know, with
those strange senses he has, and I've learned to watch
him and see if he's pleased or not. If he isn't, I don't
believe the mirror, and I put it aside till another day.'

'What's a mirror?'

Celia pointed to the box on the table. The golden
wood was lined with soft black velvet, and on the velvet
lay a flat piece of stone, cut to a circle some six inches
across, and of a sort new to Jane. It seemed blacker than
the velvet, and it had been ground flat and smooth and
then polished till it gleamed and reflected — a mirror
indeed, but a black one.

'It's on the table,' said Celia, 'so you shan't see the room
reflected in it. And of course you must keep back a little,
so you don't see your face in it. Then, when the mirror's
empty, you can open your mind and see what comes.'

'What's it made of?'

'Jet, I've been told.'

'Oh? You once told me I shouldn't get my visit to London, and you were right. But you did that with tea-leaves.'

'Yes.' Celia nodded, and carefully fitted a velvet-lined lid to the box. 'I didn't know you so well then. Besides, it was Lammas and very sunny, and sun isn't good for a mirror. It spoils its power. But where's this tea?'

She turned aside to pour it, and Arcanus flopped lazily off the table to find a rug by the fire. Celia passed a cup to Jane.

'Here you are,' she said, 'and I'm glad you've come. It was a difficult morning.'

'Your corn doll, you mean? And my father?'

'And the vicar too. I wasn't expecting them, Jane, when I went through those trees. I was taken by surprise, and I may have let out too much.'

'Such as what?'

'Mainly that I think country folk should have a country god with country ways. A simple one, who's seen in the corn fields. The vicar's trying to give them a god they don't understand, one out of a book, not their own lives. There's no difference really, of course. There can be only one god, but we can have different ways of talking about him.'

'But —'

'Oh, let it pass, Jane. We needn't get tied up in this. Do you know the widow Webb?'

'Maggie? Of course I do.' It was Jane's turn to be taken by surprise. 'I mean she lives in the village, and if I meet her I say it's a fine day, or something like that. But what about her?'

'I'm not sure, yet. But I did tell you of some odd talk in the village, as if something might be stirring. My people are sure now that it turns round Maggie Webb, and that she's at the centre of it.'

'What sort of talk?'

'That's what's odd. Go back fifty years, Jane, to Alice Openshaw who was hanged.'

'The witch?'

'I don't know whether she was a witch or not, but she was certainly hanged as one, and she probably thought she was one. But she left two daughters, and the elder became the mother of this Maggie I'm talking of.'

'Oh? So she's grand-daughter to—'

'To Alice, who had a bad name and was hanged. But Maggie the grand-daughter in due time married Dick Webb. I suppose you knew him?'

'Oh yes. He died last year, just before Christmas.'

'What sort of man?'

'Dour, I'd call him. Hard, perhaps. He had a year as constable, and he wasn't much liked for it. A churchman too, in his way, but again he was dour.'

'I'll believe it. But again going back to Alice who was hanged. She had two daughters, remember, and the younger one became grandmother to Annis here, who brought us this tea.'

'So she's related to Maggie?'

'First cousin once removed is what I make it. But the point is that when Annis was a little girl she looked on Maggie almost as an aunt. I don't think she ever liked her, and as a child she was frightened of her, but she's been able to tell me quite a lot. One thing is that old Alice, besides having two daughters, had a sister who also left descendants, and one of them is Bessie Neve of the evil eye. So that's in the family too, and I wish I knew the truth about Alice.'

'What truth?'

'According to Annis, Maggie used to talk to her about Alice being a witch. Maggie is turned fifty now. She was five years old when her grandmother was hanged, and she remembers her well — or thinks she does — and she remembers her as a witch. I don't think that need be true. At the age of five Maggie could have been deceived about it, specially since they say Alice was a bent old crone who muttered and mumbled and hobbled on a stick. But one of my people, who's of Maggie's age, says that when Maggie was a girl she was always telling them she was going to be a witch herself when she grew up.'

'Celia! Do you think she is one?'

'I'm quite sure she isn't, though she may think she is. She's certainly tried to be one. I'm told that at fourteen or thereabouts she tried scrying. She had an old green bottle, and she put water in it as a mirror, but it doesn't seem that she ever saw much. A year or two later she was seen in a field, squatting over a little fire she'd made, and scattering something into it that made smoke and a stench, which doesn't look as if she was up to any good. I don't hear of her after that for another twenty years, when she'd been ten years married, and this time there was no doubt at all. She made a clay image of someone and dried it, and she was caught crumbling bits off it — and you've heard of *that*, I suppose?'

'Yes — if it's true. Do witches do it?'

'A real witch wouldn't. She'd know that you must work magic with your mind, not with bits of clay. But I think it was done by women who'd set up as witches without the proper teaching. We can count Maggie as one of those.'

'But what happened with her image?'

'Her husband caught her at it, and he smashed it and burnt it. Then he took his belt to her, and they say the whole village heard her getting it. No more images after that, I'm told. She probably hadn't changed her mind, but she *had* learned to be careful.'

'I'm not surprised, if he was still keeping an eye on her.'

'But he hasn't an eye on her now, Jane. He died last Christmas, and that might be what matters.'

'Celia, what are you getting at?'

'I don't quite know. But she and Bessie Neve don't seem to have liked each other much — till now. Bessie, of course, was doing very well for herself with the evil eye, and Maggie may have been jealous of that. But Bessie's good times have stopped. She's getting no more free food, and she must either go back to being a semp-stress or find another witch in the village — not me — who'll be on *her* side and make her eye as evil as it ever was. Simple, isn't it?'

'With Maggie, of course, as the witch?'

'Who else? She's been wanting to do it for years past. She's buried her husband, and I expect she's burned his belt, perhaps with some incantations to help him to hell. So why wait longer? This is her moment, with Bessie and the evil eye to help her.'

'But can she? Do you think she *is* a witch?'

'She isn't one in any true sense. You have to be properly taught and admitted — initiated, as we say — but she probably doesn't know even that. She thinks it all came to her from her grandmother, and that nothing more is needed. So she might try it. She could even try forming a coven.'

'In the village?'

'Why not, with Bessie to help her? It won't be hard to find a few discontented women, and they won't know that she doesn't know anything. They'll take her for what she'll say she is, and it will be as nasty as her grandmother probably was — and just when I'm trying to show that a witch can be a friend and help to everyone.'

Celia broke off, and for a moment she was staring at the grey sky and the rain that spattered on the window. Then she wandered to the hearth and dropped on one knee by Arcanus, who promptly rolled on his back for attention. She was gently rubbing his chest when the door was pushed abruptly open and Sophie appeared. She gave a quick nod of greeting to Jane, and then spoke with crisp precision.

'Celia, there's a pretty tale come from the village. That stableman of ours has just come back with it. Do you know Jack Livsey, the pedlar?'

'No.'

'He came into the village an hour or so ago, coming from the south by the track along the slope of the moor. That took him past the old mill there. You know that, I suppose?'

'Yes. A ruin. About a mile out.'

'Less, I should say. But being a watermill it's on a stream, which Livsey had to cross below the millrace. He says that wasn't difficult. But he saw some feathers on the stones, as if they'd come down the race, and he was surprised. Not a place for feathers, he said. He looked more closely and decided they were from a cock.'

'What!'

'So Livsey says, and he wondered whose cock should stray out here, and why it should lose its feathers if it did. He asked about it when he was in the village, and that did start a flutter. A delicious one, I should think. Because they'd just had the vicar round, asking if they'd seen his cock bird, which had got out of the pen in the night and gone.'

'His?' Celia's tone told nothing. 'Is there any more?'

'There is. They all had a good chuckle, and then they took Livsey and his tale to the vicar. Guess what he said?'

'Hellish rights. Sacrifice of blood. The devil in our midst.'

'My clever Celia! That's just what he said.'

'Please go on.'

'He said he must see for himself. So off he went, fearing the worst.'

'Or hoping for it.'

'Perhaps. But he took Earnshaw with him, and Joe Parker managed to attach himself, all full of zeal.'

'He would.'

'And just as they were setting out Major Ansell arrived. He'd been to see Tabby, and he was on his way back. But he stopped for a word with the vicar.'

'And he was told of this?'

'Indeed he was, and then he made the flutter worse. He said Tabby had been asking where her cock bird might be. It had got loose from its pen in the night and gone.'

'What a woman!'

'Tabby?'

'No, Maggie. And I thought she wasn't ready yet. But go on.'

'Off they went, and Major Ansell too. This was about an hour ago, and by and by, when our stableman had had his beer, he decided to come and tell us. But when he was in the park, on his way here, he saw them in front of him — Ansell and the vicar, and Earnshaw and Joe — all stepping out hot foot to the Manor House. To see John, I suppose, and you can guess what they'll tell him.'

'I can.' Celia was looking steadily at her. 'Witches' work — and witches will mean me. I'm the only one they know of, and I'll get the blame for all of it.'

'Precisely, dear. That's why I thought I'd tell you.'

14
The Counter-spell

Jane walked home to find her father sitting with Jack Ansell and discussing this affair of the cock birds. Ansell, who had been with the others to the mill, would have the facts right, but the vicar, who had now left, would have provided the comments, and Jane could guess what these had been. So she pushed herself into the talk and said that Celia had not done it. Whoever had killed the birds, it had not been Celia.

'Then who was it?' asked her father.

'She doesn't know. She says it must be someone who isn't really a witch, and is only trying to be.'

'What the devil does that mean?'

Jane explained it further, and the talk went on. Jane, more or less forgotten by both of them, was able to sink quietly into a chair and listen, and she soon knew well enough what had happened at the mill that afternoon.

The party had found the feathers below the millrace, as the pedlar had said, and then they had looked at the mill itself, old and derelict. It had been there for longer than anyone knew, but it had not ground corn since the last of its owners had died at Marston Moor, leaving no heir for that dangerous trade. One man had tried it, and had soon killed himself. He had been found under the wheel, and that had been the end. The mill had stood derelict, and corn had gone elsewhere.

But the mill was strong and solid, built for the shaking

of the wheel, and its thick stone walls had come to little harm. The roof had some holes, but it was still in place, and from a little distance the mill looked much as it had always done. Even the undershot wheel was there, looking as if it might at any moment start its groaning and rumbling if someone would open the sluice and send the water roaring down the race from the pool above. The door, at the side away from the wheel, was shut, but it gave way at once when Earnshaw put his shoulder to it. Then they entered the mill.

It was dark inside, darker even than they had expected, and then, as their eyes adjusted to it, they saw that over each of the three small windows a piece of sacking had been nailed. They ripped these down and could see the great millstones still in place, covered now with cobwebs and the dust of years. Behind them was a wide and empty space where once the sacks of corn had waited, and in the centre of this a large flat stone lay on the wooden floor, looking as if it had been dragged to its present place. In the centre of it were some bits of charred wood and the ash of a small fire, and on each side of the ash they found a little pool of wax, where a candle had burned. In front of the ash a dark stain lay on the stone, and they thought this was blood, dry and black. They stirred the ash again, and found that some of it was bone, the thin twig-like bones of a bird.

That was all, except for some crumbs of bread in the thick dust on the floor. But Earnshaw pointed out that the dust did not here lie smooth and cobwebbed as it did on the millstones. It had been trodden and pushed aside, perhaps in a ring dance, like the one at Lammas at the Sisters. The vicar, in a voice shaking with anger, told them that not a doubt was left that some hellish ritual had been done here in the night, fire and candles, a crew of women on their knees, the killing of the birds, and then a ritual meal of bread dipped in blood. The dance would follow, he said, while the birds were burned as a further sacrifice to whatever fount of evil these witches worshipped. Earnshaw said nothing. Joe Parker fervently agreed; and even Ansell, though he thought most of this came only from the vicar's imagination, had to agree that something unpleasant had been done.

They had then made their way through the rain to the Manor House, where the vicar had poured out his tale to Sir John, who had received it as might have been expected. He disliked the whole of it, and he disliked even more the suggestion that Celia, in his own family, had done it. So he answered as he had done before, that he could not, as a Justice, take notice of anything as lunatic as witchcraft, and that he did not know of any other law these people had broken, bad as their behaviour had been. It was the vicar's duty, not his, to persuade them to behave better. He stuck to that, and parted from the vicar on the worst of terms.

Some second thoughts came to him as he discussed it with Ansell, and particularly when he learned that Celia had not, after all, been involved. That was much better, and he soon began to think that a law had, after all, been broken. The taking of those two birds had been theft, and he could certainly proceed on that if he could only learn who had taken them. He told Earnshaw to learn all he could about this, and he decided to ask the same of Tabby next time he saw her. She was as useful as Earnshaw at gathering information.

He had the chance on Sunday, after he had sat through an hour-long sermon about witchcraft, unhallowed rites, invocations of evil, and the opening gates of hell. He was not in his sweetest mood when he spoke to Tabby in the churchyard, and he did not get quite the answers he expected. Tabby, however annoyed she might be at the loss of her prized bird, had not lost her forthright good sense.

'That?' she said briskly, referring to the sermon. 'I'll agree he made too much of it. I don't think hell will swallow us all next week.'

'Is that all you can say?'

'It's perhaps the best I can say. I know he ranted, and I know he's superstitious. But I can't laugh at him this time.'

'Tabby! What ails you?'

'Those birds were taken. They were taken and killed and we know pretty well how they were killed. It's revolting.'

'It was lunatic.'

'I dare say it was, but these people must have had a purpose, even if it was lunatic, and I can't think of any purpose except that what the vicar said, or more or less.'

'Heaven help you!'

'Or all of us, perhaps. I don't believe in this sacrifice nonsense any more than you do, but it looks as if we've someone in the village who does believe it and is trying it. I find it frightening, when I think what we were in my father's day.'

'Oh yes — yes, of course, Tabby. But I need to know who stole those birds, and I want you to learn what you can for me.'

'I'd have thought it was Celia.'

'It wasn't. She isn't in this at all.'

'I'm at least glad of that. But of course I'll help all I can. There's been a bit more talk than usual in the village lately, but I don't know what it's been about. If I can learn any more I'll let you know, and as soon as I can.'

But Tabby could not. She had to tell him a day or two later that she could now learn of nothing that was of any interest. Whenever she mentioned the cock birds or the mill, nobody knew anything, and everybody spoke of something else. This was new to Tabby, and very unwelcome, and she was not much consoled by learning that Earnshaw had found the same reticence. He, too, could now learn nothing he asked about. Sir John blamed neither of them, and had no doubt that the reticence was deliberate. Jane went to the Dower House and told Celia, and Celia showed no surprise at all.

'They're frightened,' she said calmly, 'frightened to talk. They all know it's Maggie, and probably Bessie too, but that beastliness at the mill has done what it was meant to do. It's made them all sure that Maggie is a dangerous witch, the bad sort like her grandmother, so it would be better now not to cross her and not to talk about her. I could have told you there was fear in the village.'

'Why?'

'It's come to me already. Do you remember Sally Parr? She was frightened of Bessie and her evil eye, and I gave her an amulet to protect her from it?'

'And Isobel too. Yes?'

'Now she's frightened again, so she came to me again. She said Bessie was at her house last week with Maggie. They looked in, and then they walked three times round the house, widdershins, muttering as they went. Then they went away, without saying a clear word, and Sally was sure they'd put a spell on her. She came twittering to me.'

'What about your amulet?'

'That was only against the eye, not a spell. Or so she said. So I said she'd been quite right to come to me again.'

'And then what?'

'I found a shoulder of mutton, the blade bone, all picked and clean, and I wrote on it, in good strong ink with a lick of varnish on the ink to preserve it. Then I went to the house and walked round it once, *not* widdershins, and I gave Sally the bone and told her to hang it by the chimney. She's happy again now, not a bit frightened, and the village is *very* interested. They all know, of course.'

'I'm sure they do. But what did you write on it?'

'Oh, a scrap from the ninety-first Psalm, in Latin. *Non timebis a negotio perambulante in tenebris.* Mysterious to Sally, and very fitting. A good text to have on your wall.'

'How about Maggie?'

'I don't like her. I've made it clear from the beginning that I'll harm nobody, and I'll help and rescue if I can, as the proper teaching is, and I thought that people were beginning to understand me at last. Now I have this Maggie pushing forward.'

'As a witch of a different sort?'

'She's not a witch of any sort, whatever she may think she is. But she's a nuisance all the same, and she'll be a worse one before she's finished.'

'How's she to be finished?'

'At present I don't think she can be. We'll have to wait till she does something really silly that the law can hold her for. She will, one day.'

Sir John, too, was finding that affairs that week did not go as he had hoped. He said again that he would like Ansell to have some talk with the vicar in a hope that the man could be persuaded that his hate of witches rose from some fright he had once had. Ansell agreed, and was three times at the parsonage, where he found a fine hospitality and an obvious wish in the vicar to respond to anyone he could now think of as a friend. They were soon at ease, and Ansell was able to guide the talk to what he wanted. In the third evening the vicar was talking freely about his early days, but he could remember no incident that had given him any serious fright. The nearest he could come to it was that a witch had indeed lived in that neighbourhood. But this was only a tale he had heard. He had no memory of her, since she had died before he was of an age to remember.

'So that's how it is,' said Ansell to Sir John. 'He can't

remember anything — I'm quite sure he can't — so we shan't be able to ease his mind that way.'

Sir John was disappointed, and began to wonder what he could do next. Ansell took it more easily, since it was not really his concern. He did not live in the parish. He had been willing to give friendly help, but first and foremost he was the Jacobite agent, and his concern was with the rising in Scotland. This was spreading. The Viscount Kenmure had raised a standard in the lowlands, at Moffat in Annandale, and in Northumberland the Earl of Derwentwater had joined with Mr Forster to head a rising near Corbridge. These were still small affairs, not yet dangerous, but the newsletters reported that Mackintosh of Borlum had been detached by the Earl of Mar to help them, and that he was marching south with some three thousand highlanders. If the three forces joined they would be formidable, especially if Borlum had command, and Ansell was following the news anxiously. He still thought that it could not in the end succeed without help from France, but it now looked as if it might give some trouble before it was put down; and this, he thought, might lead the Government to being vicious in reprisals. Ansell did not like the thought.

Sir John would have agreed if he had given as much thought to it, but he had his attention more on local affairs. Earnshaw, nosing about in the village for any hints he could get, had at last decided that Maggie Webb and Bessie Neve had between them had as big a share as anyone in the affair of the cock birds. He insisted that he was not sure, but Sir John thought it a good guess. He had never liked Bessie and her evil eye, and he quickly remembered that Maggie was grand-daughter to a witch and had been caught, years ago, making a clay image. So he was quite willing to believe it, thought he knew he had still no evidence against them. Then Earnshaw, in his carefully casual way, told him one morning that Joe Parker had hung branches of rowan above his door and had sprinkled salt on his threshold. These, said Earnshaw, were very old tricks to keep a witch and her evil out of the house, so it looked as if Joe was frightened again.

'Who's he frightened of?' barked Sir John.

'Maggie, I should think, sir, by the way you can see him looking at her.'

'Tell him not to be a fool. But what's he frightened of, whether it's Maggie or not?'

'He was in the party when we searched the mill, sir, and he thinks she'll pay him back. And of course we're well into October, coming up to All Saints', and Joe's thinking of that too.'

Sir John had already seen the point. He knew well enough the old belief that the last night of October, the eve of All Saints' Day, was a great night for witches, when all of them were said to make their greatest efforts, and when all good people stayed in their homes and barred the doors. But Sir John would unhesitatingly have called this an old wives' tale, and he could hardly understand how Joe or anyone else could take it seriously.

But people did. Earnshaw obeyed orders and called Joe a fool, and Joe went to the vicar, asking for advice and help. The vicar, certainly taking it seriously, went to Joe's house to offer prayers for protection against evil. Then he went to Sir John, asking him to do something to help before it was too late. Sir John was not pleased.

'Help?' he growled. 'What sort of help? How do you protect from witches, anyway?'

'The best protection is certainly prayer.'

'That's for you, not me. What do you think I can do?'

'As a Justice you could move against this woman.'

'What woman? I'll move quickly enough if anything's proved against any woman. So far it hasn't been, as you very well know.'

There was more of the same sort, and they parted on the worst terms they had known yet, so much so that Sir John began to think that it was a final rift between them. For the moment he was too exasperated even to ask how he could mend it, and he tried instead to forget it. But he was not allowed to. Earnshaw came back a day or two later, and this time he had a tale that with its sheer craziness baffled both him and Sir John.

About half the village, he said, had been roused soon after midnight by a loud bang from Joe's house. Some of them thought a gun had gone off, as if Joe had been trying to shoot himself. Others thought it was louder than that, but it certainly meant trouble, and a half dozen of them jumped from their beds and went to see what was wrong. They had some trouble to get in, for the door was barred and the windows shut, and Joe, when they called him, told them to go to hell. Somebody ran to fetch Earnshaw. Others began to break the door, and when Joe at last let them in they found themselves gasping in the heat of the room. Everything had been shut and the fire built high. The heat was still fierce, and there was a stench in the room that they did not like. But in the firelight they were all looking at Joe, whose face was running with blood from some jagged cuts he was dabbing at with a cloth. His wife, crouching in the corner, had had her face cut also, though not as badly, and she seemed hardly to know her neighbours. Neither of them made any attempt to explain what had happened, but when someone lighted a candle its light showed the floor littered with bits of broken glass. Earnshaw, looking carefully at everything, found on the hearth what had certainly been the base of a glass bottle, now splintered and jagged, and he was soon sure that the bottle had been in the fire until it had burst with dangerous force. Joe must have been close to it at the time, probably peering at it, and had been cut by the flying splinters.

But that remained a guess. Neither Joe nor his wife

would say anything. Nor would they explain the stench in the room. Somebody fetched clean water for Joe's face, and Joe accepted it with a nod, but when he was asked a question or two he answered only with a grunt. His wife was rather better. She allowed a kindly neighbour to lead her to his own house for the attentions of his own wife, and as she went she was heard to say 'It's her power, her power. She broke it against us' — which was mysterious, but was taken by everyone to refer in some way to a witch. Joe would say nothing, and he was so morose and unfriendly that they soon gave up their attempts to help him. They made sure that he was not deeply cut, and then they went back to their homes. Earnshaw, saying nothing, quietly appropriated the broken base of the bottle and took it with him.

He produced it now for Sir John's inspection, and he pointed out that the inside had an uneven layer of something dark, almost black, sticking to the glass.

'I didn't notice it last night,' he explained, 'with just a candle to see by. But here it is, and it looks to me like hair. A woman's hair, I'd say.'

'What!' Sir John held it carefully to the light. 'It does look like it. But what the devil for? And there's a foul stink in it too.'

'Yes sir.' Earnshaw nooded. 'It's the stench you might get if you left a chamber pot in a room for a week and didn't empty it. And kept the room hot.'

'Oh!' Sir John sniffed cautiously. 'You're damnably right, Earnshaw. So now you can go further and tell me what Joe was doing.'

'Just what I can't say, sir. Joe's saying nothing and we just have to guess.'

'What's your guess?'

'His wife's not saying much either. But she did let out something about someone's power breaking it against them. I think she must have meant a witch, and Joe seems to think he's bewitched, or going to be. He's had the parson down there, praying for him, but he may not have thought that was enough. And if he still thought Maggie was putting something on him, he might have tried to do a bit of witching himself — to hit back at her, I mean, and made himself safe. That's the way Joe might think.'

'It seems far fetched to me.'

Far fetched Sir John certainly thought it, and noisome too, but it still seemed a better guess than any he had been able to make himself; and the more he thought of it the more it seemed the only way to explain this crazy affair. But Joe *was* crazy, so perhaps it fitted. Then a thought came that the vicar was crazy too, and might therefore understand this better; and he certainly knew a great deal about witches and what they had been supposed to do. This seemed useful, until Sir John remembered that he was not now on speaking terms with the vicar, and could not ask for his help without losing dignity. He brooded on this, and then remembered Celia, who was a professed witch and should therefore be as well able as the vicar to say what Joe had been up to. Sir John thought further and then he called for Jane, who listened with a bright-eyed interest as he told her all about it. Then she got her orders. She was to go to Celia and learn what she could.

She went that afternoon, wrapped in cloak and hood against the rain which was still sweeping in from the sea. At the Dower House Celia opened the door.

'Annis is out,' she explained, 'and she's probably getting wet.'

'I'm sorry.'

'Why? It won't harm her, and I've lent her my second cloak. But I'm glad to see you, Jane, so come to my room. Or rather, go to it. I'll join you in a moment.'

The room seemed dark, this wet afternoon, but it was warm from the fire, and with its window looking east, away from the rain, it was very quiet. Arcanus, wide awake on the window seat, got to his feet and stretched himself. Then he flopped off the seat and came towards her, as if in Celia's absence he would receive her himself. She stopped and rubbed his head, and at once he jumped on the table and rolled his head at her in further invitation. He was still doing it when Celia came in with a tea tray.

'I've made it myself,' she said, 'since I've sent Annis out. Has he been talking to you?'

'In his own fashion.'

'He's restless today, and won't settle anywhere. He's trying to tell me something. Jane, is there any news from the village, any trouble?'

'Haven't you heard?'

'I've heard nothing. But Arcanus has picked up something he doesn't like, and he's been trying to tell me so all day. He's so pushed it at me that in the end I sent Annis out to learn what's happened.'

'I've been sent to tell you.'

'Oh?'

Celia turned aside, and in silence she poured the tea, handed it to Jane, and waved her to the window seat. She took the other corner herself and Arcanus jumped up between them. Celia waited, still saying nothing, and Jane told her the whole story. Then in her turn she sat back, waiting for Celia, who was in no hurry.

'We go from worse to worse,' she said at length. 'I sometimes wish I'd never started it here, just kept my beliefs to myself. I never expected *this*.'

'But what is it? Was Joe making a spell?'

'Trying to. But not with any knowledge. It's just a bit more nonsense from the bad old days when most of them were taught nothing. They hadn't a chance to be, and they believed any tale they heard. And with a lot of them, the nastier it was the better they like it. More impressive, I suppose.'

'But it's Joe I want to know about, and this bottle he had.'

'It's a well known one. If you thought some woman was bewitching you, you might call in a second witch to help you. You'd have to pay her, of course, but when you'd agreed on that, this is what she might tell you to do. Or she might come to your house and do it for you. All right, love.'

She broke off as Arcanus began to chirp and push his head against her. She stroked him and went quietly on.

'You had to start by getting something that belonged to the woman who was bewitching you. This was to guide your counter-spell to the right woman, so the more personal it was the better. Hair combings were reckoned as good as anything, and they must have been pretty easy to get. You can always slip into someone's house for a minute when you know she's out, and I expect that's what Joe did. Or his wife did it for him.'

'That being the hair in the bottle?'

'Yes. Then you needed something personal to yourself, so that the spell would benefit you, not someone else, and I'm afraid, Jane, that this is how they got the stench. How did Earnshaw describe it?'

'A chamber pot you hadn't emptied.'

'I think that's just what it was. I've told you people liked it nasty. Joe would first put the hair in the bottle, and then he'd get his chamber pot and pour some of that into the bottle too. Yes, I know what you're thinking, but you could hardly have anything more personal, and if Joe was in fear of his life he wouldn't be squeamish. Not that he is, anyway.'

'No, but go on.'

'The next thing would be to find a piece of cork and cut a stopper for the bottle, and after he'd finished that and pushed it in, he must tie it down with thread. Then he's ready. He must wait till after midnight, build up the fire and put the bottle into it. And then no one must speak.'

174

'Celia, this is mad.'

'I don't believe in it myself, but a lot of people did, and it looks as if Joe did too. But it went wrong.'

'What should have happened?'

'As the stuff in the bottle boiled, Maggie should have started boiling too — inside. Mind you, I'm just telling you how the old tale went. It must be very unpleasant to be boiling inside, and the only way Maggie could stop it would be to run to Joe's house and ask forgiveness for bewitching him. And that, of course, would end her spell and Joe would be saved.'

'Go on.'

'If she didn't do that, the bottle would go on boiling, and it would soon blow its cork out. The thread would break and the cork go whizzing somewhere, and that would be even better because it would kill Maggie.'

'The cork would?'

'No. I think she was supposed to dry up inside, and die of that.'

'She hasn't done it yet.'

'But this is where it went wrong. The cork didn't blow out. The bottle burst, and that's different. Joe being a cobbler, I suppose.'

'What's that to it?'

'Wouldn't most people use sewing thread to tie the cork? But Joe, wanting to do it well, might have used his shoe thread, which would be stronger. It held the cork, and the bottle burst instead.'

'And what would that mean?'

'When it broke, Joe's counter-spell would break with it, and he'd be worse off than when he started. And that's what his wife must think, if we can guess from what she said. She probably meant that when Maggie felt herself getting warm inside she did a quick spell of her own, and it was strong enough to burst the bottle. Poor old Joe!'

'Poor wife too, perhaps.'

'Oh yes. They must be in a dreadful state, both of them. Is anything to be done, I wonder?'

'When Sally Parr thought she was bewitched, you put her right with your amulet and your mutton bones. Could you do it for Joe?'

'But Sally believed in me, and when I said I'd protect her she was sure I could. That's what did it.'

'Wouldn't Joe believe it too? He believes in all witches.'

'But he also hates us all. He might believe I could, but I'm not sure he'd believe I would. But it's a useful thought, and I'll see what can be done. I'll have to.'

'Why?'

'Jane, what's coming next? Joe must be nearly frantic now, when he thinks he's put himself in Maggie's power. He's sitting in that cottage with fear and hate streaming out of him, and I don't wonder he picked something up and turned all restless.' She meant Arcanus, who had lifted his head again. 'Suppose Joe tried to kill her? Or even managed to do it, if he can for once do something properly?'

'Celia!'

'I wouldn't put it past him, in the state he's in, or soon will be. We're only ten days from All Hallows.'

'And what does that mean — here?'

'Anything. You won't have trouble from me, mind you. My meeting will be in this room, and private. There won't even be anything to gossip about. But Maggie's trying to set up as a witch, and one who's to be feared by everyone. Bessie likewise. So on Hallowe'en they must do something bigger than they've done yet, and then let the village know about it. That's its purpose, and it's only ten days away.'

'But Joe—'

'He's wrong about most things, but he does know that Maggie will do her worst that night. And if he thinks it's going to be against him, he might think his best chance is to kill her first. Such things have happened, and they could happen again. So you can't wonder that I'm worried. Or *we* are.' She leaned forward to fondle Arcanus again. 'Joe's a fool, but I don't want him hanged.'

Sir John, when Jane told him of all this, looked worried and said that Celia might for once be right. Joe at his best was daft enough, and there was no saying what he might have in his head by this time. The vicar was surely the man to deal with this, since his own beliefs about witches might make him the one man Joe would listen to. But there was still the difficulty that Sir John was not on speaking terms with the vicar, and could not with dignity approach him for help. He gave this further thought, and then hit on what seemed a happy solution. He sent Ansell to the vicar, to tell him about Joe and hint that help might be needed. Sir John had some hopes of this, but Ansell, when he returned an hour later, quickly removed them.

He was looking worried himself as he explained it. The vicar, he said, had known enough of witchcraft to guess what Joe had been doing in the night, and had already been to see him, but not with sympathy and understanding. His view of it had been that Joe's proceedings with the bottle were themselves no better than witchcraft and came under the same condemnation, and he had said so without mincing words. Joe, who hated witches as fiercely as the vicar did, and thought they should be put down by any means that offered, including boiling them, had been first taken aback and then infuriated, and the resulting argument had become noisy enough to alarm the neighbours. And there, said Ansell, the matter rested, neither of them now speaking to the other. Sir John listened gloomily and then said they now seemed to be stuck fast, with nobody speaking to anybody.

Jane wondered if Joe was now speaking to Celia. He

had always been savagely hostile to her, as no better than any other witch, but she had said something of offering him help against Maggie; which might have made a difference. Jane had this in mind when she went to the Dower House that sunny afternoon and found Celia in the garden, potting carnations for the winter. But as usual she was willing to talk.

'I'm more or less sent out of the house,' she said cheerfully. 'Told to keep out of his sight and not upset him.'

'Upset who?'

'The vicar. He's drinking tea with Sophie. She'd a little trouble to get him because he's shy of me. A most damnable witch. Not a creature a clergyman can safely drink with.'

'But —'

'Oh, it's all right. Sophie's good at persuading men. She's had some practice.'

'But what does she want him for?'

'Mellow him. Get him talking. She says if he's to stay sane at all he must talk to someone.'

'It might help him.'

'It would. But I fancy Sophie has a little more in mind. If she can get him talking to her again, as he used to do, I think her next move will be to get him talking to *me*. Persuade him that it's safe to do so, and that I shan't boil bottles or cast spells on him.'

'Excellent.'

'But she's going carefully, not taking risks, and I'm firmly told to be out of sight and not scare the bird too soon. Hmm!' Celia firmed the last of her carnations and stood up, brushing compost off her hands. 'You know he's quarrelled with Joe?'

'Not liking Joe's bottle and pot.'

'I didn't like them myself, and I've fallen out with Joe too. Or he has with me. All because I tried to help him.'

'Against Maggie?'

'Yes. I went to his house and said I'd protect him just

178

like Sally, and Joe shouted that I was a damned devil-licking witch they were waiting for in hell, and be out of his house before the Lord struck me dead. All in one breath.'

'And what did you do?'

'I'd no chance to do anything. I suppose I stood and gaped, and Joe grabbed a cooking pot from the fire and threw it at me. I must say he knew his mind.'

'But—'

'I wasn't hurt. I jumped pretty quickly, and the only hurt was to Joe's dinner, which spilled over the floor. His wife shrieked and got in his way, and while he was falling over her I got out. I more or less ran for it.'

'I'd have done.'

'Yes. But it does mean I haven't helped Joe. I don't know what he'll do.'

'Can't his wife cool him?'

'I think she tries, and I've told two of my people to give her what encouragement they can. So we'll have to hope. It's five days to All Hallows.'

'And then what?'

'Make your own guess. But by then it should be Maggie's move, and I don't think it will be one we'll like.'

15
All Hallows

Monday was grey and cold, with hardly wind enough to clear the morning mist. Everything seemed strangely quiet. But then some drops of rain began to fall, and Earnshaw, who had come to see Sir John, said he did not like the look of it. Then he told of the arrangements for the night. Once again there would be a patrol in the village, and this time, after the affair of the cock birds, it had been easier to get volunteers. None the less there was a difficulty.

'It's the moon,' he explained. 'We're three days after the full. The vicar's got an almanack, and he says it will rise about half past six. These nights it's dark by six, or earlier if this goes on.' He jerked his head at the grey sky and spatter of rain. 'So we could have about two hours dark before the moon's worth anything, and that's going to be difficult. But we'll do our best, and when the moon's well up it won't be too bad.'

'All right, Earnshaw.' Sir John took his hearty and decisive tone. 'I'm sure you'll do your best. But who'll be with you this time? The vicar, I suppose? How about Joe?'

'He's coming, sir. He's that scared that the innards are near dropping out of him, but he's coming. Says you can only die once, so he might as well. Oh, and there's one little thing, sir, that might have put a bit of heart in him. It's the widow Pilling. She's well on in years and her eyes

180

aren't good. But last week she lost her wedding ring. It had always been on her finger, one day it wasn't, and she was near frantic. She turned her house upside down for it, all the places she could think of and a few she couldn't, but she didn't find it. And someone told her to ask Maggie.'

'What's Maggie to do with it?'

'It's expected of a witch, sir. She's supposed to have the sight, and be able to see where things are.'

'I've said this is crazy.'

'Yes sir. So she went to Maggie, and Maggie couldn't do it. She cleared the fire and threw something into it that stank, and then she squatted down and peered at the smoke, and after a lot of fee-faw-fum she told her to look under the dresser, where she'd looked about six times already. That's all she got from Maggie, and it cost her a shilling to get it. She wasn't pleased.'

'No? But what next?'

'Someone said go to Miss Bancroft, because she's a proper witch.'

'A what?'

'I'm just telling what they said, sir. So she went to Miss Bancroft, and there wasn't any messing with the fire at all. Miss Bancroft just sat her at the table and put a sort of black mirror on it. Then she sat opposite and put her hands on the mirror with the widow's hands over hers. Oh, and that cat of hers jumped up too and sat on the table, and put his paws on the thing. The widow thought it queer, and she couldn't keep her eyes off him after that. He was a proper witch's cat, she said, and—'

'Damn the cat. What happened?'

'Miss Bancroft asked if she had a feather bed. Then she said go and look if there's a little tear in it, and if there is, look inside the tear, because it might be there. And that's how it was, sir. The widow looked at her bed and found it was a bit torn, just where her hand might come at night, and just inside she found the ring, mixed up with the feathers.'

'What!'

'I know it's far fetched, sir, but the widow swears to it. She's telling everyone, and of course what she says is that Miss Bancroft is a proper witch and Maggie isn't. And that's put a bit of heart into Joe. Only a bit, mind you, but he did seem to think last night that Maggie mightn't be quite what she thinks she is. Not quite the devil almighty, so to speak.'

'Good. And send for me tonight if you need me, Earnshaw. At any hour, if it's needful.'

He was in a good enough humour to go to the door to see Earnshaw from the house, and the rain was no longer in spatters. It was a light rain still, but it was steady, and a wind was rising too, coming from the sea. Sir John looked round the sky, noting how even the moor was blotted out.

'I don't like a rain that starts like this, Earnshaw. You might get wet tonight.'

'Aye.' Earnshaw looked round also. 'We shall and all.'

He went off. Sir John returned to the fire, and over his wine he may have given some thought to the widow Pilling and her ring. He told the tale at dinner, and his wife looked as puzzled as he.

'I don't know,' she said slowly. 'It could be a lucky guess. But there *are* women who see odd things in teacups and pools of ink, and I suppose Celia could be one of them. I've never believed in them, though.'

'I'm not believing in them now. But it's odd. Jane, if you like to go to the Dower House this afternoon, I'll be glad if you'll find the truth for me.'

'Of course I'll go.'

Jane answered cheerfully, but an hour later she had some doubts. The rain was a downpour now, steady and persistent, and the patter on the grass had become a hiss. The wind had risen too, and was strong from the west, driving the rain in waves across the park. It hit her face as she opened the door, and she had to clutch her hat. She was wetter than she liked to be when she reached the Dower House, and once again it was Celia who opened the door.

'I've sent Annis out,' she said briefly. 'I'm glad to see you, Jane, but I'm surprised.'

'So am I. But I've been wet before.'

There were some puffs of smoke from the fire in Celia's room, as if the chimney did not much like the wind. Arcanus, stretched in front of it with his head between his paws, looked up indignantly as the opening of the door brought another puff. He gave a chirp of recognition, and let his head go down again.

'That's what he thinks of it,' said Celia. '*Not* his weather. But what brings you?'

'That,' said Jane. 'At least, I think so.'

She was looking at the mirror on the table. Its case of polished sycamore was open, and there it lay, black and shining, on its bed of velvet. Near it, on the table, was an empty teacup.

'I got nothing,' said Celia. 'Or nothing I could make sense of. Even *he* gave it up. But how does it bring you?'

'Old Mrs Pilling and the ring she'd lost. I don't understand it.'

'You've seen the mirror. You know how I use it.'

'I didn't know you found lost rings for people.'

'Oh yes. And lost anything else. It's expected of you, once you're called a witch. That's why she came to me.'

'She'd been to Maggie first.'

'So she told me, and I was pleased by that. I've said all along that Maggie's been taught nothing.'

'But the ring?'

'I'll admit that I was lucky, though I shan't say that

183

to anyone else. She came to me, and I knew I must help. I must succeed too, if she wasn't to think me another Maggie. So I sat her down and looked in the mirror, but all I saw was a mass of grey, pale grey, and at one place a dark line on it. It made no sense at all, and I might have given it up and said wait a day if it hadn't been for Arcanus. He started purring his head off as if he knew it was right. It was so unexpected that I sat back and looked at him, and as soon as I came out of the mirror, into my ordinary mind, I remembered a ring lost years ago in Ireland. I didn't find it, but one of the elders did, and it was just like this one, in a rip in a feather bed. Of course I guessed at once, and when I looked again I could see it *was* that. So it was easy, and the widow thinks I'm wonderful.'

'So she should.'

'Yes. But scrying's like that. You see something in the mirror, and you aren't always sure what it means. I'm not sure now.'

'Now?' Jane looked again at the gleaming mirror and the empty cup. 'You've been seeing in it?'

'Trying to.' Celia answered shortly, with her eyes on the streaming window and the mist of rain. 'There's a mist out there, and I can't see across the garden for it. And when I look at the stone I get the same — a mist. It seems to be rising and falling, and I don't know why. I think there's a madness about. Even Arcanus has given it up. Jane, do *you* know of plans for tonight? What about Earnshaw and Loveday? Do they walk the village again, as a Watch?'

'It's planned, but I think Earnshaw has doubts. He says they'll see nothing if this goes on.' She glanced again at the window, and a thought came of a sundial and a sunlit terrace. 'He's probably right, so I suppose that will suit you? Maggie too, perhaps?'

'Don't be silly, Jane. Oh, I'm sorry. I didn't mean to

sound cross. But do you think a witch is protected from weather? The wind's rising too.' She listened for a moment to the patter on the window. 'If a witch goes out in this, she'll be as wet as anyone — and that's the trouble. It's important that we should meet tonight. Power is greater tonight than any other night, and I've called my people here, to this room to raise a cone of power.'

'What's that?'

'It's a ritual we can do — and Maggie can't. She doesn't know how. Think of it as a protection we can raise for everyone against whatever's going to be let loose on us.'

'By Maggie?'

'Or by anyone else. But if this rain gets worse how can I expect my people to struggle across the park in it — heads down, pitch dark, feet slipping in mud, and *this* battering in their faces? Most of my women aren't young, one or two are infirm, and I couldn't expect it of them, power or no power. What would it do to them?'

'They mightn't all get here.'

'Some of them wouldn't. So I've wrapped Annis in everything waterproof I can find, and sent her to pass the word to all of them that they're not to attempt it. We must do what we can another night, but I'm not having half my people in bed, and perhaps a death or two from chilling of the lights.'

'That can happen, on a bad night.'

'I know it can, and if Maggie likes to lose her coven that way, well and good. But I'm not going to. And I think, Jane, it's time *you* were getting home while there's still some light. You'll be wet enough when you get there.'

Jane was. She got home drenched with rain and out of breath from her struggle with the wind, and she had to change her clothes before she could do anything else. Then she went to her father and told him briefly about

185

Celia and the missing ring. Celia had certainly looked into the mirror, she said, but she had remembered the earlier ring in a feather bed, and had advised accordingly. This pleased him, and he in his turn advised accordingly.

'What I've said all along,' he told her. 'Don't be gulled by this mirror nonsense, Jane, or by tea-leaves either. You'll always find a tale like that behind it if you look properly. And witchcraft is the same. It's either plain moonshine or it's deception. What will she do tonight, I wonder?'

He flung the question suddenly, and for once she felt able to tell him.

'Celia? I don't think she'll do anything tonight. Just stay at home and go to bed.'

'Don't you know it's a witches' night more so than Lammas?'

'But it isn't witches' weather. Lammas was.'

'Eh? Oh, I see.'

'Nobody will go to the stones in this, or anywhere else, and Celia said she'd sent word to her own witches that they were to stay at home and not go out at all. It's getting worse.'

She was looking to the window behind him. The light was fading now, and it was time to bring candles, to close the shutters and forget the dark of night. Nothing could be seen through the darkening window, but the battering of the rain seemed to fill the room. Behind it was the drone of the wind and a rattle or two from the window, and then a sharp crack as a flying twig was hurled against the glass. Sir John gave his grunt.

'Aye,' he declared. 'You're right, Jane. They'll not be out in this, and I'm glad Jack's safe home.'

Ansell had been with Tabby to dine with a neighbouring gentleman whose house was near the Preston road. He had come in, looking as wet as Jane had done, after riding through the village to take Tabby home, and he had found it quiet and empty, all doors shut, and not a soul to be seen in the rain. But at supper he had a scrap of news for them. He asked if they knew Lord Widdrington.

'Who?' Sir John tried to remember. 'A Northumberland man, isn't he?'

'Yes. They told me of him at dinner. He was there on Saturday, it seems, just for a meal and to bait horses.' Ansell glanced at the door, as if to be sure it was shut. 'He was one of the first to join Derwentwater and Mr Forster when they put their standard up, and then he was sent to Manchester to learn what support could be expected there. Now he's going north again, to report.'

'And what will he report?'

'More than I'd have done. He seems to have it in his head that Derwentwater can pick up twenty thousand men or so in Manchester and thereabouts.'

'I don't believe it.'

'Nor do I, and I've done some inquiring myself. Twenty thousand who'd drink a health — that's possible. But to join in arms — no. But we've always suffered from agents who'll promise the moon, believing what they'd like to believe.'

'You don't think that Derwentwater will take this seriously?'

'I don't see how anyone could, and in any case it's probably Borlum in command by now, and he's said to have some sense.'

The evening wore on, and Jane wondered more and more what was happening in the village. Most probably nothing was. Even through the curtained window she could hear the roar of the wind and the drumming of the rain on the shutters. Celia's women would be in their homes, comfortable by the fire, and thankful for that considerate message. Nor did she think that Earnshaw and his men would be out. He had more sense. It was only of Maggie that Jane had a doubt or two. She could certainly do nothing out of the village. That lonely mill, a mile away, would be as impossible tonight as the Sisters. But if, like Celia, she had planned something in her own home, it might be different. The women who had joined her were in the village too, less than a hundred yards away, and most of this could be done in the lee of other houses. This might be possible, but Jane did not think it likely. If Celia was right, Maggie needed something more flamboyant than a quiet meeting in a house.

Jane gave it up and went to bed, and in the dark the hiss of rain and the howl of the wind in the trees seemed to merge into one unending roar that was monotonous and therefore soporific. She woke to hear the clock at the foot of the stairs striking seven, and when she pushed the shutters open the storm was blowing out. A grey light was in the sky, the clouds were low and still scudding above the trees, but the rain was nothing to what it had been. The lawn below her was a litter of leaves and broken twigs, and the path at the end of it, where she had once seen Annis in the light of a summer morning, was a wet and muddy swamp. But that was past and gone, and this was no golden August morning. It was November, and it looked it.

Sir John was in a growling mood at breakfast. He complained of noise in the night, and asked why no one was raking the leaves up yet. Then he said that Earnshaw ought to bring him a proper account of what had happened in the night, damage as well as witches. Jane, whose curiosity was not less, offered to go out herself in search of news, and to her surprise she was told to get on with it and stop wasting time. She took him at his word and was away in ten minutes, walking on wet and spongy grass under cloud that still spattered rain from time to time, and she went first to the Dower

House, where again the lawns were strewn with leaves. A chimney pot had come down too, and smoke was swirling untidily across the roof in a wind that was still from the sea. Annis, looking harassed, took her to Celia's room and hurried away. Arcanus, asleep by the fire, rolled over to acknowledge her existence, and went to sleep again. Jane waited, and thought she had come at a bad moment. But Celia, arriving a moment later, did not seem to think so.

'A little difficulty,' she explained. 'In the night we lost a chimney pot from the kitchen. It spoils the fire, and that spoils the oven. And that's the difficulty. We've the vicar for dinner.'

'Oh?'

'Aunt Sophie. I told you she asked him here to drink tea.'

'Oh yes. And you must keep out of his sight.'

'Just so. He must have liked his tea, because today he comes for dinner, and this time I'm to be *in* sight, and with orders to be sweeter than honey. So I'd better see that the dinner's good.'

'You had.'

'My good name hangs on it. So it *would* have to be the kitchen chimney.'

'Is the oven much spoiled?'

'It won't do a chine of mutton, or not soon enough. And in the kitchen they were just standing helpless, all three of them. Not a thought of what to do.'

'What did you tell them?'

'I told them to wake up. Put it on the spit and have the thing turning, quick. So it should be all right now. Roasting's quicker than baking. But what brings you?'

'To learn what happened last night.'

'Nothing did. I had a blameless evening and went to bed. Did anything happen anywhere?'

'We don't know. I'm to learn what I can, but you'll probably learn first.'

'Why?'

'The vicar. At dinner. He's sure to know.'

'Ye-es. I wonder if that's why Sophie chose today for asking him. I wouldn't put it past her.'

Jane went on through some blowing rain to the village, and she was no sooner on the green than she was sure of something wrong. Across the green, and set well back from it, was the church, and in the churchyard she could see a clutter of people round the south-west door, all trying to peep in. Jane hurried. She pushed through the clutter and strode into the church.

It seemed very quiet and empty, and in spite of the lime-washed wall the light was dim. Five men were standing by the font, the vicar, the two church-wardens, the parish clerk, and a watchful Earnshaw, and she glanced first at them and then round the church, seeing nothing wrong anywhere. It was all quiet and orderly.

'What's wrong?' she asked briefly.

'We do not know. But we fear for something.'

The vicar answered gravely, and then he turned slowly to the font behind him. He stared at it for a moment.

'Here,' he said, 'a candle has burned. It has guttered, and you may see the wax on the stone. So the church has been entered in the night. This ewer, too, has water in it, though we had no baptism last week.'

He meant the brass jug that stood by the font and was used to take water to it. Then he turned again, looking up the empty church to the pulpit. Its ledge had a pair of candles in wrought iron holders, to give him light in a winter afternoon.

'Those, too, have burned,' he said. 'They're an inch or more lower than when they were quenched on Sunday. So who has done it? And why this?'

He had taken a pace or two up the nave and was look-ing at a sprinkling of earth on one of the stone flags. Near

190

it were some traces of mud, perhaps from wet shoes, but this was dry and powdery.

'Why?' he said again. 'We do not know what it means, but the church has been used for something, and I much fear there has been a desecration. Who should do this at night but these sisters of evil who have arisen in our midst?'

'Yes.' She nodded, quite understanding him. 'But I can at least tell you that it was not Celia Bancroft. She has just told me that she did not leave her house last night, and had told her people not to.'

'I am glad to hear it.' He considered it for a moment. 'I have seen a little more of her lately, and of her aunt, and I do begin to think that she intends no evil, foolish and misguided though she is. But gentlemen, it is time to go to Sir John. As the Justice, he must be told of this.'

He led out of the church, and in the porch the parish clerk stopped to lock the door, which was not usually done. He hurried after the others, and Jane went slowly down the familiar path and through the gate. On the green she became aware of someone following, and when she turned she saw Joe Parker hovering behind her as if he wished to speak. She stopped at once, and saw that he was pale and strained, and seemed unsteady, very different from the truculent fellow who had come to this same green to bawl abuse at Celia. Jane stood staring, shocked by the look of him, and wondering whether she could help him.

'Joe,' she said impulsively. 'What is it? What's wrong?'

'It's what I want to know. In the church there. Couldn't you tell me?'

'It seems nothing much.'

'Oh, don't put me off like that. Can't you just tell me? Was it witches, and a spell, one of those blood spells?'

'Joe!'

She was startled, and then suddenly she understood.

Joe was frightened, terrified for his life; and her thoughts darted back to that preposterous spell with a heated bottle. It had burst, leaving him, as he had supposed, quite in Maggie's power, and Celia had even thought he might be driven to killing her. He had not done that, but the fear was still with him, and he was desperate to know what she had done against him now.

'Joe—' Jane spoke again, and was surprised at her own calm. 'There was nothing in the church to be frightened of. Candles had been lighted, and there was some mud and soil on the floor. That's all, and it isn't very dreadful.'

'Oh?' He stared at her, trying to understand this, and again she felt pity for him. 'Only that? But what were they doing?'

'I don't know.'

'And that's the way with witches. You don't know. Nobody does, and they could have been doing any—'

'Joe!' She cut in, sure that he must be dealt with firmly, and hoping that she would be able to do it. 'Don't jump at the worst. There's no reason to think they did anything. It didn't look like it, and I think they were quite likely disturbed before they had time for much.'

'But you don't know that. And—'

'Pull yourself together, Joe, and leave this to me. I don't know what they were doing, but I can perhaps find out. Then I'll tell you. But for the present, do nothing — and leave this to me.'

She gave him no chance to talk further. She turned about and walked quickly across the green, and through the gates into the park. Then she made for the Dower House. If anyone could make sense of this it would be Celia, and Celia was therefore going to be disturbed again, in spite of a chimney pot and dinner for the vicar. Jane thought it urgent.

16
The Preston Road

Celia evidently had things in hand at the Dower House, and she made no difficulty about hearing what Jane had to tell her. Then she looked thoughtful.

'Witches do at times meet in a church,' she said. 'There's usually no other building in a village where they *can* meet if the weather's bad.'

'It's not because a church — *is* a church?'

'Not now. I don't know about the old days.'

'But with Maggie?'

'Who's to say? She seems to work on any tale she once heard. But we must certainly tell the vicar that using a church is just a matter of weather. It might calm him a little. But what's this about Joe?'

'He's frightened, and I'm sorry for him.'

'So am I, and I'll even forgive him for what he shouted at me.'

'He wants to know what was done in the church, because he thinks it was done against him. So what can I say?'

'I don't know. It does look as if, just for once, Maggie has managed to get something right. For almost any magical ceremony you must have the four elements. That's air, earth, fire and water, and you can see how she did it. The air was all round them, the earth would be that dry earth on the floor, fire was in the candles and water in the ewer.'

193

'But what was it *for*?'

'It could have been for almost anything, but I shouldn't think it was for much, because Maggie doesn't know much.'

'Then what am I to tell Joe?'

'Oh — tell him that if it had been directed against him she'd have needed something of his to link him with it, some hair or a bit of clothing, and since there wasn't anything it can't have been against him. That's at least half true.'

Jane went home, and found that the vicar and the others had left and that her father was far from pleased. He had strong feelings about a church which he thought was more or less a part of his estate, and he was muttering about the impudence of people who thought they could use it as they pleased without leave from anyone. His annoyance was the greater because he did not think he could do anything.

'I had to tell him so about twenty times,' he said to Ansell. 'Of course he's sure it's witches, but he doesn't know who they were, and I don't either. Besides, what have they done? It isn't a crime to go into church if you want to, and it doesn't seem they've done any damage. So what can I do?'

'What did he say to that?'

'He kept on saying it was witches, must have been, and the church had been desecrated. So I told him to consecrate it again, and he said he couldn't. It needs a bishop.'

'I suppose it does.'

'There aren't any bishops in winter, and he knows there aren't.'

No bishop was in his diocese during the winter. They were all in London, ready to vote for the Government in the House of Lords. A bishop who neglected this would have no hope of translation to a better see, and few bishops did neglect it. Only in the summer could a bishop be in his diocese, and even then it was by no means certain that theirs would come to them. They were a long way from Chester, and not an important parish.

'Then where are we now?' asked Ansell.

'I don't know where we are. He's gone to dinner with Sophie, and I hope she can put some sense into him. I can't.'

Jane decided that her own first business of the afternoon must be to put some sense into Joe Parker — if she could. She found him in his workshop, and did her best to explain that nothing found in the church need mean anything against him. But she had to admit that she could not say this positively, and though Joe listened carefully, and even thanked her, it was plain that he was far from satisfied. He looked a little easier than he had done, but that was all.

Jane went next to the Dower House, for the third time that day, and soon learned that the vicar, too, had been far from satisfied.

'He enjoyed his dinner,' said Celia, 'and the mutton was ready after all, properly roast. But that's the best I can say. Sophie worked hard at him, and so did I, and we kept telling him the church had been used only because of the weather. I think he believes it now, but it hasn't done any good. He keeps saying that evil has been done in it and he'll have to reconsecrate it.'

'Himself?'

'He won't get a bishop, and he thinks that what he can do himself may be better than nothing. I don't know what some others will say to that.'

They heard the next morning what Tabby was saying to it. She still had an aggressive disbelief in witches, and she was more than usually forthright about it. Any ceremony they might perform must therefore be silly and empty, and could do no possible harm to the church; and

195

the vicar's thought of reconsecration rose only from his infantile fear of them. In any case this was work for the bishop, and not for a man who was so far from the Christian faith that he thought witches could run about as cats. She became so pungent that Ansell interevened, telling her bluntly to stop ranting. What mattered most, he added, was to keep the peace of the parish.

But his interest in this was cut short. On Thursday afternoon a letter came to Sir John, by special messenger, from a Justice in Preston who was also a Deputy Lieutenant for the county. The rebels near Dumfries, it said, had abruptly changed their plan. On Monday they had turned suddenly about, marching eastward through Longtown to Brampton, and thence, avoiding Carlisle, to Penrith, which they had reached on Wednesday. The Cumberland militia, on Penrith Fell, had fled as soon as they saw the rebels, who had then occupied Penrith, seized the Excise money, and proclaimed King James III. It could hardly be doubted that they would continue to march south, and their only road would be one through Lancaster and Preston. Sir John must therefore expect them near his house, and do what he could to prepare for this. In particular he was to seize at once the arms and horses of all papists living near him, and of anyone else who might join the rebels. He might also be wise to hide his silver, if he had any, and perhaps his horses.

Sir John was aghast. He shouted for Jack Ansell and thrust it at him.

'What the devil!' he burst out. 'Weren't they for Dumfries? Wasn't it sure they were?'

'Ye-es.' Ansell was already in his Army mind. 'But this was always possible. Lord Widdrington was going north to them, you'll remember, with a tale of twenty thousand men who'd join them in Manchester.'

'Bounce and moonshine!'

'Certainly. But someone here—' He tapped at the sheet.

'— may have believed it all the same. When did they turn from Dumfries?'

'Monday, it says.'

'The day he'd have reached them. Are they mad, I wonder?'

'Bewitched, more likely. It was All Hallow's Eve. What can we do now?'

'Hide your horses, all but perhaps one. How about these papists you're to take horses from?'

'There aren't any.'

'Others well disposed?'

'None of those either.'

'Except, of course — me.'

'Eh?' Sir John sat erect. 'What the devil are you saying?'

'I'm not quite sure. But I did ask some men to join this when it came. I pressed it as a duty and a loyalty.'

'And then you went back and told them not to.'

'Not quite. I told them to be careful, for their own sakes and their families', and not to join if they thought it hopeless. But this force at Penrith is stronger than I'd expected, because they have Borlum and his highlanders, at least a thousand of them, and some men could think this a conquering force.'

'And you don't think so?'

'No. These Scots can give some trouble, but not for long. I know the Army and the battles it has fought. But men who don't know could be misled. They could put it all to the hazard and join. And could I, who recruited them, stay safely here and not join? In honour, could I?'

'Ugh! You're over-nice in your scruples. It does you credit, but you go too far. What would Tabby say?'

'I think Tabby has very loyal sentiments.'

'I've a few of them myself, and sentiments are all very well. But riding off to join, just because someone else might have done, is plain crackbrained. Have the witches had you?'

They went on arguing and settled nothing, each sticking to his point. The most Ansell would concede was that if he did have to go, it would be only to find and warn the men he felt responsible for; and when that was done, and he had persuaded them to leave while they safely could, he would himself leave also — again if he safely could. Then he went to tell Tabby of his predicament, and Sir John, who thought he might soon be in a predicament himself, began to think about his money and his horses.

Ansell came back, looking much upset, to say that Tabby had taken it very badly indeed. She had had no patience with what he said honour demanded, and instead of reluctantly agreeing, she had told him that he was a fool and evidently cared very little for her, whatever he had lately said. He had protested vehemently at this, and she had retorted that at Lammas, after seven years' absence and then a minute in the park, he had ridden away without another word to serve this Jacobite nonsense, and now meant to do the same thing again; and if he felt like that about it, he had better not trouble to come back, since she now knew where she was with him. Ansell related this unhappily, and Sir John said it might not happen. The rebels might not be coming south. From Penrith they could go east over Stainmoor to attack Durham and Newcastle.

But they did come south. They kept to the main road, Penrith to Appleby and thence to Kendal, where they again proclaimed King James and seized the Excise money. This was on Saturday, and word of it came to Sir John on Sunday afternoon. The Deputy Lieutenant added that the rebels had perhaps thought it prudent to be commanded by a protestant, and were now under the Northumberland gentleman Mr Forster. Also, they were not as strong as they had been, since at least five hundred highlanders had deserted at Langholm, refusing to go into England at all. Ansell commented that they had shown some sense. As to General Forster, these men must be out of their minds if they had superseded Mackintosh of Borlum by a rustic foxhunter who had never seen a skirmish. But it was done; and Major Ansell, looking hard at Sir John, said that excuses were no longer possible. He could see no end to this but disaster, and if his persuasions had brought men into it he must now get them out of it if he by any means could; and if he could not, he must share it with them. He could not be moved from this by anything Sir John and his wife could say, and he rode the next morning, making for Lancaster where he expected to find the Jacobites.

He had not even seen Tabby, who had seemed to be hiding herself from everyone. He had hoped to see her at church on Sunday, but for once she had kept away. She had told her neighbours that she would not give countenance to what she called the vicar's foolish and improper attempt to reconsecrate the church, but even Sir John had thought she might also have been avoiding Jack Ansell. Nor had the vicar made things happier. It had been expected that after his reconsecration he would preach about the abomination of witches that had made it necessary, but he had evidently changed his mind. He was a strong Whig, as befitted a Low Churchman, and he gave most of his time to this wicked invasion by papists, as he called it; which, if it should succeed, would put them back into the days of King James, when only King William of happy memory had delivered the nation and Church from papist tyranny. He grew fervent about it, saying everything that was obvious, and none of it pleased Sir John. Only from Aunt Sophie were there some hums and nods of approval.

It had some further consequences. Up till now the

village folk had taken little notice of the rebellion. It was an affair in far off Scotland, and not their concern. But an army at Kendal was another matter. If it took the Preston road it would pass only seven miles away, and tales of earlier invasions came to life at once, tales of carts and horses taken, of foraging parties seizing corn and hay, of Scots let loose to take what they pleased from fields and houses. True or false the tales were believed, and soon horses were being taken east to any farm that could stable them. Wheels were removed from carts, and parcels of small possessions were buried on the moor. They they had time for talk, and the sermon had given them the topic. Most of them had no strong views on politics, but Sir John was Tory and High Church, and for years they had been used to a Tory and High Church vicar. They did not much like Mr Loveday, who was the opposite, and they would therefore lean to the High Church side and look tolerantly at this rebellion — if it would only go somewhere else. But a few, whose grandfathers had fought and died for Parliament and Protector, had very different views. They detested the House of Stuart, and they were heartily for King George, little though they knew of him. They were as fervent as their grandfathers had been, and they would give any help they could in putting down this rebellion. Of this party the leader was the vicar, and second to him in fervour came Joe Parker. The village divided into two squabbling factions, and when Maggie Webb declared herself on the High Church side Joe said this was natural, since High Church was half papist and papist was half witch. Jack Earnshaw, taking it more calmly, said it was a deal more likely that Maggie had thought it better, just now, to keep in favour with Sir John.

The march of the Jacobites continued. They were at Lancaster by Monday afternoon, and were hospitably received, particularly by the ladies of the town, who invited the officers to a tea-drinking. They stayed through Tuesday for this, while sergeants beat drums for recruits and got only a dozen papists. They marched again on Wednesday, and the Horse rode through to Preston; but the Foot, late in starting, stopped for the night at Garstang, eight miles from Sir John.

He soon knew about it, for a man had been waiting in Garstang through the day to bring him news. He came back in the dusk, and Sir John heard his tale and then sent him to the kitchen for a drink.

'The Lord be praised!' he said to Earnshaw, who had been waiting with him. 'We'll be spared the rogues.'

'Eight miles, sir? It's none so far.'

'It wouldn't be for the Horse, but they've passed along. And do you think the Foot will roam so far?'

'No-o. No, I don't think they will, at the end of the day.' Earnshaw nodded his agreement. 'Of course we might have the odd one, sir. Even a horse or two that's straggled.'

'We could deal with that. All the same, we won't take risks.' Sir John took his decisive tone. 'You'd better get back to the village and tell them to get their shutters fast.'

'No need to tell 'em sir. They've done it.'

'Good. But make sure there isn't a light showing anywhere. Complete darkness is what we want. There's no moon, and with all this cloud it should be as black as pitch in another hour. A stranger will never even know there's a village here. But of course, if he sees a light—'

'I'll see to it, sir. Though I don't think they'll need telling.'

'They shouldn't. Call at the Dower House as you go, and give them their orders. Then get into your own house and stay in it.'

'Very good, sir.'

Earnshaw went off into a night that was already dark

enough, with heavy cloud and some spatters of rain, and Sir John made sure of his own lights and shutters. Then, through the evening, they waited, all of them alert for a voice, a footstep on the gravel, or any other sound that broke the night's silence. But nothing came. All was quiet, and by ten o'clock Sir John was feeling safe. No one would come now, he said. Everyone would be getting some sleep before the next day's march, which was a good example to follow. Everyone could go to bed.

The night stayed quiet and the morning was grey and cold, as so many mornings had been of late. But it was still quiet, and before Sir John was even at breakfast he had Earnshaw to report all quiet in the village. Shutters were open now and chimneys smoking, and it looked as if they would be back to normal when the horses and buried possessions had been retrieved.

'Good,' said Sir John emphatically. 'We've been lucky, Earnshaw, and I think we'll stay lucky. They'll be on the march by now, and clear of us by tonight.'

'That's it, sir. I'm sorry for Garstang, though. There won't be much left there to eat when the Scots have gone.'

'They'll get over it, and it's Preston's turn tonight. I wish I could know what's happening there.'

If he had known he would perhaps have been surprised. The Jacobite Horse had entered Preston the previous afternoon, and had had time enough before dark to see that this was a pleasant town which could offer pleasant entertainment. They had liked Lancaster, but this looked even better, and now, on this Thursday morning, the Jacobite gentlemen were meeting the ladies of Preston, who knew that their town had a name for hospitality and diversions. There was talk of tea-drinkings, of concerts of music, and even of dancing; and to the gentlemen, after their weeks of marching, this was enough to take the mind. Nobody, not even General

Forster, was giving much thought to the affairs of King James III.

Generals Carpenter and Wills, who commanded for King George, were doing much better. General Wills, with three regiments of Dragoons and three of Foot, was already at Warrington, and was waiting only for two more regiments to join before he advanced on Preston. General Carpenter, with an equal force, had left Newcastle as soon as he knew where the rebels were, and was already on the high Yorkshire moors, on his way to Clitheroe and Preston. Nothing had reached the newsletters, and Sir John did not know of these movements.

'Good,' he said again to Earnshaw. 'We should be safe now till they pass again.'

'Again, sir?'

'They'll go home some day, I suppose. Still, they mightn't stop at Garstang, so we'll leave that till it comes. What are they talking of in the village?'

'This.' Earnshaw was terse about it. 'Who likes King George and who doesn't. That's about it, sir. Oh, and Major Ansell too. There's talk about him now.'

'The devil there is! What are they saying about him?'

'Just asking where he is and what he's doing. And whether he'll come back safe.'

'Damn their impudence. I don't like this, Earnshaw.'

'It's mostly pretty friendly, sir. And I don't think you can stop folk talking.'

'No.' Sir John nodded, as if he knew this all too well. 'Leave them to it, if it's no worse than that.'

Earnshaw left them to it, and for the next two days the talk went on, Garstang, the Scots, King George and Major Ansell. It held everyone's interest, and no one even mentioned witches. In these great affairs they had forgotten witches. But they were soon to be reminded.

17
Breaking Point

It began on Saturday afternoon, when Joe Hindley, the parish clerk, went into the church to make sure that all was ready for Sunday. This was properly the work of the sexton, but Hindley had not forgotten All Hallows, and he decided to look for himself. He found everything very decent, the floor swept, the books and kneelers in their places, and the candles trimmed and ready. These were important in the dark November days, when Evening Prayer would have been impossible without them, and up and down the church there were a dozen of them in their wrought iron stands. Hindley looked carefully, making sure that the sexton had trimmed the wicks and taken away the spilt wax, and then he found that at the back of the church two candles were missing altogether. The stands were there, but not the candles.

Hindley went to the sexton, who could say only that he had done his work as usual, and that the candles had certainly been there. Hindley accepted this, and was sure that the two candles had been deliberately stolen. He thought of witches, and set off to report to the vicar. Then he remembered that theft would be more a matter for the constable, so he went to Jack Earnshaw instead.

Earnshaw took this seriously. He still thought that Maggie had intended something at All Hallows and had been stopped by the weather, and that whatever she had done in the church had been merely a hasty substitute. So perhaps she had now done what she had meant for All Hallows.

'We didn't think of this on Wednesday,' he told Hindley, 'and perhaps we should have done. But it was just the night for Maggie, when you do come to think of it, everyone clapped indoors, shutters fast, and told to stay there.'

'We were thinking of Scots, not witches. You mean a few women slipped out, quiet like?'

'We'd not have heard 'em if they did. There was wind enough for that.'

'Then where were they going to? I don't think it was the church.'

'No. And it wouldn't be out of doors either. It was too wet. And if they needed candles, that means under cover.'

'Then where?'

Earnshaw went on thinking, and remembered the old watermill at the foot of the moor, where the cock birds had been killed at Michaelmas. No one had looked at the place since, and Maggie might have thought that she could now use it again. Earnshaw took his time as he considered this.

'She might have done,' he said slowly, 'and I don't know of any other place they could have gone to. I think, Joe, I'll walk out there and have a look.'

'I'll come with you, Jack.'

So to the mill they both went, and they found it lonely and deserted in a grey drift of rain. They pushed the door open, and inside it was as dark and empty as they had expected. It was utterly quiet, and they could hear nothing but the splash of the stream and the thin patter of the rain. Then Hindley drew attention to a trapdoor that showed in the floor boards, heavy and solid, and Earnshaw looked surprised.

'I've not seen that before,' he said.

'The shaft from the wheel will be down below there, and this is how you get to it.'

'But I didn't see it last time. Of course there was dust and muck over everything then, and I suppose it must have hid the thing. Hid the chinks round it, I mean.'

'You can see 'em now.' Hindley stared at it, and then his voice sharpened. 'Do you think someone's lifted it?'

'I do. So we'll just have a look down here.'

A ring in the trap let them heave it up, and Hindley pointed to a smear of grease on the hinges.

'Someone,' he said briefly.

'Maggie,' said Earnshaw. 'Let's go down.'

A short ladder, bolted to the side of the trap, took them to the lower chamber of the mill, where the shaft from the wheel was linked by two cogged wheels to the vertical shaft that drove the grinding stone above. There was no window, and the only light was from the hole pierced in the wall for the shaft, and even this was blocked by the wheel outside. But they waited, and their eyes adjusted to the gloom.

'Good God!' said Hindley. 'What's that?'

'The devil, I should think, but I can't see properly. No, leave it alone. I'd like Sir John to see it. What's down here, on the floor?'

'Is it an image of someone? What's it made of?'

'Clay, by the touch of it. No, leave it alone. I'm going for Sir John, and a lantern too. And if this is Maggie's work, I don't like it.'

'Plain daft, if you ask me.'

'It's Sir John I'll have to ask. Leave it alone, and come along.'

Sir John was none too pleased when Earnshaw asked to see him. He had had a disturbing day already. News had come that General Wills was now at Wigan with at least six regiments and seemed about to advance on Preston, and Sir John, thinking of Jack Ansell, did not like this at all. Nor would Tabby, and he was still wondering how she would take it when she came to the house to ask about it. She had dropped pretences now, and in place of high words she was showing an open anxiety. She wanted any comfort she could get, and he had little to offer her. He did his best and then passed her to his wife; and he was still trying to get his breath back when he was told that Earnshaw was asking to see him.

Sir John turned testy. He guessed at once that it would be something to do with witches, and that was about the last thing he wanted to talk about just now, with his head full of Tabby and Jack Ansell. It was half-past four of a wet Saturday afternoon, with dusk already on them and the rain getting worse, and it was no time at all to talk of witches.

'What is it?' he barked at Earnshaw. 'Witches again?'

'Looks like it, sir. It came from Joe Hindley. He'd been looking round the church—'

Earnshaw told his tale, and Sir John tried to be patient, knowing that Earnshaw was right to report to him like this.

'What do you mean by a devil?' he asked. 'What sort of devil? And where was it?'

'Against the wall, sir. There was an old shelf against the wall there, shoulder high, and pretty rotten, and this thing was on it. Call it an image, sir, or a figure, about three feet tall, with horns.'

'Horns?'

'Two of them, and they might have come from a goat, glued on. But it's hard to say, with the light so bad. We could hardly see the shape of things. But it had cloven hooves as well, from a sheep, I thought, and it had been dead quite a while by the stink of 'em. Can you have a bitch devil, sir? Because if you can, this one wasn't.'

'What the hell do you mean?'

'A dog devil, this one. That was plain enough.'

'How?'

'A carrot, sir, a good thick one, stuck on in just the right place.'

'A pretty thing you've found, Earnshaw. Are you saying Maggie and her crew did this?'

'No, sir. I can guess, of course, but I'm not saying.'

'Not yet.' Sir John began to sound judicial. 'Is this devil the image you were talking about?'

'No, sir, quite different. There was a big flat stone on the floor, in front of this devil thing, and a cloth over the stone, and the image was on the cloth. At the devil's feet, you might say.'

'What sort of image?'

'About a foot long, and done in clay by the feel of it. We couldn't see properly, but it was meant to be a man. Pretty rough and ready, but that's what it was, a man.'

'Just any man, do you mean? Or could you put a name to him?'

'I'm not sure.' For a moment Earnshaw hesitated. 'You couldn't tell from the image, sir. It was much too rough. It was a man and not a woman, but you couldn't say more than that. But it had a yard or so of thread wrapped round it, quite loose. We couldn't really see it, but it felt thick and strong and all waxy — cobbler's thread, perhaps, for sewing shoes.'

'Shoes?' Sir John stared at him for a moment. 'Are you saying that Joe Parker —'

'I'm not saying he made that image, sir. I'm quite sure he didn't. But I did think the thread might be saying it's an image of Joe.'

'But what are you coming to? I'll agree it sounds like witchcraft, and it's about as nasty as it's silly, but you know I can't proceed on that. So what are you asking for?'

'I don't know, sir. Of course we might see more when we go back with a lantern. We've left it just as it was, sir, for you to see.'

'Me? Go to that mill, do you mean?'

'I thought you'd wish to, sir.'

208

'I've no wish to at all. Still—' Sir John was beginning to understand that he would have to. 'Very well, if you think I should.'

'It would be as well, sir, and we'd best take a lantern each. I'm afraid it's raining, sir.'

'What! Go out there tonight, do you mean? Don't be so stupid.' He glanced at the rain splashed window, where the glass was darkening as the November night closed in. 'I'm *not* going out there tonight, and nor are you. Leave it till daylight.'

'Very good, sir. Tomorrow then?'

'Tomorrow's Sunday, and I don't deal with this sort of thing on Sunday. You know very well I don't. It can wait till Monday.'

But it did not wait till Monday. Joe Hindley was the parish clerk. His duty was to the vicar, and when they had parted in the village he had gone straight to the parsonage, making exactly the report that Earnshaw was making to Sir John. Its reception, of course, had been very different from a man who had no doubt whatever of the reality of evil behind that figure with the horns, and who now thought that his worst fears had come true. He could see no hope for his parishioners, in mind or soul, till this was utterly stamped out.

He gave the whole of his sermon to it the next morning, and Sir John sat aghast and angry. He had thought this a matter between himself and Earnshaw, to be kept quiet until he had decided what to do, and now he heard every detail of it given out, with dire warnings of what would follow if nothing was done. Sir John frowned, grunted, scraped his feet, and did all he could to make his feelings plain, and the vicar took no heed at all. He had no thought of prudence left. He went on to tell them openly that if the law would not help them they would have to help themselves, and he used at last the notorious line from Exodus, *Thou shalt not suffer a witch to live*. Sir

John tried to get to his feet, and his wife clung to his coat to pull him down. The congregation was seething, and the vicar took no heed of that either. He turned next to the image of clay with thread wrapped round it that had been placed at the cloven feet of that horned devil, and to Jane's consternation he identified it plainly as an image of Joe Parker. The cobbler's thread showed that, he told them, and they must all understand what would happen if nothing was done. Little by little the witches would crumble the image, and as they did so Joe would crumble too, in strength and health, till death and the devil took him. Jane, forgetting all rules of conduct, turned in her seat to see Joe at the back, white faced and shaking, while his wife put her arms round him to help him. She turned back, furious that he should have been put in such fear, and she could only suppose that the frenzied vicar would do that or anything else if he could only rouse his people. She turned again, heedless of a slap from her father, to see Celia sitting with a face that could have been carved from stone.

Afterwards, on the path, and regardless of the rain, it was worse. Sir John, standing on the sodden grass, was speaking his mind without restraint to a vicar who was answering as angrily. Sophie was in hot talk with Lady Mallinder, and seemed for once to be agreeing with her. Jane moved aside, and Celia quickly joined her, looking angry and determined.

'The man's impossible,' she burst out. 'Was there ever such a crazy sermon?'

'It was wicked. Have you seen Joe?'

'I did see Joe, and it was the sermon that put him into fear. He'll think—'

From near the churchyard gate a high shrill scream, fear and pain together, cut through everything and stopped all talk. Jane, with no thought left of Sunday dignity, jumped to the border stone of the nearest grave, and could see better. Down by the gate Maggie was on her back in the grass and mud, writhing and screaming, held down by Joe with a foot and all his weight. She was trying frantically to keep his hands away, and he was frantically scratching and clawing at her face with his finger nails. An instant later a half dozen men were pulling him off and holding him fast. Others hauled Maggie to her feet, and she sagged in their hands, panting and moaning, with blood streaming down her torn face. Earnshaw was gesturing for quiet, as Sir John went pushing through the crowd. Jane stayed on the tombstone.

'What is it?' she said to Celia. 'Is he mad?'

'It's a bit more from his grandmother. They'd a wild belief in those days that if a witch put a spell on you, you could break it by getting blood from her.'

'It's not true?'

'Everything his silly grandmother told him is true to Joe. What are we to do with him?'

'Do?'

'You see the state he's in. He'll either go mad and kill himself, or he'll kill somebody else. So we must get him out of fear at once, and that means this afternoon.'

'*When?* But can you?'

'I hope so. But I'll need your help, Jane, because I shan't get him without you. Can you come to see me after dinner?

'Yes, if you want me.'

'I do. And after Joe there's the vicar, who's at break-ing point too, if he could preach that sermon. He's as deep in fear as Joe, and he's worse because he doesn't know he is. He'll be more trouble than Joe.'

'But he doesn't listen. There's no way with him.'

'I'll have to find one, because no one else will. Come to me after dinner, Jane. And dress for getting wet.'

211

18
The Burning Coif

The cloud seemed lower and the rain even heavier when Jane set out after dinner, with a little fluttering feeling inside herself as she wondered what was coming. The park was empty, as if no one but herself was out this Sunday afternoon, and in the quiet she could hear the patter of the rain on the squelching grass. The Dower House looked lonely, as if it had retreated into the rain, but Celia was in the hall, cloaked and booted, and surprisingly cheerful.

'So far it goes well,' she said. 'I asked Sophie to get the vicar here somehow, and she said she'd already done it. She'd guessed he'd be near frantic, so she'd asked him for talk and a dish of tea.'

'And how did he take that?'

'Pathetically grateful, according to Sophie, and I'm not surprised. He must think everyone is against him now. So then it will be for Sophie to keep him till we have dealt with Joe, and I've asked her to get him somehow — any tale she pleases — into my room, not her own big one.'

'Why?'

'I've a ball that hangs there and reflects the light, but never mind that. It's Joe first, and I think he now trusts you but not me. So get him, Jane, as quickly as you can. I don't mind what you say to him, but you must persuade him that if he'll trust me for an hour I'll make him safe from Maggie forever. Can you?'

'I'll try.'

212

'You may find it not too difficult, because he's frightened enough now to grab at any help that's offered. Then bring him to the well, the one we dressed with flowers at Michaelmas, and I'll be there to meet you, with lanterns.'

'Lanterns?'

'For the watermill, where the image is. It's said to be dark. But remember, please, that what matters is to get the fear out of Joe, and what tale I tell him doesn't matter at all. So don't look surprised. Now, the sooner the better.'

Jane set out again, and the village was grey under the rain, as quiet and empty as she had expected it to be. She had seen no one when she came to Joe's house, though she did not doubt that her passing had been seen through several windows. They would perhaps think she was on some errand of charity.

It went as Celia had foreseen. Joe was at first up in arms at the suggestion that he should trust himself to a witch, but he had been grateful to Jane of late, and he was now willing to listen to her. And, as Celia had said, he was frightened and almost without hope. He did not think his scratching at Maggie's face that morning had been enough. He had been pulled away too soon, he said, and Jane promptly told him that he would therefore be mad to refuse an offer of help that might not come again. He hesitated, and his wife reached for his cloak and hat and told him not to be a fool. But he was still looking frightened as he struggled into his boots.

They could barely see across the green for the mist of rain when they set out together. Once, when Jane looked round, she thought she saw someone, but it was a mere darkness in the mist, and when she looked again there was nothing. Then they were past the houses and at the well, where the water dripped from the stones and the pool quivered with rain rings. Celia was waiting with the lanterns and a bundle of something wrapped in canvas which she did not explain. She spoke to Joe at once.

'Joe, if I'm a witch, I'm not the sort you once told me I was. So don't think of me as a witch. Think of me instead as a Wise One, and you'll be near the truth. I should never put a harmful spell on you, and since it seems that someone else has put one I'm going to take it off again. Or rather, I'm going to turn it round. Do you know what that means?'

Joe, visibly upset, managed only a shake of the head, and Celia went firmly on.

'It means that with your help I'm going to turn the power in the spell away from you, and send it back to the witch who made it. It will hurt her, not you, and you'll be safe from her for ever. But you'll have to do yourself one or two simple things I shall tell you about. They aren't harmful and you needn't be frightened of anything. Now come along. We're going to the mill.'

She gave a lantern to Jane, and the canvas bundle to Joe, who clutched it as if it was filled with gunpowder and had a candle in it. But he carried it as Celia turned into the grassy track, now muddy and squelching, that led along the foot of the moor. They had nearly a mile to go, and they could see nothing of the village or the moor or of anything but the track in front of them. They plodded steadily on, in a silence broken only by the gurgle of water and the patter of the rain, and when at last they saw the mill it seemed unreal, a dark loom in the mist that had no right to be there. Jane found it eerie, and wondered what tremors it was giving Joe. Even Celia seemed to hesitate, standing by the stream that at Michaelmas had been too low to wash away those feathers, and was now a splashing torrent. Then she led up the path that skirted the race, and with a hand on the door she turned to Joe.

'Now come with me,' she told him, 'and remember that I have a greater power than the other, and that nothing she has done can do you harm while you are with me.'

The hinges creaked as she pushed the heavy door, and Joe gathered himself together and went in after her. Jane followed, and it was so dark inside that she could hardly see the others. But Celia had brought a tinder box, and already she was striking at the steel with a flint. A spark flew, and then she was blowing the tinder to a glow and lighting the match from it. Soon the candles were burning in the lanterns, and then she looked round. She found the trap in the floor, and Joe helped to lift it open. Jane held a lantern to show the ladder.

'I'll go first,' said Celia. 'Light me to it, please.'

She went carefully down. Jane followed, feeling a little nervous, and Celia called a word of cheer to Joe. Slowly, and plainly not liking this at all, he came down to them, looking as if he expected the devil to appear at any moment. With both the lanterns high they could now see fairly well, and nobody paid much heed to the shaft that ran across the floor from the wheel outside. They were looking at the end wall, at the shelf that ran along it, and at the monstrous figure there, with horns and hooves, *cum ingente priapo*. Celia took it calmly, at first showing no surprise, and then she suddenly went closer, peering closely at it.

'Do you know this thing, Jane? Do you remember it?'

'I've never seen—'

'Yes you have. You saw it on Sophie's terrace, and it was a statue of Adonis then. Venus, you remember, was broken, and Sophie told them to be rid of this one too. I wonder how Maggie got it.'

'Just what she wanted.'

'Ready made, and she'd only to add to it. Those are the missing candles, by the way, the ones from the church.'

They were on the shelf, left and right of the figure, and wax had run from them to show they had been burning there. Celia stood silent for a moment, and then lowered her lantern, lighting now the flat stone on the floor and the image, roughly wrought in clay, that lay upon it, wrapped round with a length of thread. Joe recoiled from

215

the sight, stepping back and trembling visibly. Celia went to him at once, passing her lantern to Jane.

'Joe—' Her voice was soft and gentle, but incisive too. 'Joe, you are not to fear anything, not even the image. You'll soon see why. But just to make double sure—'

She felt in the inner pocket of her cloak and came out with a thin disc of wood, smooth and polished, and carved to the shape of a star. Jane, looking closely, saw that it was the five-pointed star called the pentagram that she had seen before in an amulet. It had a cord attached, and Celia hung it quickly from Joe's neck.

'There,' she said. 'Keep that always, and it will make you double safe. It's rowan wood, cut in berry time, and that's as it should be. Now—' Her voice changed sharply. 'We've work to do, and I can't do all of it for you. Is that your thread there, round the image?'

Joe looked carefully, none too willingly, and said it was. Celia nodded.

'Being round the image, it makes the image mean you. So take it off. Unwind it, I mean, and carefully. Whatever you do, don't break the image. That's right. Now put the thread aside. Don't lose it. Now do you remember this?'

From her cloak she had produced a white linen coif, the simple head-covering that a village woman would always wear in church and often out of church. This one was wet and filthy, heavily daubed with mud and showing some blotches which even in the lantern light looked like blood.

'It's Maggie's,' said Celia. 'She was wearing it this morning, and when you pulled it off her it was trampled and forgotten. I picked it up, and now it's going to be useful. Wrap it around the image, Joe, and again go carefully.'

Slowly and gingerly he did as he was bid, and Celia nodded her approval.

'That's right. The thread meant you, and the coif means Maggie, and much more strongly because it has her blood on it, and you can't get closer than that. Now, where's my bundle?'

She meant the one wrapped in canvas, and Joe had to scramble up the ladder to get it. In it were thin dry sticks and the stubs of three used candles, and she piled the sticks on the stone and dropped the stubs between them. Then she looked up at the horned god.

'To this god,' she declared, 'the image in the thread was offered, and therefore in the fire to this same god do we offer this same image, wrapped now to mean another. And there is no evil in that, because —' She turned, looking for a moment at Joe, and then, perhaps for rather longer, at Jane. '— because there is but one god, no matter what shape we give him, and when no evil is offered, none can return.'

She stood silent, and seemed to withdraw into herself. Then she spoke briskly to Joe, and he, under her directions, laid the thread on the prepared fire, and put the image, wrapped in the coif, on top of it. Again she felt under her cloak, now bringing out a small wooden box, from which she turned into her hand a little heap of what looked like tiny stones. She put them carefully upon the image, and then Joe, again doing what she told him, took a thin splint of wood from the fire and lighted it from a lantern. With it he lighted the stolen candles on the shelf, and the horned god grew bright between them, as it had been meant to do. Joe looked at it with a shudder, but he still had himself in hand, and at a further nod from Celia he thrust his flaming splint into the waiting fire. It burned at once, the dry sticks flaring and crackling as the candle stubs added their flame and heat.

Soon it was a mass of flame, fanned by a draught from the hole where the mill shaft entered, licking round the image of clay, and all but engulfing it. The coif turned a scorching brown, then burst into flame, just as the top of the fire collapsed, letting the image sink to the reddening

217

heart of it. At once the smoke turned to a thick pall that drifted through the open trap above, and an overwhelming scent came into the room, sweet, sickly and fragrant. Jane moved back, guessing that Celia's tiny stones had been incense. But it affected her none the less, and she felt an excitement building up within her, and some wild fancies seemed to shoot through her mind. Joe, pressed right back against the wall, looked as if he expected marvels at any moment, and she wondered if he, too, was seeing pictures in the shadows from the billowing smoke. Over it the horned god presided fitfully, now lost in the smoke, now glowing in the reddening light, and taking an expression that to a heightened fancy was sinister. Joe began to quiver.

But already the fire was dying. The heart of it lost light, and then collapsed into ash and glowing fragments, with only some wisps of blue smoke rising. The coif and thread had disappeared, and the image, lying in the ash, was brown and scorched, though still of clay. It had not been fired into a glaze, and Celia seemed satisfied.

'You're quite safe now.' she said to Joe. 'The image is Maggie now, not you, and if it's crumbled it will work at her, not you. It's too hot now to touch, but tomorrow I'll bury it where it won't come to harm.'

'Bury it? But can't we—'

'No, Joe. We can't. I didn't come here to work evil, even on Maggie, so we are *not* going to crumble it. But I think you will find that something has already worked on Maggie, and that the fear is in her now, not in you.'

She picked up her piece of canvas and led them up the ladder, leaving the image in the ash. They shut the trap and then, from the eerie shadows and the smoke and reek of incense, they went out into the November afternoon, where the air was cold and wet, and the rain as heavy as before. Jane shivered and pulled the collar of her cloak a little higher, thinking that it was time to be going. Already the light was fading, and a solitary pine tree beside the track, which before had been stark and lonely, was now almost in the mist. Celia looked at it, perhaps with the same thought as Jane, and then came back to affairs.

'All right, Joe. You're quite safe and happy now?'

'Oh yes — yes.' For once he seemed almost shy. 'I'm sorry I said all that about you at Lammas. I am really.'

'We'll both forget it, Joe, and that's how quarrels ought to end. But now get home, and quickly, and tell your wife all's well. She doesn't know where you are or what you're doing, and she must be tearing herself in pieces, wondering if you're safe.'

'Aye, that's true, and I'll go if I may. You don't know what a time she's had, and what a help she's been to me. Of course it's you that's—'

'Never mind that, Joe. Get back to her at once.'

Joe went off at his best speed, only too willing to be with his wife again, but after some fifty yards, as he approached the pine tree, his walk stopped abruptly. He seemed to stare at it, and then someone moved behind it and could be dimly seen hurrying into the mist. Joe gave an exultant yell, and at once he was running in pursuit. Celia, still by the millrace with Jane, spoke in surprise.

'Was that Maggie?' she asked.

'Yes. She must have followed us here.'

'But—'

'I did think I saw someone as I crossed the green with Joe. I suppose she saw me through the window when I was going to his house.'

'Joe's house? That *would* set her wondering. So perhaps—'

An uproar of voices, loud and angry, from somewhere beyond the tree, cut her short. There was nothing to be seen in the rain, but it could only mean that Joe had caught her. Celia glanced at Jane, and then stepped out briskly.

'It doesn't sound to me as if he's frightened,' she said easily.

219

'It sounds to me as if Maggie's frightened. And about time too.'

In a few yards more they met, and it was indeed Maggie, held tight by Joe, and pushed along by frequent jabs of his knee into her back. He was talking to her, noisily and triumphantly, but he turned to Celia as she came close.

'Here she is,' he shouted. 'The proper devil witch, and her power's gone. Hiding behind that tree she was, and you know why? She had to come to me. A witch always has to come when she's made a spell and it's broken. She has to come to you and ask—'

'Ask nothing,' said Maggie. 'You'll do the asking yourself tomorrow, when the Justice has you. Let go, will you?'

She twisted suddenly from his grip glaring venomously at him. She was certainly not subdued, but she made a pitiable sight, cold, out of breath, drenched with rain, and with a dozen vicious scratches all too plain on her face. But the force was still in her, and she turned it now on Celia.

'Your little pet, isn't he?' she shouted. 'What's he paying you for it? Come to the green tomorrow and you'll see him in the stocks — and whipped first, if he has his rights — and *I'll* play hell with him when he sits, him and his—'

'That's enough,' said Celia, and the cold certainty in her tone cut Maggie short and left her staring uneasily. 'Think instead of where you've put yourself. *You* made that image of Joe.'

'What if I did? I'd have made a worse one if—'

'If you'd known how, but you didn't. You didn't know anything, but that can wait a moment. Joe, if you do find yourself in trouble for scratching her — though you shouldn't have done it, mind — just remember that she stole two candles from the church, which is certainly a matter for a Justice.'

220

'Ha!' said Joe, and Maggie was all but snarling at him. But Celia had more to say.

'She also stole a statue belonging to Mrs Mallinder, Sir John's close kin, and I don't think *that* will please him. She might be wiser if she didn't go complaining, but that's not my affair. Now I still think you should be home at once to your wife. She'll be fretting even worse for you now.'

'Aye, aye,' said Joe, and suddenly he turned and spat at Maggie. She jumped to avoid it, and before she could do more he was hurrying away. He disappeared into the mist, and for a long moment there was a deep and soothing silence, broken only by the hiss and patter of the rain. Then Celia spoke again.

'Maggie, you've been a fool. You're not a witch, and you know you are not. You've never been taught, and you know nothing except some silly tales from your grandmother. With no more than those you styled yourself as a witch. You even set yourself to lead a coven, and you did this only for what you could get, or thought you could get. I suppose that's the one thing you were right about.'

'What is?' Maggie was sullen now, and not shouting.

'You thought you could get something, and you have done. It's with you now, and closing on you.'

'It isn't. What do you mean? I—'

'I can see it. And it's nothing to be surprised about. Witchcraft is not a sport for fools, and if you push into it, knowing nothing and thinking nothing, you're likely to find more than you expected. You can bring company you do not see, and would not like if you did see.'

'It's not true. I—'

Maggie had sounded frightened, but she stopped short, looking round almost in relief, as the sound of a horse broke in. It was at first faint, the hoofbeats deadened by the rain, but a horse it certainly was, coming from the south at a slow and weary trot, and they were standing in silence as horse and rider came from the mist, gathering shape and detail. Jane was the first to recognize Jack Ansell.

'Jack!' She spoke impulsively. 'What's happened at Preston? Is all well?'

'No.' He shook his head gravely. 'We didn't even make a fight for it.'

He seemed sunk in thought, as if he had not yet brought his attention to them. Then he recognized Celia, and at once he swept his rain-soaked hat to her.

'What in the world do you do out here?' he asked.

'Village affairs. Don't concern yourself,' said Celia. 'It's you we ask of.'

He nodded, and belatedly he dismounted. Maggie, seizing her chance, slipped away into the rain, and no one even watched her go.

'What is it?' said Jane urgently. 'What's happened?'

'Oh —' he sounded weary of it. 'Forster had command, and I didn't know the world held such a booby. Derwentwater knows nothing, and nobody heeded Mackintosh, who does. We were in Preston on Wednesday, and from then till yesterday nobody did anything but drink tea and the like with the ladies. Not a thought of war. Nobody joined us but some few papists.'

'How of the gentlemen you were seeking, to warn them?'

'They'd taken heed and they weren't there. But it took me till Friday to be sure of it.'

'And then what?'

'A sorry tale.' He seemed to brood on it for a moment. 'Yesterday there was still not a thought of war, not a defence prepared. Wills and his regiments arrived at noon, and Forster didn't even know they were coming. Even the bridge was undefended, and Wills took it at once. Then he surrounded the town, all but one point which he forgot. Then he pushed his dragoons up Wigan Lane to the bottom of Church Street, and the highlanders shot them to pieces. They lost a hundred men at least, and that was all for the day. But this morning General Carpenter came with another three thousand or so of men, and that made it hopeless. In another half-hour Forster had given up and was sending a Trumpet for terms of surrender, and I didn't wait for any more. I didn't think I had a duty to, and I just rode away.'

'But could you?'

'Wills had forgotten to guard the marsh below the Friargate, and beyond it are two good fords across the river. So I got across, and only just in time. Two squadrons of Horse were on the marsh when I looked back.'

'And then?'

'I didn't linger. But I was on the wrong side of the Ribble, the south bank, and I must cross again before I could come here.'

'Oh!' said Jane, quickly understanding this. 'You'd have to go to Clitheroe?'

'Almost, before I found a bridge, and it's a long way round, with the ways as foul as this. My horse is tired, poor beast.'

'Never mind. We'll rest him, and you too.'

'I don't think you can, Jane. It wouldn't be safe.' He spoke quietly, but with the firmness of a man who has his thoughts clear. 'I wasn't the only one to escape by those fords. There were hundreds before me, and once they've made sure of Preston the generals will start a hunt. The cavalry will be out, and the dragoons, and I should *not* be safe if I were to stay here. Nor would your father, if I were taken in his house, and I must not do it.'

'Oh? Then what?'

'I'm glad I've met you, Jane. I'd meant to stay out here till dark, and then creep in and ask him for a change of horse.'

'I'm sure he will.'

'But would you do it for me, if I stay out here? It will be safer if I do.'

'Then tell me what to do.'

'Take this horse home, and arrange for someone to bring me another, and perhaps a bite to eat.'

'Someone?' said Celia sharply, and paused for a moment. 'I think that's work for Tabby, and she'll like doing it.'

'Oh?' He sounded as sharp. 'I'd wondered if I could by any means see her.'

'Not at her house. She has peering neighbours, so we'll get her out here. Leave it to us.'

'Gladly. You'll take this horse with you?'

'No. It would be the wrong saddle for Tabby. You'll change horses here. Now —' Celia sounded briskly in command. 'Jane, get home as soon as you can. Explain to your father, get your own saddle on a good horse and ride him to Tabby's. Meanwhile, I'll see Tabby. She can take the horse from you, and bring him here, and return this one to stable. That—' She turned quickly to Jack. 'That will give you chance for a word with her.'

'I'm grateful.'

'Don't say it. But when you have the horse, what then? It's near dark, and you must be tired too.'

'I've known worse, in war, and I'll do well enough. I must work north of Bowland and then turn east, into Yorkshire. I've friends there I may lodge with, and if I stay for perhaps a month it will be all over and I may return here safely — to Tabby and all of you. I'll speak my thanks then.'

'Again you needn't. But we'll be as quick as we can, and if I were you I'd shelter in the mill yonder. Now Jane, let's be off.'

They set out together, walking briskly, and they got no further than Joe had done. As they reached the pine tree they found Maggie hiding behind it once again, but this time she did not run. She stood in front of them, and she was now looking pleased with herself.

'I can keep my mouth shut when it's worth while,' she said.

'You?' Celia's answer crackled, and Jane stood silent, angry that they had forgotten Maggie and let her learn too much.

'Aye,' said Maggie. 'They're looking for him, aren't they, with a bit of rope handy. But I haven't seen him, of course, if you've some sense.'

'I doubt if *you* have.' Celia sounded smooth and quiet. 'I told you you were a fool, and now you've perhaps killed yourself.'

'Me?' Maggie sounded alarmed, and much less sure of herself. 'What do you mean now?'

'Where's your coif — the one you had this morning, with the blood on it? You'd like to know? I put it round that image of yours, and burned it in. I burned it into the clay, Maggie, burned the blood in, with ceremonial fire. Do know what that has done?'

Maggie made no answer. Her lips moved as if she would mutter something, but no sound came. She looked too agitated, and Celia's tone became even smoother.

'I'll tell you what it has done, Maggie. It has made that image *you*, not Joe Parker, and the evil of hate that you heaped upon it is ready to return to *you*. You don't know much, but I think you understand that.'

Maggie stood shaking, staring wildly at her. Again she tried to speak, but all she managed was a croak. Celia stood poised for a moment, and then made an end of her.

'Speak two words that I don't like about Major Ansell, and I'll start to crumble that image. I'll start with its throat, and there'll be plenty of time after that for the rest of it, just a little each week, not hurrying. Are you listening, Maggie? Are you?' Again Celia hung on it for a moment. 'I've told you it isn't wise to play at being a witch when you don't even know what isn't safe. So next time you think of calling a meeting of your people, just remember that someone else may be at the meeting too, someone you don't see. That's all. Now Jane, we must go.'

She stepped out at once. Jane fell quickly into step with her, and neither of them spared a backward glance to see where Maggie went. The light was now so bad that they had to watch the track for pools of water, and in one of them Jane went sliding and stumbling. That broke the silence, and she had a question for Celia.

'Was it true,' she asked. 'what you told her about the image, and what it will do if you crumble it?'

'I don't believe much in this image magic. But Maggie does — from her grandmother — so I don't mind making use of it against her. She had to be stopped.'

'She looked frightened enough to me.'

'I hope so. And it's the same with Joe, of course. You don't make magic that way, but Joe thinks you do, and now he's out of fear. As for Maggie, she'd better remember what I told her — all of it.'

'Why?'

'The image was nonsense, but not that last bit, about witchcraft having dangers if you don't know anything. That's entirely true, and she'd better remember it. Now forget Maggie.'

They came to the beginning of the village, and by Tabby's house Celia stopped.

'You know what to do,' she said. 'Bring a horse here as soon as you can, and see that he's a good one. I'll deal with Tabby, and she'll be another we're taking out of fear today — fear for him, of course. But she'll fret till you have the horse here for her.'

Jane hurried. She marched into the house expecting to find her father half asleep, and she found him awake and ill at ease, plainly with the same fear as Tabby. Then there was argument. He wanted to hear again what Jack had said about General Forster and affairs in Preston. Jane said she must hurry, and her mother supported her. He grumbled, but perhaps he agreed, for he went himself to the stable to choose a horse and see Jane's saddle put on it. Eventually she got away, with the horse, a bag of bread and sliced cold beef, a bottle of October ale, and — at her own suggestion — a little leather bag of twenty-five golden guineas. She was doing her best.

Dusk was on them now, darkening fast, and she rode carefully, trying to make no more noise than she must as she passed through the village. Tabby's house was in darkness, not a light showing, but Tabby herself, in her boots and riding clothes, was ready and waiting. She seized the bridle as Jane dismounted.

'Thank you,' she said fervently. 'I'll remember this, Jane.'

'Remember these instead.' She handed Tabby the guineas, and showed her the meat and ale in the saddlebags. 'And you'll return Jack's horse to the stable? They're expecting him.'

'Yes.'

Tabby waited for no more. She went away, and was lost in the dark. The hoofbeats faded and were gone, and Celia came quietly to Jane.

'All's well,' she said cheerfully, 'and Tabby's a new woman for thinking that she can help. It was well thought of, and we can trust her to get him safe away. But what an afternoon!'

'A useful one.'

'Oh yes. He'll be back in a month with hue and cry forgotten. Joe is out of fear, and I don't think he'll make more trouble. He's too happy to make it.'

'And Maggie?'

'Maggie is in fear, which is where she ought to be. I can tighten the screw a little if I have to, and between one thing and another I don't think we shall hear much more of her as a witch. A useful afternoon.'

'But I'm glad it's over.'

'It isn't. Don't forget the vicar.'

227

'Oh!'

'He's in fear too, Jane, and he can't help himself. It's too old and deep, so we'll have to try, wet as we are.'

'But how?'

'I once saw it done, and this may be our lucky afternoon. Come along.'

19
The Sleep of Memory

The Dower House was quiet under the rain, a dark shape in the dusk, but it was a friendly refuge from the night, and Annis looked glad to see them back. In the candlelit hall she helped them with their cloaks, and she did not wait for Celia's question.

'He's still here,' she said crisply, 'and they're at the second dish of tea. But they're in your room, not the great parlour.'

'Good. Do you know why they went there?'

'Wet soot was what Mrs Mallinder said. Falling in the chimney, and it made the parlour fire smoke.'

'And did it really fall?'

'About a spoonful.'

'Excellent. Then a third dish of tea, Annis. For us. We'll take five minutes, Jane, to dry ourselves a little, and I'll lend you some slippers.'

'They stretched it to ten minutes, and they were at least feeling better when they went into a room that once again looked different. Jane had not seen it in candlelight before, and it had always meant Celia to her, but now Sophie was there with the vicar. The fire was red and quiet, but candles were on the mantelpiece and another on the table, leaving the room as bright as it was warm. Fresh tea was on the table too, and Celia went to it at once. But already the vicar was on his feet, looking uneasy.

'I must not intrude,' he said to Celia. 'This is your room, I'm told, and—'

'Sit down, please.' She cut him short and looked him in the eye. 'Mr Loveday, I won't pretend to misunderstand. You are uneasy of me, because you've been told I'm a witch.'

'Are you not one?'

'Not as you know the word. Do you find me in the least like Maggie Webb? Or Alice Openshaw? Do you?'

'I suppose I do not, for what that is worth. But—'

'Good. And this is indeed my room. You are now my guest in it, and I think no guest of mine has ever come to harm. Also, I have some news which I think you will welcome. So please sit down.'

He stood uneasily, his wish to be courteous plainly in conflict with his deeper fears. Celia stood waiting, and for a moment he turned his head, glancing round the room as if he felt trapped and was looking for escape. Sophie caught his eye, and at once she had a reassuring smile.

'Yes, do,' she told him. 'It's quite safe, in my house. I'll vouch for that.'

He gave a slow nod of acquiescence. Sophie leaned forward, turning his chair so that it faced more into the room and he sank into it, still looking suspicious. Celia moved forward and began to pour the tea, still seeming calm and at ease, and when she handed a cup to Jane she motioned her to the empty window seat. Jane went to it thankfully, and found Arcanus lying against one of the cushions. He gave a little chirp as she moved him gently aside, and then he settled next to her, pressing against her leg, quiet and watchful.

'And what, pray, is this news you have for me?'

The question came quietly, and Celia, still standing by the table and enjoying her tea, took it with careful ease.

'Yes,' she said as quietly. 'I must tell you. But first, Mr

Loveday, I am going to agree with you, or largely agree with you, about Maggie Webb.'

'That woman? Do you not know what she is?'

'I know better than anyone what she is, and on all counts but one we are agreed, you and I.'

'Oh?' He sounded wary. 'And what is that count?'

'She has set herself to be a witch, and not of a good sort. She has gathered others round her to make a coven. She would have power, and make herself feared. She killed the cock birds, and when Joe Parker spoke against her, she determined to strike him down. She made an image of clay—'

'I know, I know. I have said—'

'And I agree. But, Mr Loveday —' She paused for a moment, holding his attention. 'She is not skilled and dangerous, as she would have you suppose. She is no more than a silly untaught woman, and now she has cause to know it. You may heed her antics no longer.'

'What!'

'Cannot a witch be ignorant? Is she so peculiar?'

'When the devil teaches—'

'Does he teach truly? Is it his nature to be true?'

'No, indeed. But—'

'If he taught Maggie anything — which I much doubt — he taught her no truth. She set herself to strike Joe Parker down, and she made her spell so badly that with no great trouble I have turned it round upon her. She knows now that if that image is crumbled it will be she, not Joe, who is stricken down. She is in fear, the fear she meant Joe to be in, and I think you will hear no more of her.'

'If I could believe *that*?'

'You may. She went into what she knew nothing of, and she found what she did not dream of, as others have done before her.'

'Ah!'

231

Celia stopped, leaving him to think of it while she drained her teacup, reached for Jane's, and carefully refilled both of them. He sat silent, looking at nobody, and she waited patiently till at last he looked back at her with something of gratitude in his eyes.

'Thank you,' he said quietly. 'This will help.'

'I hope so.'

It sounded merely courteous. But then, very slightly, the note changed; and Jane, with every sense alert, thought that Celia was coming at last to what she wanted.

'Would you now do something for me, Mr Loveday? Tell me please, have you ever, apart from Maggie, had dealings with a living witch, or even seen one?'

'I saw Jane Wenham, in Hertfordshire, before I came here. I sat in the Court of Assize when she was tried for it.'

'Did she look very evil?'

'I cannot say she did. But the devil may so hide his—'

'No doubt. But that was only a year or two past, and you must have had your beliefs about witches for much longer than that.'

'I have known their evil and fought against it for as long as I can remember.'

'From what age, do you think?'

'Five or six, pehaps. I do not well remember.'

'But what gave you those beliefs?'

'The scriptures, of course. Do you not know what is written?'

'I did not know it at the age of five, and surely you did not? The scriptures do not mean very much at that age.'

'Then it must have been my father. He was always strong against witches, and he warned me often. That, at least, I remember.'

'Ah, yes.' She nodded, and her tone changed, becoming quiet and soothing. 'But forget it now. You are tired, and that is very right.'

'No. Not tired.'

'Very tired, and you are growing sleepy. Of course
you are. You have had great trouble, which is very
wearying, and you have to hold it off, and off, and off.
But now the trouble is lifted. Tiredness comes back, and
sleep comes with it.'

'Not yet. I am—'

'You are sleepy, and a pleasant feeling it is. So let your
eyes close, just for a minute or two, and then you will
be able to help me.'

'How?'

He sounded vague and drowsy, as if this thought of
sleep was becoming truth, and Jane sat very still,
wondering what purpose lay in this. A purpose there
must be, for the thought of sleep had been Celia's, not
his. She had firmly put the thought into him, and he had
taken it as his own. She had made it sound pleasing and
proper, which would no doubt be in her purpose too.
The room was very quiet, and Jane could hear his slow
breathing as if he was indeed asleep. But then, even more
drowsily, he spoke again.

'What help?'

'It's nothing.' Celia moved closer to him. 'But try,
please, to remember your father telling you about
witches. Was he a clergyman, like you?'

'An attorney.'

'Oh?' For an instant Celia seemed surprised. 'But the
day he told you first about witches — you'd be five years
old, you say?'

'Or four.'

'Try, please, to remember that day. Try to think you
are *in* that day. So what's he saying?'

'Oh — that I must be wary always of them. It's wrong
and foolish to be sorry for a witch, and only because—'

His voice died away, as if nothing more would come.
Celia tried gently to persuade him.

'Yes? Because of something?'

'It's gone. I don't remember.'

'It doesn't matter. Let your eyes close more, and your head go back. Here's another cushion.'

She slipped it behind his head, increasing his comfort, and he was sleepy enough to do as she had said. His head sank into the cushion, and he was near to sleep. Celia stood back, watching him critically, and Sophie, who had been sitting still and silent, turned and slowly nodded, as if in agreement. For a further moment Celia waited, standing as if she were gathering force, and then she turned to the curtained window and the silver ball that hung above it, and could sway and dazzle in a summer light. Arcanus, who was still lying against Jane, came suddenly to his feet as if he knew about this. Delicately, and without a sound, he jumped to the floor and sat by the cushioned chair. He looked up, and broke into a deep throbbing purr.

Celia took the single candle from the table and carefully, with some upward glances, put it on the window seat. Jane got up, and at a sign from Celia she went to the other side of the room. Sophie sat watching as Celia went to one of her tall presses and took from the top of it a book, a spacious volume of folio size, bound in leather. She opened it, and for a fleeting moment Jane wondered if it was some dark *grimoire* filled with charms and spells. She leaned forward, and saw that it was only an apothecary's herbal, listing his flowers and fruits. And Celia did not even read it. She merely stood it, opened in the middle, on the window seat in front of the candle, which it hid completely. She stepped back, seemed satisfied, and went to the hearth to quench the candles on the mantelpiece.

The room sank into darkness, with only the shaded candle and the red glow of the fire, but suddenly the silver ball had come alive, glowing and shining once

234

again. It was not dazzling, not hurting the eye as it had done in summer sun, but gentle in the candlelight that was flinging up to it from behind the standing book. Jane found herself looking at it. It held the eye, and she could look at nothing else till she made herself look round again to see what Celia was doing; for she had not a doubt that Celia had deliberately placed the candle and the book to do exactly this.

But Celia for the moment was doing nothing. In the cushioned chair Mr Loveday had not moved. He was looking very comfortable, relaxed and resting, but his eyes had opened, as if he too must watch this ball of light. Celia had returned to his side, standing still and silent and seeming to wait for something. They all waited, and in the darkened room the steady purring of Arcanus seemed to take a power of its own. It was loud, rhythmic, monotonous, and perhaps sleep-inducing.

In the hearth the fire fell suddenly together and a flame shot up. It died, and the room was dark again, but with a difference. The glowing light from the silver ball was no longer steady. It had begun to shimmer, and Jane saw the shimmer grow stronger. It became a twinkle, and soon she was sure the ball was moving, gently swaying and turning as it hung. It had done so before, in a summer wind, but there was no wind now, and for an instant she had wild thoughts of Celia doing some secret magic to turn a ball that no one touched. Then she remembered the stream of heat that must be rising from the candle below. It might be enough for so slight a movement.

The twinkle held the eye. It was soft and gentle, and it demanded to be looked at, even more than the steady light had done. And it meant nothing. It conveyed no thought, and it took attention so completely that it killed all other thought. Jane had to wrench her attention from it, knowing that she had been slipping into a world of nothing else. She looked down, away from it, and at once she was aware again of that throbbing purr from Arcanus. It was blending with the twinkle, reinforcing it, doing to the ear what the twinkle did to the eye.

She looked round, and saw Mr Loveday already under the spell. He was lying back to watch the light, and he had sunk his head back into the cushion as his eyes looked up. Celia, watching intently, had moved closer, and was standing behind him. She spoke quietly, in a tone that was both firm and soothing.

'Watch the light. It brings help, and is good, and pleasant too. Watch the light. It will help.'

She waited while perhaps another minute passed. Then his eyelids began to flicker as if he had had enough of this comfort, and at once she spoke again.

'Now shut your eyes. Quite easily. Just let them shut. You will like it. Yes, you are sinking into sleep, a happy sleep. It is getting deeper.'

She put her hands upon his forehead, pressing gently, and then she began to move them up and down, monotonously stroking his head. He showed no sign that he felt her fingers or had even heard her voice, but soon he seemed deeply asleep, wholly relaxed and comfortable. Celia looked closely at his face and then lifted one of his arms. It lifted limply and she put it at his side again. Then she took a pin, and after a moment of hesitation, she pricked it firmly into the palm of his hand. He showed no sign of knowing of it, and Celia stepped back. Arcanus had stopped his purr, and Celia looked at Sophie.

'I think so,' she said, and Sophie nodded.

For another long moment Celia waited, standing with her eyes shut and her hands clasped together, as if she were again gathering a power, or perhaps invoking it. Jane standing forgotten in the shadows, wondered what was coming, yet found that she was at ease and fearing nothing. Whether invoked by Celia or not, there was something in the room that banished fear and said that all was well. If this was Celia's witchcraft, it was a world away from anything Maggie had dreamed of, or Alice either.

Celia spoke again, in the same quiet and insistent tone.

'You will help me and I shall help you. Peace is coming.'

She waited, as if to let that sink in. Then, very slightly, her tone sharpened.

'It is the day when your father is telling you that you must beware of witches. You remember it well. He says you must not be sorry for a witch. Do you remember?'

'Yes.'

The reply wsas prompt and firm, and Jane all but gasped in surprise. She had been quite sure he was asleep, but it was no ordinary sleep if he could hear, and understand, and answer. She looked again, and was still sure he slept.

'Who was the witch you must not be sorry for?'

The question was in the same quiet tone, and again he answered promptly.

'Mother Ashe.'

'Who was she?'

'She lived in the village. A cottage that backed on the common. She had hens there.'

'You liked her?'

'Yes.'

'Why?'

'She was good and kind. Always a friendly word.'

'Why were you sorry for her?'

'I — I don't know. I can't see.'

'You are four years old, and your father is speaking to you. Go back in time another week, and tell me what you see. Think of Mother Ashe.'

'I don't see her.'

'Go back yet another week.'

'Oh!' He had apparently adjusted to this at once, and

237

he sounded startled. 'She's in a cart, a dirty old cart, and she's being driven away. She's lying on straw, and her feet are tied with rope. They're hooting at her, and throwing stone and clods of earth.'

'Why?'

'No one tells me. It's dreadful. I like her and I want to help her, and I can't. I'm pulled home, and I'm crying.'

'Do you sleep that night?'

'I keep thinking of her, and I'm frightened. It was dreadful. They say she's wicked and deserves it. All witches do.'

'Who says that?'

'My father. He's very angry. He fetches his Bible and reads to me from it. *Thou shalt not suffer a witch to live.*'

'Did she live?'

'I don't know. I'm not told.'

'Come forward again in time, till when your father was saying you must not be sorry for her.'

'Yes.'

He answered at once, as if this had given him no difficulty, and it passed Jane's understanding. It was not possible, but it was, and it must be witchcraft. It was Celia's witchcraft, done with light and a silver ball.

'Come forward another month. Move about in time, a little each way, and tell me what you see.'

'Ah—' He had come to it at once. 'My father is speaking to me again. He says she was taken to the prison at Lancaster. She was to be tried at Assize and hanged, but she died in the prison. My father tells me that the devil would wait for her no longer. She was his, and he came and took her.'

'What had she done, that she was taken as a witch?'

'My father says little of that. Only that his horse had died, and he knew she had overlooked it.'

'When he tells you that, do you understand him?'

'Not well. I am very frightened. He is in a great rage

that I said I was sorry for a witch, and he tells me much about witches and the hurt they do. He says the devil takes them all, and the devil will come for me too, if I do not hate them. He tells me about it.'

'And do you hate them?'

'I try to. But I keep remembering Mother Ashe in the cart, and I see her eyes as she looked at me. She'd been good to me, and I wish they hadn't taken her. I know I do, and it's wicked. The devil will come for me if I think like that, and I'm too frightened to sleep.'

'Come forward yet another month, and tell me what you remember.'

'It's no better. The vicar came to see us, and he told me more about hell and what the devil will do to me if he takes me. And Mother Ashe keeps coming to me. I see her at night when I'm in bed. I see her in the cart, and I don't want to. I want to forget her and I can't. I want to forget all of it, and I'm trying to, but I can't. And I hate it all. I hate it.'

His voice died away, and for a long moment Celia stood in thought. Then she spoke again.

'Come forward in time five years. You are nearly ten now. Do you remember Mother Ashe?'

'Who? I don't know her. Oh yes — I've heard of her. She was a witch, and she used to live here. She's dead now.'

'Did you ever see her?'

'She's been dead for years. I couldn't have seen her. It was long ago.'

Celia seemed to breathe deeply, almost a sigh of relief. Then she leaned over him, and again she touched his forehead.

'Now sleep again. Let yourself rest. Speak no more, but sleep now.' She lifted her hands, and her voice became sharper and more incisive. 'You will soon wake, and you will feel strong and well and happy. But you will remember all this. You will remember Mother Ashe, and you will know that it was not your fault. You will remember how your father frightened you, and you will know that he need not have done, and that you would not have been frightened at all if you had been older.'

She paused, and once again she lightly touched his forehead. Then she spoke her last word in this.

'You will not, when you wake, have fear of any woman who may be a witch. Because of Mother Ashe you will be good to her, and kind, trying always to help her. It is what at heart you wish to do, and now you will do it — always. Now sleep.'

She stepped back and breathed in deeply. Her head went back, her arms lifted, and she seemed for a moment to be giving thanks to whatever power had filled her. The room was silent, and then Arcanus came suddenly to life. He broke again into a noisy happy purr, and at once he jumped on the table, waving his tail and demanding attention. Celia was happy and relaxed as she went to him, and Jane saw it with relief. But Sophie was the first to speak.

'My clever Celia! You've done well indeed. He'll be all right, I suppose?'

'He'll wake in an hour or so, and he'll have all the thoughts I've told him he'll have. So he'll give you no more trouble. Maggie won't either, because she's too frightened, and Joe won't because he's too happy.'

'And Tabby?'

'Not long to wait. Then he'll come back to her. So all's well. Isn't it, Jane?'

'Yes.' Jane had to collect thoughts quickly. 'I think it is — thanks to you.'

'Not all to me. Something to those who taught me, and showed me the beginning of wisdom. Some thanks to them. But most of all —' She looked earnestly at Sophie, and then came back to Jane. 'Most of all — thanks be to God.'